by **Mark Bowman**

First Edition published 2018 by Slap-Dash Publishing
ISBN : 978-1-906407-31-5

Slap-Dash Publishing
St Luke's Art Project
TLC-St Luke's
c/o St Luke's Church and Neighbourhood Centre
Guidepost Road
Longsight
Manchester
M13 9HP

0161 273 1492
stlukesmanchester@googlemail.com

Available on Lulu, Amazon and Kindle

Typeset design by Rae Story
Cover Image by Jex

THE VERITY TRILOGY:

Verity

Perfidy

Certitude

Prologue

Lesana leaned backwards over the edge of the balcony. Six floors up somebody launched a firework into the sky. Lesana traced the orange spark of its flight until the rocket erupted in sprinkles of red and green. The colours seemed crude and mechanical against the backdrop of an incandescent sky. Somewhere nearby a man oohed and aahed. A woman close to him giggled.

A tongue of turquoise unfurled across the sky, tasting the edges of space and silhouetting the jagged peaks. As the first wave of the aurora quivered out of existence, it was replaced by fresh threads of blue-light. Other, unnamed colours, teased the edges of Lesana's visual perception.

The Festival of Light erupted into life on the crest of cheering crowds.

The city itself was strung-out along a valley. The most agile buildings clung to the edge of a caldera, offering their residents the best possible view of the Northern Lights. Other buildings jostled for position on the gentle slopes worn smooth by an extinct glacier.

The festival was the turning point of the year. Tomorrow the city would begin the long migration back towards sea-level and the relatively mild climate of the coastal planes; pushing south as far as the land allowed in search of a few extra minutes of sunlight each winter's day.

The man next to Lesana nudged her with his elbow. "Now do you believe me?"

Lesana agreed obediently. She spoke quickly, each word wrapped in a puff of steam.

Her neighbour was energised by the light show. "You need to use your own eye. Let the raw nature of it soak into your soul. The moon will rise soon. The sky won't be dark enough. Enjoy it while you can."

Lesana shivered and tried to remember the man's name. Her tunic tightened at the cuffs and collar, trapping a little more heat. The

Rosannguaq AI had twisted the building's back to the wind, creating pockets of calm air around the freshly disgorged terraces, but the air was cold enough to sting Lesana's lips and nose. She chided herself for not investing in actively heated clothing.

"My jacket has enough power for two, if you don't mind sharing," the man offered.

Lesana looked at his face properly for the first time. His features looked expensive but understated, not like the glamorous men in her favourite splice shows. Surely it was not so dark as to conceal her meagre status. Maybe he was simply feeling neighbourly.

"I have a girlfriend!" She clamped her mouth shut, confused by her own lie.

The man laughed without any signs of embarrassment. Lesana felt blood rush to her skin; angry first with herself and then him for his part in the situation.

A fresh wave of aurora danced across the sky, threading the mountains into a tapestry of light. Energy surged though the crowd. Lesana fixed her eyes on the sky.

Half an hour later a dip between two easterly peaks started to glow. The Moon clambered into sight. For a moment it sat huge and heavy between the mountains, before launching itself free into the sky.

The gasps of wonder were quickly stained with trepidation.

"Abu al-Wafa City! It's dark." People were pointing at the Sea of Serenity. The blocky glint from the solar farms was gone, faded into the liquid grey of the lunar sea.

Lesana was still digesting the missing lunar city when someone pulled her attention back to the aurora with a new cry of confusion.

A dark hole opened in the lights. It was artificially circular, like a hole punched in coloured paper. A few people pointed and fresh questions swirled around the balcony.

The hole in the aurora healed but something glinted reflected light as it descended towards the ground.

"Talk about inconsiderate," a deep voice complained some way behind Lesana. "Who'd perform an orbital insertion during the festival?"

"That's not a ship," a woman's voice asserted.

One of the more officious buildings directed a pair of search-lights at the object. The reflected aurora was washed away in brilliant white. The beams narrowed and tracked the featureless silver-grey sphere as it descended just slower than free-fall. It hit the ground without slowing, and Lesana waited for the sound of impact to reach her.

People began to fidget. Somebody called out and waved a direction. One of the search lights swept back across the point of impact. A dome of distorted light was rising from the ground. It became a hemisphere and then began to grow, slowly at first and then in disturbing leaps.

Nobody reacted.

The hemisphere swelled towards the edge of the city, its growth stilted by the rugged terrain. Its surface reflected and distorted the colours of the sky. Half-formed shapes coalesced then decayed before Lesana's brain could make a connection, like waking from a nightmare over and over again.

It reached the first building and there was a pause. The hemisphere, now several stories high, partially flowed around the lower half of the structure, more like a viscous liquid than a solid body. Tendrils grew from the surface and probed the building. Lesana got the strong impression of a lizard tasting its environment.

There was a moment when the building was both there and gone; a conflict in the underlying structure of reality. Lesana's mind floundered at the contradiction.

Lesana blinked.

Reality reset.

The hemisphere was expanding again. The building was gone. Fresh figures joined the half-imagined nightmares that formed a film between the world outside and inside the invader.

A squall of icy air gambolled among those stunned into silence. A man cried out a name and broke the spell. Pandemonium took hold of the crowd, scattering people in random directions. Lesana was swept from the balcony and into a stairwell. The building responded to the stampede by undulating the stairs. It started to evacuate itself; transporting each person away from the crush and catching those who fell.

Lesana fought against the flow of people and the gentle insistence of the building. She felt betrayed by ground; the thing had originally fallen from the sky, but it had then risen from the rock. She did not want to leave the building and expose herself as a tiny morsel for the thing that devoured buildings in seconds. Lesana made it past her own floor and up to the executive levels. The flow of people subsided. Every door was fully retracted, offering glimpses into palatial suites of profligate extravagance. At the end of a corridor Lesana saw a cluster of people cramming themselves into a transport drone. The overloaded vehicle emitted a pitiful klaxon of distress. Lesana got closer and she could hear people arguing about who should get off. Several people gave her threatening looks. She turned and fled back to the staircase.

The next two floors were deserted; no people or means of transport.

The upper six levels were single suites for people Lesana considered to have more calories than sense. Lesana chose one at random. She stumbled through a tropical jungle and into an atrium of turquoise light. Green-eyed mermaids peered at her as she skirted around an aquarium bigger than her apartment.

Beyond the living area Lesana could see a private hanger containing an assortment of sophisticated vehicles. She entered the space and turned on her heels, trying to find something she recognised. The deferential voice of a simple AI leaked from an oval craft, finished in black and augmented with dozens of engine blisters. Lesana ran towards an open hatch just as it started to close. She caught sight of a man's face, made ugly by fear. She held his eyes and pleaded as the pressure seal closed between them.

Lesana hammered on the hull even after it lifted from its moorings and started to rotate. An aperture dilating in an external wall of the building, revealing a night-sky peppered with fleeing pods. Dozens of buildings were missing from the usual skyline. The dome had grown so that it loomed over the remnants of the city.

Lesana crunched her knuckles against the metal of the lifting pod. Tears and pleas mixed in her throat making her choke.

The pod paused at the exit. An arm was thrust through a narrow opening. Lesana grabbed hold with both hands and was dragged inside.

Humanity was on the move.

Like gas in interstellar space, people began to clump and cluster. Within days some started to organise, lead or simply follow. On Earth's greatest continent, a refugee city formed around two renegade buildings. These dark towers had a will, and that will wanted to survive. They supported a motley collection of buildings on a desperate flight south.

The four great corporations of the Cartel lost their hold on everybody's

11

lives and faded into irrelevance. A disparate group of humans, Martians and others emerged to lead the exodus and mount something like a resistance to the Eidolon invasion.

Chapter 1

When the Reset started, it grew faster than a man carrying a child could run.

The Reset was already hundreds of kilometres across when Nomia and José lead a dozen Nodes in a counter attack. Squatting on the ground they closed their eyes against the turbulence of humanity's exodus. The fragments of their minds residing permanently in Verity Space started to build a barrier against the invading reality.

A thunder clap announced the collision of two immutable forces. Fleeing families paused and watched as the edge of the Reset slowed to walking pace, stopped altogether and finally started to creep back a centimetre per heartbeat.

The seated circle of frail figures glowed with the friction generated by a spectrum of conflicting realities. A gawking man with soot-grey skin started to applaud. A young woman, with a red-fern tattoo spiralling across her cheeks, cheered. The noise grew into a chant as one word took root and flourished. The chant expanded into an anthem.

"Satyagrahi! Satyagrahi!"

The crowd started to sit down, believing that the Reset could be defeated by passive resistance. Dozens of men and women squatted or sat cross-legged in concentric rings of defiance. Every mind was focused on the retreating wall of the Reset. A hush descended, born from awe and respect, but maintained by a static charge building behind suppressed probability.

Something darker and slicker than blood oozed from the ears of one of the Nodes.

Somebody in the crowd gasped.

The Reset shuddered and halted its retreat.

Another Node fell backwards and lay motionless.

The man sat directly behind, managed half a scream, before they both vanished.

In their place was a squirming sphere. The human-sized version of the sphere which had landed in the Arctic was new to Earth, but horrifically familiar to José and Nomia.

People started to climb over each other as they fought to find their feet and run at the same time. José stood up and faced the sphere. One of the Nodes joined him. Nomia and the remaining Nodes continued to resist the Reset.

As José slipped back into the unseen battlefield of Verity Space, he pushed a single word into every mind in sight.

"Run!"

Then the screaming and crying started again. The Reset resumed its growth and pursuit of the fleeing men and women. Only now the screams were not consumed mid-breath. Its advance was relentless but slower. The rout had become a battle of endurance. A massacre reduced to a war of attrition.

*

Yakini turned her back on the Reset. She clamped a hand to the back of her neck, but the fractured reality continued to charge the skin along her spine.

The migrating herd was getting strung out again. An octagonal block of executive suites was drifting to the left. As she watched, its deranged cartwheel finally stretched the feeding tether to breaking point. Even before the building shuddered to a halt, it had started haemorrhaging refugees.

Yakini pulled herself up onto tiptoes, trying to get a glimpse of the black spires of the Generals. Earth's gravity pulled on her gangling frame, making her shin bones ache as much as her lower back.

"Stupid planet," she muttered for the thousandth time.

A gap opened up between two residential towers, and Yakini caught a glimpse of one of the Generals. The contorted nightmare tower was the architectural equivalent of a malignant tumour. Decay and cannibalistic growth competing and cooperating to distort and contort the structure. The only uniformity was the empty black of its surface.

Yakini leant over the edge of the roof. A thin stream of refugees were heading towards the street entrance, thirty floors below.

"Alyona," Yakini said without turning around.

"Yes," came the mechanical response.

Today Alyona's perfunctory manner would not annoy Yakini. Today Yakini lacked the strength for empathy, charisma or inspiring leadership. She simply needed things to happen.

"Tell the ground-floor militia we have incoming refugees. Redirect them to the Tesla and Arlington buildings. See if we can muster a couple of ground vehicles to help."

There was a pause and, maybe, an involuntary whirring sound, before Alyona replied. "Done."

Yakini mouthed a silent thank you. She appreciated not having to explain herself. Thinking about losing two buildings in one day was bad enough, having to explain it would break her. She missed Bergur. He would have got stuff done as efficiently as Alyona, but with bonus hugs and more. Or Sera; another tower of strength and resourcefulness, but this time packaged in the most beautiful Martian woman she could imagine, and Yakini had a hyperactive imagination.

An image flashed behind Yakini's eyes. Herself writhing ecstatically under Alyona's brutal beauty: thrusting pistons, screeching servo systems and hand-crank manual overrides.

"This war is playing havoc with my libido," Yakini choked.

"What?"

Yakini turned away from humanity's flight. "Let's get started," she said.

Alyona was facing the Reset, her face impassive against the advancing wall of tortured reality. "The rate of advance is increasing," she stated without inflection.

"Of course it is. The Nodes are exhausted. We need a relief team from the Suparna."

"Do you want me to send another message to Kaamil Sillah?" Alyona offered.

"Not now. We'll retreat to a General. Give the boys and girls a few hours rest."

"We'll lose more buildings without their efforts."

"This is a war of attrition. It's not about winning, it's about surviving. We'll keep fighting, even if we're reduced to carrying each other, on foot."

"As you say. Survival is something the Ж are taught before we crawl out of our first airlock."

Yakini tried to smile. "Don't worry. We'll get you back into a hard vacuum just as soon as Nomia and José come up with a plan."

"Save the false bravado for those who need it."

"Just practising."

"On your six," Julienne ordered.

"My what?" Mex flashed as he turned.

Julienne thrust out her arm, brushing the end of his nose, and fired point blank at a hole in reality. The hole was held within a person-sized sphere of prismatic eddies. A dozen tentacles retreated back into the sphere as it digested the pellet of biotechnology.

Mex fired three more pellets into the sphere for good measure. "Six what?" he repeated, over the hiss and thud of the pneumatic gun.

"It means, there is a target approaching from your rear. Three is to your right, and nine is..."

"But six of what?"

"Something to do with time. Forget it. Just stop talking."

"Yes Ma'am."

"You know what I mean. Concentrate on protecting the Nodes."

Mex talked more than he used to. It was not entirely to annoy Julienne, even though it did add a certain masochistic thrill. When he stopped talking he could hear the other chatter; the continuously circulating data flow between his half of the brain and her half. Some parts of the experience were extremely cool. Like, for example, Arcade Mode; another phrase of his own invention and guaranteed to get a frown of exasperation from Julienne. And, when they found time to be intimate it was truly mind-blowing, and every other over-exercised cliché used by normal folk. Monopols, as Mex had started calling those unfortunates who had one mind each. Yes, he was truly blessed, even if he talked a lot more than he used to.

"Engage Arcade Mode," Mex injected into the shared canvas of their minds. In response, an image of a man being flayed alive materialized behind his eyes. The features were indistinct, but the mop of black hair identified him uniquely.

Julienne and Mex's shoulder blades kissed briefly as they moved to stand back to back. The spheres were materialising from all directions. A slight gasp of defied probability heralded each sphere's arrival. As soon as reality's objections were thoroughly overcome, the sphere started to taste its surroundings. Tongues of Verity Space made conscious, slithered amongst the probability strands of the local reality, looking for human influence. The Nodes were like beacons to the spheres, or, maybe, catnip. Inexorably drawing spheres closer, while the tentacles writhed and drooled. The virtual saliva corroded human history on contact. Searching back through moments in quantum history, to the probability fork marking the point of contamination. Then history was reset, as if humans had never existed.

Actual, physical, humans were hunted and erased.

Nodes caused a feeding frenzy.

In the first days of the Reset fear had driven many to reject the Nodes. The spheres hunted apparently randomly, offering the illusion of safety in numbers. That is, unless a Node was around. Then they converged like sharks on a dying whale, devouring anyone nearby.

After the Nodes became the Satyagrahi, every refugee in the migrating city revered and treasured each of the surviving thirty-eight Nodes. Many had sacrificed themselves to save a Node, hoping their death would help to save loved ones. So, they nurtured the Nodes within their city, even though it brought the spheres to the threshold of their home.

Mex had his eyes open, but his concentration was turned inwards.

Wrap-around perception. Perfect peripheral vision.

This was Arcade Mode.

Two pairs of eyes and ears created the basic canvas, and painted it with targets and assets. Additional sensors, of more esoteric and less natural design, augmented the scene with strategic texture. At the centre of this landscape a four armed composite creature danced a lethal waltz. Mex had never been particularly ambidextrous or, really, any kind of dexterous, but two of the arms belonged to him. Each was armed with a pneumatic fléchette gun, and he never missed.

An Oikake – Mex's pet name for the Eidolon spheres and a homage to an era when computers offered little more than pixelated entertainment - drifted towards the huddle of Nodes from the South. Mex brought it to a flailing halt with two pellets of biotechnology. At the same time, his right hand was tracking another Oikake floating indecisively a hundred metres above them. Chromatic tentacles writhed from the surface of the first Oikake, and it started to advance again.

"Shit", Mex thought.

"I see it," Julienne thought back.

As one, Mex and Julienne swivelled a quarter turn and she pumped a different strain of fléchette into the sphere.

"They're definitely developing an immunity to the original Martian strain," Mex worried.

"That means they communicate, or they are elements of a larger organism."

"Lovely, but it still means my gun doesn't work any more."

"Don't exaggerate." Julienne chided. "There is no useless information. The tactical subsystems are already adjusting for a multicellular enemy with limited cooperation."

"If you say so." Mex mentally shrugged.

The aerial Oikake was on the move. It sank towards a lone pair of refugees. The man and woman dragged each other South, away from the distant Reset. Mex and Julienne positioned themselves between the fleeing civilians and the sphere. The undulations of its tentacles became agitated and the Oikake accelerated its descent. The Mex/Julienne composite viewed the reality nullifying sphere with an overlay of tactical projections. At ten metres they raised all four arms and pumped one of each fléchette strain into the sphere's surface.

The entry wounds formed a perfect diamond as the sphere desperately attempted to implode around the pellets. Tunnels of determinism burrowed to the heart of the sphere, where they coalesced into an amorphous blob. The Oikake shed globules of reality, and lost any coherence of shape or motion. Destroyed realities oozed from the fragments: entire genetic lineages compressed into a pleading face, hierarchies of civilisations flowing like molten rubble and historical eras agglomerated into a discordant scream.

The fragments flailed for a few seconds before dissolving completely from sight.

"Did we win?" Mex thought.

"No. It just retreated back into Verity space."

"I'll take that as a win."

"The Nodes have selected a target."

The five Nodes were sat in a rough circle amongst the churned soil and rock. A hole was starting to form at the locus of their concentration. The hole was in the air a metre above the ground; a speck of vacuum sucking at the dust laden breeze. A corona of scintillation marked the boundary between sanity and unreality. The speck grew into a funnel, which squirmed and mutated with the strain of existing in only three dimensions. At the centre a miniature Oikake appeared and started to grow.

Mex blinked hard as the perspective shifted. The Oikake was not growing. It was approaching from a distant place, but never moving from the very centre of the Node circle.

At full size, the Oikake obscured or replaced the funnel between spaces, and mostly filled the circle. Suddenly, the sphere came alive and lunged towards one of the Nodes. There was a dark flash and the leading part of the sphere flattened against an invisible barrier. The sphere recoiled, rotated the oblate face downwards and lunged again. Like a trapped bird behind a window, the sphere continued to batter itself against the barrier. Progressively, it lost coherency and became a ragged blob.

After five minutes, the Oikake retreated to the centre of the circle and started to withdraw from this universe, back to its masters in Verity space. The Nodes inhaled as one, and the level of reality manipulation jumped a gear. Without using Julienne's donated implants, Mex could feel existence and certainty surrender control to the five minds sat before him. Even from ten metres, pairs of pi electrons in his neural tubulins were losing entanglement. As the Frohlich condensates lost coherence, the brain's gamma-wave synchronisation faltered. His consciousness fragmented into discord. Mex was still struggling to adapt to his mind being linked to Julienne's, but when the Nodes did their voodoo he gained a momentary insight into full-blown schizophrenia.

The bits of his mind Mex could identify as his own, tried not to think. The others whispered random insults and insidious lies. Or maybe, they were pure gibberish, that he chose to interpret as malicious.

"Please die quickly," Mex whispered towards the Oikake.

The sphere answered with a strangled groan of twisted physicality, before admitting the absurdity of its existence and fading into nothingness.

*

Lesana drifted towards consciousness, the morning news stream merging with her own dreams. Slowly, the mixture of celebrity gossip and product placement condensed into discrete images. A familiar morning fatigue drifted up from her body. She groaned and rolled over, burying her face in the coolness of her pillow. The splice feed vanished as the lasers lost contact with her eyes and she enjoyed a few moments of tranquillity.

Mistaking her stillness for sleep, the building A.I. chimed. A calm, but passionless, voice drifted down from the ceiling. "Lesana, I'm sorry to intervene," it lied, "but you instructed me not to let you sleep-in again."

"I know, I know," she grizzled into the pillow, before rolling her legs to the ground, and dragging her body upright. She had a fleeting vision of a pair of stars sinking into a sea blue horizon, and then her eyes acknowledged the waking reality of her grass-green cubicle. "Ross, can we lose the grass and trees and go for more of a beach feel?"

If the building minded her shortening its name there was no hint in the tone of the reply. "Of course, Lesana, I will reconfigure your cubicle while you are at work."

The tickling of the cool grass on the underside of her feet immediately started to fade as the floor covering withered and started to be absorbed back into the building fabric. Lesana treated herself to a stimulant from the dispenser in the kitchen, and promised herself she would not waste her calories on any more that day. At least she now felt able to face the day, and the hours of tedium it presented.

At lunchtime she left her office building, and walked blinking into the bright yellow of the sunlit street. Her eyes felt sore and slightly square from a morning of bureaucratic splicing. She had reconciled two database irregularities from customers who decided to change their names to avoid a calorific debt. People never learnt how minor a name was amongst the metrics of the corporate customer profiles. Someone could download into a completely new body, and she would be able to spot them by their spending habits within a month. Still, it was soulless work, and not even remotely interesting from the featureless perspective of statistical data.

She spent a few calories at a new sandwich bar, freshly imprinted in her consciousness by the subliminal hoarding of a taxi drone. Lesana sat chewing thoughtfully in the comforting warmth of summer. Her mind drifted back to the splice show she had fallen asleep to last night. Two of the main characters, whose names remained just beyond the reach of her tongue, had been about to reveal their mutual love. She could not remember what had happened. She had a vague feeling of cosmic irony intervening at the last moment, but nothing specific. Maybe it was a cliff hanger, and she would find out tonight, but more likely she had fallen asleep at the wrong moment, again. The building had recommended a sleep therapist but...

"Everybody out!"

Lesana opened her eyes to a world dimmer than her dreams.

"Abandon building!" the same voice demanded, without a hint of irony.

Lesana's spirit plummeted into the reality of her tired and hungry body. She tried to stretch her curved spine. Her legs jutted from the small blanket, and leached heat into the cold floor. She became aware of dozens of other bodies around her: coughing, moaning, crying and pleading. She couldn't tell where her skin ended and her clothes began. In an idle moment, between bouts of terror, she had tried to decide if, given the chance, she would kill for a hot shower.

With barely a coherent word, they each wrapped whatever counted as precious in a sleeping blanket, and poured into the corridor. There they joined the other refugees with slack-jaw, dead-ahead stares.

Lesana stumbled on a lump of freshly scarred sandstone. The man walking next to her reached out a steadying hand, before jumping across the shallow trench. Lesana grunted her gratitude, and stopped to catch her breath. The disturbed ground snaked left and merged with the engineered slab of a building. The logo of the MynCorp Administration Division was frozen, mid-cycle, on the rear façade. The bread crumbs of churned soil and rock lead from the base of the building, passed Lesana, and were swallowed by the wall of the Reset. She had heard people claim that inside the Reset history was erased. The building's trail would be expunged, along with any other building whose ruins lay under foot, any crops grown to feed people, right back to brick and steel houses of the pre-corporation era.

Lesana had no idea how history could be undone. Covered up, or hidden, maybe. If something she knew was erased from history, would she still remember it? Or them? Was it truly not erased until she and any other witnesses were also eliminated? Surely, everything had to be changed in one instant. Or at least, at the speed of causality. Was that what the Reset was? The speed at which reality could rewind?

And how did anyone know what was happening inside?

She made herself look at the Reset. It emerged from the ground and rose high into the sky. It looked less like a hemisphere these days, as if the centre was sinking into the Earth under the weight of so much destruction. The surface itself was hard to look at. Realities writhed within its confines. Infinite images of people and things coalesced and degenerated too fast for her mind to grasp. Her sight seemed to slide right off the surface and fall to the ground, or fling itself up to the sky. There was nothing for her mind to grab hold of. It was visually frictionless.

Lesana could see the ground being swallowed up as the Reset advanced. Boulders and bits of static structures were engulfed with barely a ripple on its surface. A small copse of trees gave it a momentary pause for thought. Lesana had seen this before. Living things, non-people living things, were obviously harder to unwind from human history.

She still had a kilometre walk to the nearest mobile building and it was already level with her position. Lesana dragged air deep into her lungs and rejoined the exodus. The first wave of people had arrived at the base of the nearest building. They were congregating around the main entrance, but Lesana couldn't see anyone going inside.

Lesana began to hear raised voices when she was still two hundred metres away. A few people broke away and started to head towards the main herd of buildings. A more urgent tension fuelled their stride. The main gaggle of people was radiating agitation.

"Those who are able," shouted one of the militia from the top step of the entrance, "should head to Tesla and Arlington buildings."

"We'll never make it," pleaded voices from the crowd.

The militia man raised his arms in the air. He probably thought it was a calming gesture, but the gun swinging from its shoulder strap twisted it into a threat. "This building is losing ground. We're about to commence evacuation. Those who cannot walk, form a queue. We're bringing in a couple of vehicles."

"No way. You're lying." a male voice shouted. "There are Nodes inside. It must be safe."

Lesana had seen it happen a few times over the last weeks. When frightened people gathered in a big enough group, any suggestion of persecution rapidly led to panic. She often felt it herself. Her life was so dependant on the few souls able to fight back; people whose thought and decision processes were so removed from her own. They must be making the kind of decisions she would never be able to make. Including, who to save and who to sacrifice. Everyone in the crowd hoped and expected the impossible, but paranoia was rife. One poorly chosen word, and suspicion became confirmation of betrayal.

Another figure appeared on the steps. The cries and pleas of the crowd were strangled into silence. The woman was almost two metres high and radiated immutability. Black metal traced neural networks across the skin of her skull. As it vanished into the collar of her tunic, it turned into hard steel, as if the inorganic black was an attempt to blend in with Terran humans; a vestigial concession to mortality. Even without an obvious weapon, she was more intimidating than the militia squad.

There was a whirr, like a Gatling gun spinning up. The female automaton spoke."The Nodes will stay until we have cleared the building. The longer you linger, the more you risk their lives. If they die…"

She did not need to finish the sentence. There was some grumbling, but the crowd turned on its heels and gathered momentum. Lesana moved away with them, carried forward by the energy of fear.

A woman nearby spoke to the man who held her arm, "Arlington has been turning people away for days, and I left Tesla because it was too overcrowded."

"We need to move faster. Get to Tesla before they start turning people away. We're not all going to make it."

Lesana felt more tears rising from her throat. Liquefied futility, they burned hope from her cheeks. A single drop fell to the ground. She watched the spot of earth turn ferrous red.

Lesana struck out on her own.

The refugee party was fragmenting anyway. Lesana could hear the fear in their voices. Exclamations and strangled whispers preceded each splintering. When they had evacuated their previous home, uncertainty had drawn them into a singe huddle, but now each mini collective was hoping to improve its survival chances by out-thinking the rest. Each time a group broke away Lesana felt a jitter of uncertainty pass through those who remained. Eventually, certainty was eroded to nothing and the exodus became a free-for-all.

Lesana had made a decision while staring at the tear-stained clump of dirt. With reality unwinding all around her, she was determined to become the engineer of her own destiny. She reached the spiralling tuber of the Tesla building and moved on without breaking stride. After an hour of forced march her legs felt like lead. In her mind, humans simply were not designed to walk so far. Her hips and joints were specially evolved for riding: acceleration couch, taxi pod, zero-G cradle or even the back of some animals.

Frustration was an effective anaesthetic. Lesana pushed on deeper into the main herd of buildings. The valley breeze did not reach into the heart of the herd. The air was still and only disturbed by a moan leaking up between the grains of soil. Deep underground the churning heart of each building was dragging at the soil and rock, pulling itself away from the pursuing threat. Lesana could not be sure if the buildings or the Earth were making the groaning sound. She felt like she was walking on the surface of an ocean filled with particularly melancholy whales.

The only other sound was the creaking of feeding tethers. The black ganglia formed a cat's-cradle forty metres above Lesana's head. Mostly the buildings marched in haphazard formation, but sometimes a building would start to slow or meander drunkenly, adding another knot to the web.

Most of the buildings had stopped talking, but rumours were rife. The residential habitat brains had never been designed for extended periods of energy deprivation. They seemed to be drawing from a reservoir of simple instincts. Despite the unsustainable energy drain, they continued to move away from the Reset. Lesana tried not to dwell on whether the buildings were attempting to save the occupants or running blindly to save their own existence.

The lack of aerial activity, birds or taxi drones, reminded Lesana of the other rumour. As far as she knew, carnivorous eating habits were limited to the more military-minded buildings. It was too hard to contemplate; the home that had nurtured her since birth, might become desperate enough to consider her as food.

Lesana shuddered. Imaginary digestive juices crawled across her skin, burning under the trace of her finger tips. She had to ask herself why she was searching for the heart of the web. Why was she making her way towards the two buildings absolutely known to eat anything, including people? Before she could counter the doubts, a vista opened up through the city. One of the Jefferson Buildings cut a putrid wound on the horizon.

Jefferson A and B had flitted on the edges of her awareness for as long as she could remember. At one time they had been identical twin towers; domiciles for the aspirational. So advanced they were rumoured to have used the Nexus to calculate resident's desires before they were even aware of them. The pinnacle of decadence, reserved for MynCorp's highest energy generators. Some said the buildings had become disgusted at their sybaritic existence, or developed an ego sufficient to rebel against corporate servitude. A brave few suggested a deliberate act of terrorism by an anti-corporate programmer.

Officially, the buildings were simply defective. The fact that MynCorp had never shut down and dissected the buildings told Lesana the more esoteric explanations were unlikely.

Defective or not, the towers terrified Lesana. Regardless of their true nature, there was something about them that tapped into her fears. Fear of decay, malignant growth and predatory hunger. Yet, she was slightly more scared of being erased from history; a pointless death versus a pointless existence.

Lesana acknowledged an indignant sense of injustice stirring in the festering pit of toxins that had replaced her stomach. She swallowed hard before it could erode her determination.

"Been there. Done that. Bored with feeling sorry for myself," she chanted.

Lesana looked straight at the Jefferson tower. She did not turn to stone or melt into a nutritious soup.

"You're not so tough."

Lesana picked up her flagging legs and marched directly towards the mutilated spires. The buildings flanking her path seemed to moan in despair at her folly.

*

When Romany Eight stepped into the pod, Sardon felt a grimace take hold of his face. The fluid grace of her stride had leached away with the deceptive youthfulness of her face. Her movements were now jagged, like accelerated video of duelling plants. In Terran terms, her face had aged by a decade in just a few months. For a DogStar affiliate she must have lost closer to a century.

Pimlico spoke while Sardon was still bringing his facial muscles back under absolute control. "By the red dust, you look rough. Whatever you're taking, Romany, it's killing you."

For once, Sardon envied the Martian's straight-talking parochial charm.

Romany Eight smiled carefully, causing a cascade of unnecessary muscle spasms. "I have found it necessary to accelerate my body. The situation is developing more rapidly than I am used to." Her speech was clipped and left her breathless.

"If it's any consolation, things are happening faster than any of us can deal with," Sardon acknowledged.

Pimlico said nothing. His evolving face had passed from androgynous to masculine since the last meeting. His shoulders had squared and residual breasts were still fading into the background chest muscles.

Romany did not look soothed by Sardon's admission.

So much for solidarity in adversity, thought Sardon. Everything was out of kilter. The natural order of things had been seriously disturbed. MynCorp was no longer the dominant force in the market. The cartel itself was unbalanced without ▨; the collection of metal space rats had crawled inside their asteroids and turned out the lights. Either that, or they were all dead. Sardon knew one of them still lived, but Alyona Semanov had abandoned her seat in the cartel in favour of playing soldier with the anti-corps.

Sardon reached out a steadying hand as his stomach reacted to a change in the pod's altitude. There was the slightest of vibrations as the structure adjusted its figure and picked up a fresh thermal. Pimlico gave him a quizzical look.

"The pod's mind is on a starvation diet. It makes its reactions somewhat..." For a moment Sardon struggled for the right word. "...mechanical."

"From what I hear, MynCorp is a little short of minds, starved or otherwise," Pimlico casually breathed during a routine fingernail examination.

"We had to move to secure the Nexus during the current hostilities." Sardon replayed the sentence, checking none of the shock at losing the Nodes showed through. There was no point denying the shut down of the Nexus. The other corporations had been the biggest account holders. Processing data on scales beyond rationality, and paying with the tiniest morsel of each transaction. An accumulation of data, which made MynCorp the most powerful institution in human history. A reservoir of data made worthless by the absence of the Nexus to store or interpret it. The most valuable asset in the Universe, and Sardon had stood helpless and watched it being unplugged, one Node at a time.

Pimlico smiled. "Of course," he said.

Sardon decided he had preferred the Martian more when he was female.

"And how are things on Mars? Any trouble being accepted back after Durga Corp abandoned the population to their fate?" Sardon countered.

"We have found a new equilibrium with the people."

"Of course," Sardon retorted.

Romany Eight rose from her seat. "Must we?" Impatience and frustration tainted each word. "Can we get to the point?"

Sardon felt his world lurch another degree away from true. DogStar traded in patience. It had always been their unique selling feature. They played the long game. Romany Eight had never had a hurried thought or uttered an impatient word in her very long life.

Until now.

Pimlico laughed. "I thought the whole point of these meetings was to make cryptic comments while trying to prize a little information out of each other."

"Have you seen what's happening on the surface?" she said with open exasperation.

Sardon watched her face carefully. Entrenched fear, and whatever drugs she was taking, had stripped away her strategic caution. She was ripe for exploitation.

"Any news from home?" he asked with just the right level of compassion.

"You know it will take years to find out anything."

"Sorry. How thoughtless of me. I'm sure the colonies are far enough away to escape this madness and destruction. They'll probably be helping us rebuild, once this is all over."

"If we bother," Pimlico said.

"Quite," Sardon said through thin lips. "Let's just hope the Martian reprieve is not a temporary state. We'll need Durga's resourcefulness before too long."

"So," Romany said.

"So?"

"So, what's the plan?"

"Ah, the plan," Sardon said sagely. "MynCorp are working on counter-measures to the quantum anomalies."

"And?"

"We are making progress."

"What about evacuation plans?"

"We're not ready to flee just yet."

"Not for you. For the population."

"Evacuating the population is completely impractical and offers very little opportunity for profit."

Pimlico laughed again. It was starting to sound a little manic to Sardon.

Romany took time to collect herself. Eventually, she managed to say, "You know what I see? I see MynCorp looking increasingly irrelevant. The anti-corp group, which have been causing us all so many problems recently, seem to be doing more to fight the invasion than all of our combined resources."

"What you see as irrelevance. I see as strategy," Sardon bluffed.

"So why are we here?"

"You asked to be kept abreast. And to be honest, if we are talking about relevance, DogStar are not really bringing much to the table just now."

"We're doing what we can."

"Aren't we all."

Chapter 2

Kaamil floated at the epicentre of the Suparna's new habitation zone. A swan-white jumpsuit hugged his gaunt frame. His bare feet pointed straight down like fins. Combined with his skeletal ankles, they looked useless as load bearing appendages. Tendrils of indigo metal emerged from his neck and left arm. They swayed on unseen currents, completing the aquatic illusion.

Six concentric spheres spun around him. The smallest was four hundred metres in diameter. The largest was almost twice as big. Partly as a tribute to the original Chinese generation balls, circular apertures in each jade green sphere provided a clear line of sight through to the neighbouring spheres.

As Kaamil watched a rare alignment occurred in the spinning spheres, and he caught a dazzling glimpse of a cloud wrapped Earth. The alignment lasted a few seconds, before a city of accommodation blisters and snaking conduits truncated his vision.

A momentary flash of pride energised the air in his lungs. The ship, his Suparana, had responded majestically to all that had been asked of her. A few months ago she had been drifting rudderless through the solar system, surrounded by a cloud of her own glistening innards. After weeks of self-repair, she had limped back into Earth orbit. She would probably never return to interstellar space, but she was back in control of her destiny. Since then, she had completely redesigned herself. Any vestigial indication of her deep space heritage had been swallowed up as she embraced her new role. Kaamil's Suparna was now the command and control centre for the human resistance against an alien force bent on genocide.

Earth's last hope.

An old fear leaked from Kaamil's joints and drained the warmth from his skin. His nemesis was stirring in its lair.

Pride.

Arrogance.

He only had one lifetime to repay an immeasurable debt. Humility was the currency of his redemption. The Suparna had no such debt and yet she was serving others with total dedication and devotion.

Kaamil surrendered his pride in the Suparna, and instead drew inspiration and determination.

He felt a distant gasp of injected air linked to a release of complex volatile compounds associate with dirt, adrenalin and blood. A team had returned from the Earth, and were being triaged on the underside of sphere three. Kaamil experienced the familiar knot of dread contort his stomach, but he was glad to have something outside his head to concentrate on.

With the slightest manipulation of the structure around him, Kaamil's body started to drift from the ship's epicentre and fall towards the inner surface of the first sphere. He fell head first, accelerating sluggishly. A makeshift medical bay passed underneath. The facilities on the inner sphere were reserved for the most seriously incapacitated. Some had physical injures, but most were broken at a fundamental level beyond medical help. The scalps of two nurses bobbed beneath him as they tended patients. A young man lay flat on his back, eyes open and staring. For a moment Kaamil felt a strong sense if he fell into the Nodes eyes he would be swallowed whole.

The shell continued its rotation and Kaamil passed through the centre of one of six circular holes. He immediately started to slow. Looking back between his feet at the uninhabited outer surface, a wave of metal passed underneath. Kaamil let the aggregation of mass slip back towards uniformity and removed the meagre gravitational field within the inner sphere.

The second shell was spinning about its own axis, tilted at a giddy angle from the first. Kaamil's eyes told him he was tumbling uncontrollably while his inner ear insisted he was stationary. He was grateful his stomach had no opinion, despite the recent introduction of solid food into his diet.

Kaamil passed through the apertures in each shell, slowing more rapidly each time. Each shell had a different direction and rate of spin except the final outer shell. As Kaamil emerged from the fifth shell, the bustling sixth shell appeared to be almost stationary above him. He was 'falling' at walking pace now. With ten metres to go, Kaamil tucked himself into a ball, flipped his major axis and landed with barely a grimace. His feet slipped half a metre as friction removed a residual discrepancy in angular momentum.

"Kaamil, its good to see a friendly face," Nomia smiled and touched his hand with hers. Strips of ivory coloured fabric hung from her arms. Similar coloured strips of various size were draped over her shoulders and wrapped themselves in loose knots around her hips and legs. Impossibly fragile feet and hands, the colour of finest porcelain, projected from the folds. Since Kaamil had first met her, she had allowed blond hair to grow in poorly controlled waves which roamed her shoulders. A smear of blood tinged dirt crossed her face like war paint.

"General Nomia, are you okay?"

"General? I don't think I like that."

"Sorry. I heard people use the title. I assumed... I'm sorry."

"It's okay Kaamil. It's just too brutal a reminder of all the people depending on us."

Kaamil felt a flicker of jealousy at the thought of sharing her care; another residual arrogance in need of dissolution. "People need someone to believe in."

"I don't want to be responsible for false hope."

"It's better than no hope."

Nomia laughed. Aeons of pain fell like dust from her face. "When did you become the sagely one? You sound like José."

"Where is José?"

"Still down there." She nodded towards her feet.

Kaamil instinctively allowed telemetry from the Suparna to mingle with his vision. He saw the space directly below their feet. The Earth was indeed drifting past as the habitation sphere spun on an axis perpendicular to the Suparna's orbit. It was entirely possible Nomia was tapping into Verity Space, and could see the space about her even more clearly than his artificially enhanced senses. But Kaamil was gradually becoming aware that ordinary people often used such gestures symbolically rather than to impart specific information.

"How goes the fight?" he asked.

"Not much of a fight. All we can do is slow the slaughter."

"To what end?"

"You should be careful of the company when you ask such questions, but I know what you mean. If there is no hope then what are we fighting for? The answer is, I'm not sure." Nomia was somewhere else for a few moments. When she returned she asked, "how is the Suparna coping?"

"We are short of a few raw materials, but the major refactoring is complete. The inner habitation shell is finished, and the most seriously injured are being moved into the specialist care facilities."

"And the cloaking? Is it effecting her operations?"

"Nothing we've detected. As victims of causality, I'm not sure we could notice."

"Good. We're all grateful. You could have both run. Maybe even have escaped. It means a lot to me you stayed."

"It never occurred to us to leave." It was the truth, but she laughed as if he was lying.

"Thank you," she said again.

"So, what is the plan?"

"Time."

"Time?"

"There's an ongoing dialogue with the Eidolons."

"You're talking to them?"

"Nothing as linear. It's like a court case where the questions and answers are mixed up."

"And where the prosecution, judge and jury are the same."

"Well, there is that. Our greatest hope really comes from the fact they didn't wipe us out instantly. If they had come at the Earth like they did on Mars, we wouldn't be having this conversation. What they're trying to do is abhorrent to the Universe. Unravelling so many millennia of entrenched quantum collapses, stretches the definition of improbable. Add in the complexity of their new found moral affinity for non-human life, and they really are fishing in the shallows of reality's river."

Kaamil nodded. He understood very little, except that there was the faintest of hopes. It was enough.

"When was the last time you slept?" he asked.

"I'm asleep now."

"What?"

"I wanted to talk to you, but the war doesn't seem to respect personal time. Eventually, even you and I have to sleep."

Kaamil opened his eyes again. It was dark. He was alone with his rasping breath.

Light and telemetry flickered into life, like an erratic neon light.

*

There was a point of perfect calm. Nomia stole a breath. At that moment, it was the loudest force on the Suparna.

Nomia held the breath as ransom against the fates. A second later a thump of displaced air heralded her reward.

A huddle of exhausted bodies appeared in front of her. Their ankles surrendered to a sudden shift in inertial reference frame. They collapsed to their knees in a posture of abject surrender. One of the figures was bigger than the other five – a tension around Nomia's heart released as she counted six living returnees – his skin was without the pallid purple blotches of the others, and he had black hair which turned from wavy to curly as it spread towards his chin. Grey was starting to leech colour from the strands behind his ears. This unkempt beast was her José. Nomia's feelings were much simpler than love; she simply would not exist without him. He had died once, and she had fought on. For a while she believed she might survive, but it had been soul wrenching. In truth, José had never really been far away. He had simply hidden from death in a secluded probability crevice.

Nomia wanted to ask José how he had come by the cut under his left eye. She needed to run her fingers through his hair, to brush away the flakes of congealed blood that dulled the black. Touching her forehead to his and sharing a stolen moment, felt more important than the battle to come.

Their minds met a millisecond before their eyes. The flicker of a connection would have to be enough, for now. Her turn had come around again.

Nomia breathed out.

The sound was lost amongst dust, screams, mayhem and death.

Nomia's team materialised in tight formation on the trailing-edge of the city. The enemy was on them instantly. Even this was a victory of sorts. As long as Nomia and the five Nodes by her side were in the vicinity, the spheres would ignore humanity.

The rest of humanity, she reminded herself.

Six Nodes was the critical number. Any fewer and the loss of one would be catastrophic to the others. Her team were Cretheis, Teledice, Ethemea, Chania and Oinoie. All names from mythology. All nymphs of one kind or another. Three of them were physically male, but they had all chosen nymph names in misguided homage to Nomia. Since their liberation from the Nexus, they had found time and individuality enough to chose names, but their gender and sexuality would have to wait. The Nodes were physically mature, but in all other respects they were child soldiers. If they had not been fighting for the very existence of humankind, the guilt would have overwhelmed Nomia.

They remained cross-legged where they had materialised. There was no strategically advantageous high ground in this battle, and the enemy would come at them indefinitely.

Towering above them was a stationary building. Refugees emerged from the entrance in dribs and drabs. They braced themselves against the chaos of battle. Their eyes were wide with adrenaline, fear and expectation. As they moved clear of the building's shadow, everyone of them stole backward glances at the Reset. Without exception, shock robbed their faces of expression. The Reset rose high into the sky like a mercurial tsunami. It hung above them all, threatening to crash down when fickle whim dictated.

The first sphere was on them in seconds. The honey in their trap was a construct styled on the human consciousness. A representation of the Downey engine; a quantum decision-making machine of theoretical perfection, inspired by the Carnot cycle heat engine in thermodynamics. Such a distilled representation of humanity was irresistible to the Spheres, triggering a primary directive and overriding all other pursuits. The jaws of the trap were made of hardened determinism, forged in the mind of each Node.

The first sphere took the bait, shimmering into physical space at the centre of the Node's concentration. A shell of tempered reality isolated the sphere from Verity Space, the source of its existence. The effect was instantaneous. There was no writhing battle or barrage of improbable missiles. The sphere was erased from existence and had probably never existed.

There was no jubilation. The trap had been sprung, and could not be reset on the battlefield. Moments later they were fighting for their lives armed with only their will.

Nomia, Chania and Oinoie targeted the first sphere to attack. Collectively, they set about dismantling it, layer by layer. Nomia and José had learnt much from the battle on Mars. The sphere's weakness was its determination to recreate a single reality, by unwinding all the state changes caused by humans since their inception; returning a point on the world to a virgin state free of human corruption. Its tentacles felt out points in physical and Verity space, looking for an untainted solution. The three nymphs countered each attack with closed loops of causality, trapping the sphere is a series of tiny prison of looped probability. The defence took total focus and trust.

Cretheis, Teledice, Ethemea fought to keep the other three nymphs safe. They formed a defensive cordon, repelling any other sphere which approached. The defence was not elegant or particularly damaging to the spheres, there was no time for tactics. Teledice led them in a furious repulsion, trashing out with blades of discontinuous probability. Cutting, slashing but always falling back, being pressed harder and harder against the single battle at the core of their circle.

Nomia we have to jump, Teledice thought. There are too many this time.

Nomia tried to answer, but she could find no power left to create words. She could feel tremors criss-crossing her body and sweat collecting in her eyebrows. The sphere was adapting to their attack, randomly jumping from one probability stream to another to prevent stagnant cycles. They were struggling to contain the sphere, It might even break free.

Nomia, Teledice screamed. We can't hold them.

Okay, Nomia relented. Focus on defence. Teledice jump us back to the Suparna.

The world around the circle became intangible. In the last moment before they jumped, the sphere's lost interest in the Nymphs and fell back, leaving Nomia free to take in the scene. She was horrified by the scale of the battle. While she had been concentrating on a singe sphere, Teledice and the others had been fighting off a dozen more.

Oh my god, Teledice, how could you fight so many? Nomia projected.

There was no answer.

Teledice? Nomia pushed her focus back along their probability stream, bridging the new reality and old. Seeing the five nodes on-board the Suparna and the six which had been on Earth. But there were only five.

Teledice existed with zero probability. She had been erased.

*

"Stop looking at me like that," Sera complained.

"Do you prefer this?" A translucent eyelid closed horizontally across Bergur's eyes.

"I'd rather you didn't stare at me at all."

"Sorry, after a couple of days I got bored looking at this blinking red light."

"Watch Ben, he might appreciate the attention." They both looked at the Node. His face was slack and vacant. Sera grimaced and massaged her neck. "I'm too uncomfortable to be bored," she complained. "How are you even standing?"

Sera followed Bergur's gaze down to his pylon thick legs. He had little in the way of a neck, so he flexed his upper and lower back to get a clear view. The pose made Sera think of a rhino. Bergur was a distinctly odd purple colour, and there was no horn between his multi-flapped mouth and the double eyelid eyes, but still there was something of the rhinoceros about him.

"You're staring at me again," she noted.

"So, are you sisters?"

"Who?"

"You and Yakini."

"Sisters? No, that would be all wrong. We don't look remotely similar."

Bergur shrugged.

Sera gapped. "Don't tell me, all Martians look alike."

"I've only met two. What do the males look like? Do they have some sort of display crest on their heads?"

"What?"

"To attract females."

"You're teasing me. You are teasing me?"

Muscles tensed in his shoulders in what Sera chose to interpret as a shrug. His mouth flaps fluttered with pulses of air.

"So, you're not sisters."

"Yakini really hasn't talked to you about me."

"She's been a bit busy saving humanity."

"Convenient."

The roar of the engines and rattling of the ship's superstructure seemed even louder in the wake of conversation. A few minutes later the Node opened his eyes. He was obviously in severe and prolonged pain. His eyes were wet and shot with red.

"We are in imminent danger."

Except in direct response to a question, it was the first time he had spoken in three days.

Sera looked at the utilitarian bulkhead above her. It had developed an annoying rattle that was threatening to unhinge her sanity. "Is this pile of off-cuts finally going to shake itself apart?"

"No, the threat is external and intelligent."

There was a momentary pause in the crushing acceleration. The engines continued to whine and pour white-fury into space, but it was like there was nothing to push against, or reality had temporarily abandoned attempts to conserve momentum.

It didn't last long. Sera's spine barely had time to straighten before she was once again being compressed into Terran proportions. The Node's eyes were closed again, but his head lolled, rolling with the shaking ship.

"Ben, are you okay?" Sera asked.

Bergur moved across the narrow space and gripped the Node's face in once hand.

"He's out cold. I'll brace his neck before it snaps."

"What do you think happened? Are we still in danger?"

"The ship reported a momentary dislocation in astro-navigation."

"Meaning?"

"Meaning, we jumped about a million kilometres in no measurable time."

"We avoided something"

"Presumably."

"What I wouldn't give for a window," Sera growled. "This ship is so primitive. Who builds with dumb metal in this day and age?"

"⍰ corp."

"I was being rhetorical."

"I like it. Reminds me of home. And if Alyona hadn't leant us her shuttle, we would barely be out of Earth orbit."

"They should have sent you and Alyona. You could have spent days locked up together, testing each other's mettle."

"I don't think Yakini would like that."

"You'd be surprised."

"Anyway, you think Mod solidarity stretches that far?"

"Que?"

"Just because I've had a few weak bits genetically erased and Alyona has had them surgically removed, do you think your Martian chums would welcome us with open arms?"

"I know why I have to be here, but it doesn't stop me complaining about it."

"Just enjoy the ride."

"The ride that is slowly crushing me to death? By the time we get there, I'll be no taller than you."

Bergur ended the conversation with a dismissive grunt. Sera performed another visual tour of the shuttle. It was not much more than a hollowed out missile. The three of them were the payload. Everything else was dedicated to thrust. There were spaces for a crew of three. Each bay was a semicircular alcove with a number of ports and orifices. Some of them had obvious biological purpose. These did not disturb Sera; she had endured worse in long haul mining vehicles on Mars. There were other apertures that looked like the inner workings of a splice terminal. In Bergur's alcove a control console had been grafted into these ports. He occasionally used this to interact with the rudimentary brain of the ship. In the other two, acceleration couches had been mounted. Ben and Sera were confined to these. A normal Terran would have struggled to stand against the relentless acceleration. For the fragile Node and Sera's low gravity frame, it was painful enough just sitting. She had tried to sleep, but each time she woke up gasping for air. Her lungs only seemed to function awake. The pain and lack of sleep could be contributing to her general bad mood. It couldn't possibly be an irrational dislike of Bergur based solely on jealousy.

"Do you think Alyona plugs herself into these ports?" Sera pondered.

"Probably"

"Don't you find that disturbing?"

Bergur opened all his mouth flaps, revealing a perfect circle of needle shaped teeth. It might have been a grin. Whatever it signified, Sera found the ship's human-machine interface less disquieting.

Sera crossed her arm defensively and demanded, "Are we nearly there yet?"

*

Lesana's conviction lasted to within two hundred metres of the Jefferson towers. The coal-black towers creaked and groaned as they moved, swaying slightly, like a lumbering man. The wind raced to escape the flutings spires, creating a warbling lament. The spires themselves looked like the decaying ribs of a mythological sea beast.

Lesana stood mesmerised until a mechanical screech from behind broke through her reverie.

"They're not as scary as they look."

The woman's voice was coming from the shadowy doorway of a ground vehicle. Caterpillar tracks completely encased its length, with a simple hatch in the side. Even though the thing was stationary, a throaty grumble emanated from a pipe at the back.

"Still, I wouldn't hang around here any longer than necessary," the voice continued. "Hop aboard."

An arm extended from the shadow. It stretched towards Lesana, spanning the gap with disconcerting ease. The hand and fingers were the colour of burnt sand and impossibly elegant. Lesana was convinced the bones within would simple snap if she were to take the hand.

"Come on. We need to keep moving," the voice urged. There was an accent lapping at the edge of the voice, like the ocean at dusk.

Lesana throw off her stupefaction and allowed herself to be hoisted through the hatch.

The vehicle was immediately in motion. The noise and vibration were instantly painful.

"I'm Yakini," the woman shouted.

"You're Martian," Lesana blurted. "Sorry, I don't know why I said... I've never met a... Sorry. I'm Lesana."

"Right, Lesana. We're just going to swing round in front of Jefferson-A, drop off some bait, then we'll get you inside."

"Inside?"

"I assume that's where you were heading."

"Yes."

"You don't sound so sure."

Yakini sat next to a grinning teenager. His hands and feet were operating a series of push-pull levers. He was bouncing in his seat even more than required by the jolting progress of the vehicle.

"Fez," he said.

Lesana assumed this was his name and grinned weakly in response. Most of her senses were objecting in one way or another, but she asked, "What's the smell?"

"Exhaust fumes," Yakini explained. "This is what we've been reduced to. This thing burns petrochemicals. As in, with a real flame."

"How does that make it move?"

"Barely at all," Yakini complained. "You want to help?"

The vehicle swung to a halt, facing its own track marks. Yakini levered open another, much larger, hatch and began pulling pieces of scrap material from the vehicle onto the ground.

Lesana joined in as best as she could. Fez had the poorly connected body of an underweight teenage boy. He and Yakini were both gangly and looked like they would snap in the breeze, but with a few grunts they were shifting bits of defunct pods and other equipment and creating a rough pile on the grass.

Fez looked up at the approaching Jefferson building. "Time," he shouted.

Yakini took Lesana by the arm and dragged her back inside the vehicle. Fez tore up wads of grass as he accelerated back towards the base of the building.

Something pinged off the outside of the vehicle.

Then a second ping.

Lesana didn't dare ask, but a look of concern flashed across her face.

Yakini nodded up. "Splinters of dead polycrete," she said. "The buildings are coming apart at the seams."

"Ten seconds till drop," Fez said.

Yakini took Lesana's hands and looked directly into her face. The Martian's eyes were disconcertingly far apart. "Lesana, you need to follow me as quickly as you can. Okay?"

Lesana nodded.

The vehicle did another sliding stop. Lesana dropped to the ground amongst a cloud of fumes and dust. The caterpillar tracks rattled back into life and the vehicle was pulling away. The ground around then was dotted with splinters of black. A grumbling sound seemed to be coming from all around her.

Yakini was moving. Lesana chased after her with as much haste as her terrified legs could muster.

Lesana started to pull up. Yakini was running full pelt towards a large doorway. The depth of the shadows within and the rough carved surround made it look disturbingly like a mouth, but that was not what made Lesana hesitate. Yakini was running straight at two salt-aged planks pinned across the entrance. Three words were painted in blood-red paint.

CONDEMNED – KEEP OUT

Lesana opened her mouth to object, when Yakini went straight through the opening with barely a ripple of disturbed photons.

Lesana sighed in recognition of the continuing decline of her fortunes, and stepped out of the light.

The lobby of the building was dark and decrepit. A slab-like reception desk ran the full length of one wall. Behind it a man and a woman were furiously sorting through sheets of a flat cream material. They seemed to study something on the surface of each and occasionally prod one with some kind of stylus.

Yakini reached down to Lesana's shoulder. "You going to be okay?" she asked. "I have to get upstairs and talk to someone about a meeting. Good luck."

Lesana stammered a thank you. It seemed appropriate even though she wasn't entirely sure what for. Then she tentatively approached the reception desk.

"Excuse me," she said to the man.

He looked up and blinked a couple of times. "Where did you come from?" he asked.

"I was in Magueijo Building until this morning, but we had to evacuate."

"I mean just now. Where did you come from?"

Lesana pointed at the door. She was baffled by the apprising look he gave her.

"What can I do for you?"

"I need somewhere to stay." Lesana rushed to talk over his interruption. "And I want to help."

He put down the sheet he was holding. It was covered in static writing with many parts crossed out and alterations added between the lines.

"Every building has a volunteer work force. Believe me, you wouldn't want to live here unless it was absolutely necessary."

The other receptionist paused and gave Lesana a confirmatory nod.

Lesana tried to make herself taller. "I want to help everyone."

"Did you really walk through the shadow of the Jefferson building to volunteer?" he looked genuinely concerned.

"Mostly. Then I got a lift with Yakini."

"Yakini Akida?"

"The Martian?"

"So, Yakini Akida bought you to the Jefferson building to volunteer in the war effort?"

"I suppose."

"In what capacity do you think you can help?"

Lesana really wanted to start the conversation afresh. "Capacity?"

"What did you do before this?" he held his hand out to encompass the room and beyond.

"Nothing very useful. I studied database anomalies."

The man looked impressed for the third time. "You have no idea how short we are of decent analysts. We have rooms full of data on the Eidolons." He held up the sheets as if they represented a useful storage medium for data. "What's you name?"

"Lesana Abaroa."

He rummaged through the sheet and then scratched at it with the stylus.

"Nice to meet you Ms Abaroa and welcome aboard."

Chapter 3

Yakini rattled her knuckles against the door for a second time. The faintest of tremors reverberated back from the surface; an echo of the Jefferson building's residual desire to serve.

Patience exhausted, Yakini pushed the curtain aside and stuck her head inside. Mex was sat in a corner. He had little choice; the contorted room was almost entirely composed of corners. As barrack rooms went, it was relatively large, but almost devoid of useful space.

"Mex," she said.

Yakini tried to read his posture in profile. His head was cocked slightly towards the remnants of a sound. His hair hung in neglected rat tails, the jet black deadened to slate grey by the dust of battle. One hand lay on his knee. Three fingers twitched with something just short of purpose, but not quite pure agitation.

Mex turned to Yakini. His eyes seemed slow to focus as if his mind was stuck in a groove of atrocities. The creases of devastation sat awkwardly on his eternally sanguine features.

"Yakini," he confirmed.

"I just got a message from Sardon Lucas. He wants to parley."

"Is MynCorp finally going to join the fight?"

"He didn't say. You coming?"

"Now? I've just got back from a sortie."

"You can sleep on the way."

"With your flying?"

The mischievous grin was back where is belonged, but the tremor in his shoulders was more than pure fatigue. He coaxed his body into a standing position and joined Yakini in the corridor.

"Do you want to say good bye to Julienne?" Yakini checked.

"She'll meet us in the lobby."

Yakini had detected no evidence Mex was communing with the woman whose mind he shared. For all she knew, Julienne had been part of the conversation since the moment Yakini knocked.

The carnivorous tendencies of the Jefferson buildings had become more veracious with the exodus. Teams of volunteers worked round the clock to scavenge technology and other titbits from the surroundings. They made piles in the path of the towers, like offerings to an insatiable deity. Mex had once described it as a carrot to a donkey, a carrot and stick, or something equally anachronistic and meaningless.

Yakini just saw the building's appetite as a logistical nightmare and tactical weakness. Nobody knew exactly how the building's deranged minds detected food or how far the sense of smell extended. All the important equipment the resistance had commandeered or otherwise acquired had to be kept out of reach. Consequently, Yakini had a ten minute trot across a meadow to reach the inverted V shape of the Mickelson building. To avoid looking at the Reset, she scanned the path ahead of the mobile city. They were entering the foothills of a mountain range; tiny by Martian standards, but crammed with harsh weather and elemental adversity. Winter had passed in this hemisphere, but Yakini had no idea how dozens of buildings were going to navigate mountain passes.

It was up to Alyona to devise a strategy for the city. Years representing ▢ had made her ruthlessly efficient. She would do whatever it took to preserve the city, including sacrifices Yakini would have found impossible. Yakini was not the only person to use Alyona to make unpalatable decisions, but the woman never complained. A life forged in dimly lit asteroids had made her immune to squeamish indecision. Time and time again the former corporate executives had shown she could be trusted. Yakini hoped Alyona's example had inspired Sardon, but somehow she doubted it.

Yakini exchanged a few words of hearsay with the militia on the entrance to Mickelson building, before picking her way through five floors of refugee and fighters. The press of people triggered spasms of claustrophobia to restrict her breathing. By the time she reached the roof her lungs were aching from clenched breaths.

The rows of flight-pods spread across the roof made her hungry for a cockpit. Another former MynCorp pilot greeted her by name. Yakini vaguely remembered the man from flight-school, but nothing about him. She had been a different person then: driven and certain anything short of total dedication would prevent her from overcoming her racial disadvantage. A few times a year she allowed herself a night of inebriation, sex or both. The remainder of the time she had focussed single-mindedly on becoming the best pilot MynCorp had ever seen. A target she had largely achieved, for all the good it had done her in the end. Assuming this was the end.

Yakini tried to share a few moments of camaraderie with the other pilot, but he looked almost grateful when she asked for a flight-ready pod. She chose one with fixed wings grafted to the bulbous body. Ostensibly, the aerofoils would give them a better chance of surviving a drive failure, but Yakini was really after a more manual flying experience.

The pod bobbed in anticipation as she approached; a good sign the drive was not too depleted. Yakini climbed aboard and instructed the pod to climb vertically. Once they had gained sufficient altitude, Yakini configured the pod for simple forward thrust. The lurch in her stomach, as the pod started to tumble towards the ground, felt like welcoming an old friend.

With minimal manipulation of the wing configuration, Yakini converted the plummet into a glide. The Mickelson roof passed beneath her, and Yakini caught a glimpse of the other pilot calmly applauding. Then the side of the building fell away and she was truly airborne.

"I thought you were going to fly off without me," Mex commented later.

"I was tempted."

Yakini had deliberately overshot the agreed landing spot in favour of performing a grand circuit of the rag-tagged band of meandering buildings; a marching refugee camp of the dispossessed, survivors and an impromptu army. People formed fractured streams between the buildings in a futile hunt for more space, food or sanity.

"Up", Yakini demanded.

The pod's mind was bright enough to pick-up on her impatience. Clouds obscured the ground in seconds. Mex was counting softly behind clasped lips and eyelids. Yakini allowed a flicker of satisfaction to pierce her professional demeanour, then she punched an override. The lump in her stomach did a somersault and moved to the top of her ribcage.

The controls began to respond as they picked up ground speed. Yakini banked and reached inside her mind for the nano-compass embedded between her eyes.

"Make yourself comfortable. This is going to take a couple of hours."

Mex raised an eyebrow and prized his teeth apart. "Are you taking the scenic route?"

"We don't have enough energy for two suborbital flights. We need to use some good old fashion aeronautics."

"How convenient."

Yakini lifted the nose of the craft to climb out of a layer of turbulent air. Mex grimaced as if the manoeuvre was borne of mischief. He repeated the expression each time the atmosphere buffeted the tiny craft.

"Could we spare a little energy to increase the intelligence of the hull?" he asked. "It's going to shake itself apart."

"I'm not sure it would help that much. The Reset is starting to effect global weather patterns. It could be we're seeing the climate without human interference."

"Or, maybe, the giant, impenetrable sphere is just too big for weather to go around."

Yakini continued to talk because Mex seemed to need it, but her concentration was mostly on maintaining attitude with the few instruments she had available. "Who knows," she pondered. "Perhaps, the Earth is due another ice age."

"You're just hoping to tempt holidaymakers to Mars."

"Pale, blobby Terrans lounging next to Lake Vanuatu? Delightful."

"Actually, a bit of lounging sounds tempting."

"Doesn't it just?"

Mex gradually descended into silence. His head nodded loosely as the pod rocked from one pocket of air to the next.

"I can't believe how much I need this?" Mex said without raising his head.

Yakini didn't know if he was talking about sleep or getting away from the battle, so she didn't offer any comment.

"I'm not a fighter," he declared. "Never have been. I'm actually more of a run away sort of person."

Yakini had seen him do little other than fight since they first met on the Svargaloka, but Julienne had introduced him as a technical consultant. Rather than offer encouragement he might not want, Yakini left him to elaborate.

"I'm mostly following Julienne's instructions. Let her worry and strategise, while I pretend it's all a big arcade game."

He must have spotted the corner of Yakini's raised eyebrow, because his voice collected a smattering of defensiveness. "You have no idea what it's like sharing a mind with someone like Julienne."

"Someone like Julienne?"

"That doesn't sound good, does it? Maybe I should go back to sleep now."

The craft's fuselage cut a swath through the atmosphere, shoving air to one side, then sucking it into the churning wake. The air inside the cabin whined and grumbled in sympathy with its tropospheric cousin; white-noise cancelling the silence of the occupants.

Briefly, the atmosphere grew angry, shaking the tiny craft like a baby's rattle, then as calm as patience.

Mex drew Yakini's attention to a small cluster of isolated buildings, grown from the cliffs of an ancient quarry. People huddled together on the roof of each building, their faces and outstretched hands turned to the sky.

Yakini dipped a wing in an acknowledgement. Mex raised a hand to the canopy without enough commitment to fully unfurl the fingers. Three short flashes of orange light twinkled on one roof. A moment later, like a blow to the nose, pain erupted across Yakini's face. She swallowed. Her ears popped and the roar of the atmosphere invaded her head.

"They're shooting at us!" Mex screeched.

Yakini scanned the canopy of the cockpit and identified a ragged spot of bleached sky as the source of the cacophony. The small craft banked hard under Yakini's instruction, bringing the bullet hole in the craft's belly out of the shadows. It was already healing, the roar or air shrivelling into a plaintive hiss.

Several more flashes of light spat bullets into the sky, but the craft's new course made it a much harder target to hit. The barometric pressure in the cabin started to climb, taking with it the brick of pain behind Yakini's cheek bones.

Mex ground his teeth. "Why were they shooting at us?"

"I've no idea. Frightened people do stupid things. I'm going to gain some altitude – make for a less tempting target."

They started to climb, letting the features of the landscape blur into blocks of colour, then into grey, as the first wisps of cloud passed beneath them. Soon, endless rolls of brilliant white cumulus replaced the Earth's surface and the sky turned an impenetrable blue.

Yakini regularly checked the craft's navigation system to assure herself they were actually making progress and to break the illusion of stasis.

A few minutes later the craft shivered as they entered a strand of stratospheric nacreous cloud. The controls pinged to reassure Yakini their course was clear of other craft. As her eyes strained to pierce the gloom ahead, Yakini spotted a vertical tendril of silver, harsh against the soft contours of water crystals. Her head rocked, improving depth perception and ruling out a reflection on the inside of the canopy. Her hand snapped the control stick to the right, beating the curse to her lips by half a heartbeat.

"Something in the air."

The craft jolted a second time. The nose lifted to the sky. The engines wined and something pulsed red amongst the controls. The weight of a dozen elephants tried to force Yakini's spine out through her tail. A blast of ozone scrubbed her nose. The controls went limp and life fled the tiny craft.

There was a moment of stillness then Yakini's stomach told her that they were swinging back and forth over hundreds of metres, propelled by gravity and bullied by the relentless trade winds.

"We're dead in the water. Dead in the air." Yakini turned her ire on Mex. "How's that even possible?" she demanded.

"I suppose we must be hanging from something."

"At nineteen thousand metres? Talk sense."

"The only thing I know at this kind of altitude is the ARIA."

"The geoengineering blimp? Is that thing still floating around?"

"Albedo Reduction Initiative Airship. Yes, I think it was bought by an eccentric after attempts to alter the climate mechanically became redundant."

Mex's voice was weary-calm but bone pressed white against the skin of his knuckles. A spam of tension ran up his forearms as the craft was yanked a dozen metres higher. A patch of the pod's roof puckered outwards from the stress of whatever gripped the craft. The period of their swing shortened. They cut a churning tunnel through the upper layer of the cloud. Another yank and they were pulled clear of the cloud.

Dozens of silver tendrils hung all around, dangling from an amorphous silhouette of storm-cloud grey. It looked ponderous and impossibly heavy against the azure-cyan of the sky.

One of the nearest filaments switched.

A translucent pod swung into view. Five slender legs were grafted to the top, each articulated at seemingly random points. The overall effect was like a spider made from the body parts of every known species. The pod seemed too fragile to survive the punishing wind, as it swung closer from tendril to tendril.

A gaunt face with a scrubby ginger beard was pressed against an observation blister. The man's lips mangled a rapid series of silent words. Text started to scroll across the skin of the pod.

"You have supplies: water, food. Give them to me. Will release you after. Definitely. No hassle. Give me supplies."

Mex turned his face away from the window. "He looks just as frightened as he does hungry," he said.

"Unpredictably so," Yakini fretted. "We need to get clear before this situation gets any worse."

"We have nothing to give him."

Mex held his open hands in full view and mouthed that they had nothing to offer. Agitated words spewed from the man's mouth. The scrolling text struggled to keep up. "You must have something. Give me food. Don't lie to me. So hungry. Been stuck up here for weeks without food. Give me food. Now."

"We are leaving now," Yakini told Mex. She drew a circle the size of a fist with her finger on the roof of the canopy centred on the distortion. "About here?" she asked.

"Here what? Oh, I see. Yes, that looks about right."

Mex raised an eyebrow as Yakini drew a carbon knife from her boot. She thrust the blade into the roof. Nothing changed, so she twisted the blade savagely. The craft swung to the left. The gaunt man pressed his hands and face hard against the window, his lips and eyes pleading against what was about to happen.

Then he was gone. Yakini and Mex began a silent plummet towards the centre of the Earth. Yakini left the knife in the roof and grabbed the flaccid controls. Her pulse and breathing objected fundamentally to the uncontrolled acceleration of free-fall.

Mex was lifted out of his seat by limbs turned rigid with fear. A muted scream oozed from his drawn lips.

"Not helping," Yakini grimaced. She yanked on the controls, frustrated by their limp response. "Come on. Wake up!"

Her stomach unclenched, once they reached terminal velocity. For a minute the only sound and sensation came from her fist pounding a rhythm of desperation on the console.

The craft started to tumble. Faster and faster it spun, pressing and twisting Yakini into the side of her flight couch. Blood pounded behind her eyes.

A collection of klaxon filled the cockpit with multiple protests.

"Yes!" Yakini cheered. She found a point of view with a fixed horizon, counted to three and pushed the control column hard right. This time is offered sensory feedback. The tumbling stopped and they started a gliding descent. Two more finger punches and the engines wheezed back into life.

"You okay?" Yakini asked.

"Next time," Mex groaned. "I'm walking."

*

The engines exhausted themselves on final approach to Mars. The absence of noise stunned Sera, Bergur and Ben into silence. Sera gulped far too much air for her slender lungs to hold. She did not seem to be able to breath softly. The ship's relative velocity was too massive to be captured by the red planet. If the Martian orbital system had been incapacitated for any reason, their little shuttle would skip-off the atmosphere and head on to the outer reaches of the solar system.

Sera felt time slow down without the continuous harassment of g-force. Her arms floated into the air of their own volition. She waved her hands and feet like a marionette, and giggled. Bergur looked up from the splice interface he had been using to talk to the ship's brain.

"You're staring again," she said.

There was a groan from the ship's super-structure and lurch of g-force.

Bergur gave Sera a reassuring nod. "That's a good sign. It looks like the orbital spiders are still operational. We just snagged the atmospheric braking web. It's going to get rough for a bit," he said.

Ben tried to reach a hand across to Sera. She couldn't tell if he was seeking or offering reassurance. Either way, the rapidly rising deceleration defeated him. A low frequency roar started in Sera's stomach and spread down her legs. It leaked into the ship's structure and started to tear things apart.

"Is this normal?" she mouthed at Bergur.

He distracted her briefly with one of his shark-attack grins. Moments later she started to lose consciousness and was grateful for it.

When her brain decided it was safe to peak outside, she found herself floating down a rotating corridor of corporate orange. There was a distant hum and the murmur of nearby voices. She felt like entropy emerging into a virgin universe. She let the serenity wash over her like the pause before a sand storm.

Practicalities emerged from hiding and troubled her brain. She was lying on a stiff stretcher. She could hear hisses of escaping gas from the air-jet propulsion. Tipping her head back she could see Ben on another stretcher. He lifted his head and smiled awkwardly.

A voice percolated to Sera's brain, before bifurcating into the guttural punctuation of Bergur and the lilting waves of a Martian accent.

"Yakini?" Sera murmured.

A luridly-coloured sea-monster rose into view. "Welcome back," it barked.

"Bergur?"

"The one and only." The reality of the expression seemed to take Bergur by surprise. He blinked horizontally twice, before sinking from view.

Sera sat up. The stretcher bobbed to a halt and dropped until her feet brushed the floor. She allowed weight to flow from her body into her legs. All the bones seemed to have absconded. Muscles tensed uselessly and her knees jellied at an alarming angle. She slumped back to a prone position and muttered a collection of obscenities targeted at space-travel and the ⍰ corporation.

A couple of hours later, after the ministrations of a stim-chewing medic and a long glide to the planet's surface, the three of them stood in an ante-room waiting to be seen by a Durga corporation liaison. One wall was transparent except from the green tint of algae. Other pondweed-coloured cubes of various sizes created a cubist landscape, until a wall of red rock dramatically truncated the horizon.

Ben stood with his palms and forehead against the slick surface. Bergur and Sera were exchanging half-hearted insults when Ben started to speak.

"It mourns the necessity," he mumbled.

Sera gave him a minute to continue. "What mourns who?" she prompted.

Ben gave no indication of having heard. Sera touched his shoulder. The skin retreated from her touch, but he spoke again. "I can smell my body. I don't like it."

"I know, Ben. We all need a wash and some sleep. Especially Bergur."

"Bergur does not smell. The flora in his skin metabolises and recycles his body's waste. The chemistry sings to me in the key of G minor."

"Whatever gets your plasma fusing."

Ben turned his head from the window and fixed his gaze a metre above Sera's head. "Your body smells different. It makes me feel..." He shrugged away her hand. "It is disconcerting."

He turned back to the exterior view.

"It's not polite to tell a lady she smells," Sera teased.

A Martian male appeared at an office door. He wore a pale orange suit of simple cut. His spartan beard was trimmed almost to oblivion.

"Welcome to Vanuatu City," he said. "Sera, it's good to see you again," he added with apprehensive affection.

"Tabansi." Sera looked him up and down. "The war seems to be treating you well."

Tabansi's smile tightened. He turned to Ben and Bergur. He offered his hand to Ben, but was ignored. Bergur took it and gave it a single shake. Tabansi reclaimed his arm. He looked stunned and surprised the fingers still worked.

Tabansi let some air from his lungs and invited them into the office.

Once inside and seated he seemed to regain some of the confidence Sera remembered from when he led the Martian independence movement, the MBT.

Sera instantly fell back into her antagonist role from when she was one of his lieutenants. "So, am I speaking to the MBT or Durga corporation?"

"It is a time of war. There is no space for political division; MBT and Durga speak with a single voice of solidarity."

"You're not even pretending there's a difference, between the two?"

"Sera, did you come all this way to insult my integrity?"

"Mostly."

"Then it's time you returned to Earth."

"Gladly, just gives us what we came for."

"You mean the thing our scientists are slaving away to grow? The Martian gift to the grateful people of Earth?"

Bergur inflated his mouth flaps and interrupted. "Perhaps we should..."

Ben spoke, cutting across the conversation. "Biodiversity does not improve harmony." Sensing three pairs of eyes assessing him, he shifted his gaze from the ceiling to the floor. "Can I have something to eat?" he asked his feet.

Tabansi recovered first. "So, this is one of the Nodes, much valued by MynCorp."

"Ben. His name is Ben," Sera barked.

"Well. Ben is entirely right. It's time we broke bread together. Of course, we don't have any bread. What with the war and everything, but we can offer you a hundred flavours of algae."

"I could eat," said Bergur.

"Excellent." Tabansi herded them towards the door. His hand moved to rest on Bergur's back, but retreated as if he had touched a snake. "After you," he urged.

"Product first, food after," Sera demanded.

"Please," Bergur added with his mouth flaps open.

Ben meandered after Bergur and Sera, as if his path merely happened to coincide with theirs. Tabansi sighed something about misfits and delinquents before ushering them from his office.

As they emerged from the Durga admin cube, a wave of regret flattened Sera's pulse. The sun reflected from every rock, creating an entire spectrum of pinks. The light prized open her internal store of nostalgia, which raced to her slick eyes. She turned her face to the sky to hide the tears, letting the dusty breeze have the precious moisture.

The jaw-like crater wall chewed away at the horizon, leaving cloudy tears in the sky. As her eyes drained onto flat cheeks, Sera spotted the pale zigzag of a particular crater path. She tried to pick out the gully she and Yakini had made their own; a vantage point from which to project a dream of a free Mars and an altar to a germinating love. A hard nugget of betrayal emerged from the cave it had dug in her heart. Her mouth clenched, almost flattening the ocean-waves of her lips.

"What'd I do?" Bergur asked.

Sera was unaware she had turned her glower on the Eridanian. She wanted to accuse him of stealing her girlfriend, but Yakini was not hers to lose. "Your skin clashes with the local colour scheme," she said with a half-hearted smile.

"Am I ruining your appetite?"

"An appetite is not essential for Martian cuisine."

Tabansi stepped between them and took the lead. "Believe me, it's got worse since you left."

"Joy."

The gravel underfoot settled, but lacked the reassuring crunch of the Martian planes. The artificially constrained surface reminded Sera of the continuous frustration she had felt while living in Vanuatu City. She tried to relax and enjoy the open space; it would soon be time to clamber back inside the coffin-like shuttle for the return flight to Earth.

Tabansi led them to the same food hall Sera had eaten at since she dropped out of college and signed-on as a prospector. The most recent shift had finished a while ago and people were drifting away from the hall. Several people smiled at Tabansi and some even patted him on the back in camaraderie. Tabansi greeted each by name.

Someone, Sera vaguely recognised, said with irony, "I like the suit."

Tabansi fidgeted and said, "trying to impress our visitors." He nodded towards Ben, Bergur and Sera.

The overall-clad Martian nodded in understanding.

Tabansi offered Ben and Bergur a tray each. Sera took her own from the pile. They were presented with a meal consisting of green algae prepared to different textures: crunchy green, chewy green and sloppy green.

"Can I have some green with that?" Bergur asked one of the staff. She stared at him without humour.

Bergur tried one of his neckless shrugs and joined the others at a long table.

They ate largely in silence. Bergur kept his head down, snapping at bits of food and swallowing with the minimum of chewing. Ben appeared to be having a silent conversation with his food, pushing pieces backwards and forwards as the debate swung from point to point. Sera saw a former colleague across the room. They exchanged smiles of recognition.

"Where are the men and women from our MBT cell?" Sera asked Tabansi.

"They're around."

"Where?"

"Some are still doing shifts. Many are working in the labs, for the war effort." Tabansi raised a pointed eyebrow. "Why? Do you think I betrayed them and sent them to the Drop?"

"No," Sera conceded.

"Right. So, if we've established I'm not a monster, and I might warrant some of the respect you used to honour me with."

"Anyway, there is no more Drop," she added belligerently.

Sera swallowed the last fork of algae. She dropped the utensil into the empty dish. The tray scuttled away and stacked itself on a passing trolley.

Tabansi shrugged away the animosity. "As you say, mysteriously, there is no more Drop. And MynCorp have all but withdrawn from Mars. Essentially we won. Mars is independent."

"Yeah!" Sarcasm dripped from Sera's lips. "Let's party. No more corporate over-lords. Oh wait, who are these Durga dudes? And what's that scary sphere? Oh look, it seems to be eating all the people. Does that mean the party is off?"

"And yet you still want my help. Why did your friends think you were the best person to send?"

"Because I can smell waste-sludge even when it's dressed up in a suit."

Bergur's mouth flaps quivered. Sera noticed the state of his exposed arms and chest.

"Is it the light in here, or are you glowing?" she asked.

"This skin makes it hard to shed toxins," he gurgled. "I'll be all right in a minute. Please continue to express your disappointment in our ally. It is most … distracting."

Sera felt simultaneously disgusted, confused and intrigued.

Tabansi pushed free of the bench. "Shall we move onto the main event?" he asked.

Bergur grunted in agreement.

Ben seemed to have reached a consensus with his lunch; all of his serving of algae was pushed to the front of the tray. He coaxed a new pocket into existence at the waist of his tunic, scooped up the sludge with both hands and dribbled it in. He sealed the pocket with meticulous care, then wiped his hand clean on the rear of his trousers.

Tabansi blinked and muttered something under his breath about last best hope. A moment later his forced smile was back. "Let's get to the labs and then you can be on your way."

They trudged back towards the Durga headquarters, each drifting in their own microcosm of introspection. In the lobby, they entered an alcove. The cylindrical wall pulsed like a beating heart, pumping murky green sludge down into the bedrock. There was a faint ripple and the compartment joined the flow. They sank into the surface of Mars. The algae started to luminesce. The sickly green glow made Bergur look like a shadow. Sera felt an inexplicable fear creep through her skin.

Tabansi tapped his left foot to some internal mantra.

The cubicle deposited them on the edge of a rough cut cavern. Numerous voices and shadows spilled round an outcrop of rock. Tabansi beckoned them to take the lead.

Beyond the outcrop, the cavern opened up into a vast factory. Dozens of orange clad Martians bustled over eight identical production lines. The head of each line was a translucent pipe hanging from the ceiling like a green stalactite. Fogs of algae swirled in each pipe, drifting down to a finger-width nozzle. The dribble of green seemed to feed a complicated series of fabrication activities, which, after twenty metres and the ministrations of a dozen pairs of hands, ended in a crate. Sera recognised the crates from the munitions room in the basement of the Jefferson Buildings.

Sera was baffled for a minute. She shook her head in an attempt to clear the cloud forming behind her eyes.

Bergur spoke first, "So, you can eat it or kill aliens with it. Useful stuff."

Tabansi agreed silently.

Maybe it was the noise or the lack of air movement, but Sera was struggling to grasp the scene. The edges of the cavern slipped into shadow. She managed to articulate a question. "You make the fléchettes from the stuff we were eating? We're fighting aliens with algae?"

"Eight different genetic strains. Don't ask me how. Your man, José, conceived the process." Tabansi seemed to be scrutinising her as he spoke. "The Earth resistance batch is already loaded onto your shuttle. What you see here is the next batch and stockpiles for our own defence."

Sera decided to sit down.

Bergur moved towards her, one mouth flap askew. Was this an Iridanian look of concern? Sera felt a weight land on her chest. There was too much darkness to push it off. There was no pain, more a sense of reassurance. The world vanished under a heavy blanket of silence.

*

It was a complete and utter farce.

Lesana had started out convinced she could do some small thing to help save the human race. She bubbled like a new puppy when they led her to a room on the tenth floor of Jefferson-A. The space was roughly square but the walls, ceiling and floor bulged as if holding back a massive volume of water. Small blisters wept a fine grit, which over a few days worked into every crease of her body. Nodding and repeating each word she greeted the shelf turned bed, bucket come latrine and sheets of cellulose masquerading as analysis tools.

Within a week she knew the whole endeavour was futile, and yet Lesana persevered.

The eighth day started the same as the previous seven.

One of the communications team handed Lesana a scrap of paper with a pair of sextant numbers scribbled in barely legible handwriting. Her fingers brushed across the pencil marks without triggering any vocalisation from the inert paper.

She trudged over to the least cantankerous wall and traced her finger up the grid lines of a topographic map. The irregular texture of the wall competed with the density of contour lines to create an illusion of mountains where there was plains and impromptu waterfalls in languid rivers.

Finding the square corresponding to the number on the paper, Lesana added a blue pin to the hundreds dotted across the map. Then she stood far enough back for the individual pins to form clusters and threads. Her brain found patterns everywhere on the map, but the analyst within her rejected each and everyone.

"The sampling is so skewed it could mean anything," she complained to the man at her side. "We need aerial surveillance to get a more even sampling of the Eidolon attacks."

He ignored her repeated objection and concentrated on chewing the woody end of his pencil.

"John, you do know that pencil is a museum piece?"

He spat a flake of yellow paint onto the floor. "Tastes like it."

A woman appeared at the room's ragged opening. "Ready?" she asked anxiously.

"No."

"Yes."

John's positive answer seemed to satisfy the woman and she stepped to one side. She was replaced by a taut figure in an immaculate one-piece suit. He entered the room without his eyes deviating from far wall. He did not acknowledge Lesana or John in any way, but she felt certain he was scrutinising her just as much as the map.

She opened her mouth to offer some contextual information, but the man's assistant raised a silencing finger. Lesana stared again at the map, trying to get her spongy organic computer to mimic the behaviour of his nu-metal implant. It was futile; her brain just could not hold enough simultaneous ideas. She could construct the various models needed to remove the human bias from the data, but she could not apply the models to the map. Even the attempt felt like spinning plates in a hurricane.

The man gave the barest shake of the head and turned on his heels.

"What do you see?" Lesana called after him.

The assistant gave Lesana an incredulous glare, and then, as if a head gesture could communicate statistical analysis, she repeated the man's shake of the head.

"This is an utter farce," Lesana confided loudly to John. "I need my own processing power, not a box of pins and a pencil."

John went back to chewing his centuries old pencil.

A face sporting a lopsided grin grew from the side of the doorway. Fez's body remained out of sight, as if he could not be sure what fresh horror puberty had induced today.

"We're going hunting. You wanna come?" he asked with a tone already resigned to rejection.

"Sure, why not?" Lesana

The centipedal transporter stuttered slightly on the uneven ground, then the convoy was moving again. Lesana peered out of the fixed-form window at the deserted gates to the food factory; whomever had been left to guard the entrance had capitulated quickly, either abandoning their post or, maybe, even joining the humanitarian effort.

Fez coaxed the transport into position amongst the other hotchpotch of vehicles. He clambered down from the cab and leant against a pair of jointed legs.

"I'm going to help load," Lesana said.

He briefly looked a little crestfallen, then remembered his teenage indifference and shrugged dismissively.

"One hour," an authoritative voice squawked in her ear-bud. "This place will be Reset by the end of the day, so don't be gentle."

Lesana was assigned to a small gang of similarly conscripted refugees, and instructed to harvest fruit and vegetables. They moved towards white poly-tunnels standing in regimental rows of regenerated cellulose. Lesana picked one amongst thousands and gave the instruction to harvest. She watched through the translucent wall as an army of silver spiders started to strip the plants of red and purple fruits. Once the first parcel had been packaged and trundled off to the waiting vehicles at the loading bay, Lesana moved onto the next tunnel. This time she gave the harvest instruction without waiting to see it start. With a dozen tunnels of different fruits at various stages of maturity, being stripped and packaged, Lesana stopped.

A passing carton bleated as she stole an apple. The insides of her cheeks ached from the effort of salivating. Her stomach protested at being tormenting so unfairly. Lesana tried to savour the cleansing feel of the white flesh on her tongue, but she was betrayed by her throat; swallowing the lump, whole. It clogged her windpipe until she coughed it down, then it sat as a hard lump of guilt in her gullet.

Unable to see the value in supervising a self-sufficient community of crop-spiders, Lesana headed toward the main factory complex. There was a lot of earnest shouting coming from within. A gaggle of men and women were gathered just inside the entrance. As Lesana stepped thorough the doorway, they stopped arguing and tilted their heads upward. Lesana was aware of an unearthly slurping sound coming from above. It was fading towards the edge of natural detection, but the echo was frighteningly organic. She looked up and was immediately thrust into a giddy labyrinth of diamond-clear tubes. The pipes glowed from within with a green so intense it reminded Lesana of radioactive slime from a cheap drama.

"What's going on?" Lesana asked the nearest woman.

She turned and studied Lesana with slightly crossed eyes. Having been assessed against some internal criteria, the woman replied. "Some idiot tripped an interlock. The whole system is shutting down."

"What's the green stuff and why is it glowing?"

The woman sighed despondently, as if Lesana had just confirmed an unpleasant suspicion. "Arthrospira cyanobacteria."

Lesana shook her head.

"Really?" the woman patronised. "Spirulina to you. Or maybe just dinner? The glow is from the light-pipe running along the centre of each tube. There are solar collectors on the roof."

"And that?" Lesana frustrated by the woman's patronising tone, was pointing towards a bulbous vessel in the middle of the room.

"Yes, that's where they burn shit."

"Burn? Why would they do that?"

"To generate carbon dioxide for photosynthesis and use up waste oxygen. Only an idiot would perform agro-chemistry on this scale without controlling the waste products. The Earth would be plunged into an iceage in less than a hundred years without CO_2 absorption control. And that would be really bad for business."

"So what's the problem?"

"Problem?"

"Yes, all the shouting and foul moods."

"Oh, the system has gone into shutdown, so we can't get the food product out, and the fresh water tanks are about to become cross contaminated."

"That sounds bad."

"You think?"

"Maybe you should do something rather than yabbing to me."

Lesana smiled politely and walked away.

The factory was barren of all signs of human occupancy. Lesana's ulterior motive for tagging along on the hunt was a vague hope of finding some self-contained computing power. The factory was entirely automated; any processing power it needed was built into the fabric of the building.

Lesana wandered back outside. A procession of packing crates and food trays was snaking its way from the food-bank to the waiting transport.

Fez was just closing the cargo pods of the transport. He saw Lesana and circled a finger to indicate he was ready to leave. Lesana made a vague hand gesture and ducked inside the next building.

The food production in the second building was an all together more refined affair. Rectangular tanks with a slick, mercurial finish filled the space in three dimensions. The lattice of spaces between the tanks hummed softly from the vibrations of an intricate web of translucent threads. A small army of fist-sized bots fussed over the tanks like palliative crabs.

Lesana estimated the three stories above ground were matched by a similar space below. She advanced to the edge of a promontory cultured from a single diamond lattice and steadied her vertigo with a hand on the lip. The nearest tank has a transparent side, revealing a honeycomb scaffold of grey cartilage. The hexagonal voids were filled with a pale fibrous material flecked with red.

It looked almost like flesh.

"Meat!" Lesana declared.

For a moment she was stunned by the shear magnitude of the find. Spontaneous calorific calculations sprung into her mind, but rapidly floundered at the shear scale of the task. This one building contained more in-vitro meat than Lesana imagined was consumed by the entire planet. Someone somewhere was eating a lot more meat than she could afford.

She scanned around for some way to trigger a harvest, but the platform was purely designed to impress visitors and not to control the process. A pair of bots moved directly towards Lesana making her take a guilty step back. They stopped at the edge of the platform and lifted a small pouch in a prayer-like offering.

"For me?"

A dozen pincers performed an impatient tap-dance against solid diamond. As soon as Lesana held her hand near the pouch, the bots dropped it and sprang onto a thread and vanished.

"Lesana, time to go," Fez said from the doorway.

"I found enough meat to feed everyone."

Lesana pushed the pouch of meat towards her stomach. A pocket formed and swallowed the precious cargo.

"For all of three days before it spoils. We don't have enough energy to keep it fresh," Fez admonished.

"So, we're just going to leave it to be Reset?"

"Oh, you remember the Reset. The Reset that's getting really quite close."

Sarcasm was new from Fez; either he was getting more confident around Lesana, or he had an annoying reaction to fear.

Lesana was reluctantly turning to leave, when a sizzle of charged air echoed between the tanks. A monumental burp erupted from the nearest tank, spraying Lesana with partially cooked in-vitro meat.

Through the transparent side of the tank, Lesana watched with mounting horror as a sphere of uncertainty forced its way into existence. The surrounding lattice of meat responded with contortions. The colour darkened and the texture became rougher. In places brown fur sprouted. For a moment a leg and hoof kicked out and thudded into the side of the tank. Then it was gone, only to be replaced by a twisted horn and a yellow eye with a rectangular pupil. A mouth opened to reveal protruding teeth and rough molars. With no lungs to feed it, the scream was silent, but overwhelming.

"Run," Fez screamed.

Lesana did as she was instructed. The gift-pouch of meat bounced against her chest, like a repulsive secret.

*

The roar came first.

It reflected off the shards of her consciousness and seeped through the cracks in her psyche. Sera traced it back to her ears and, from there, into the waking world. There was a clicking sound coming from her chest. She experimented with a deeper breath. Pushing her chest out seemed harder than she remembered. She was rewarded for her effort with a spike of pain.

Now her mind was bright enough to encompass her whole body, she was aware of a uniform pressure holding her against whatever it was she was sitting on. Some kind of couch. Judging from the contours, she was sat in an acceleration couch. So, the pressure was probably her body resisting the thrust from shuttle engines. Hence, the roar.

By the time Sera was ready to open her eyes, she was resigned to another period of tedium aboard the shuttle: avoiding Bergur's unsettling gaze, trying to make eye contact with Ben and staring at blank bulkheads. She tried to calculate how many times she had been through this routine. Too many. How long should it take to get to Mars?

Sera's eyes flashed open. Bergur was slumped in the opposite alcove. She remembered being on Mars: the exasperation she felt at Tabansi's complicity, and the loathing and longing for lost home, beauty and love. Now she was back on the shuttle. Heading for where? Earth?

"Bergur?" she experimented.

His mouth and eyes were sealed tight. Sera could see no movement at all. Not even the rise and fall of his breath.

"Bergur!"

Sera kept the panic from her voice and refused to let it take root in her chest.

"What?" Bergur growled.

Both sets of eyelids were still closed. His chest settled back after ejecting the syllable.

"Are you awake?"

Bergur's outer eyelids slid back. Sera tried to read his mood through the cloudy inner lids. His chest moved again.

"I wasn't asleep," he said.

"If you say so. What happened?"

"We were drugged, rendered unconscious, ferried back to orbit, loaded in the shuttle and shot into space."

"What?"

"Which bit?"

"Any, all?" Sera pleaded.

Bergur took a breath and used it to sigh. "Tabansi betrayed us," he explained.

"I don't understand. Did he lie about the ammunition?"

"No. It's all here, but he stole from us."

Sera surprised herself by laughing. "Stole from us. You haven't even got a shirt on your back."

A neat stack of munitions cases were stacked in the third alcove. Sera scanned the pile waiting for her brain to fight free of the fog. "On no! He wouldn't."

"He did."

It became a reality as soon as she said the name out loud, "Ben's gone."

Chapter 4

Sardon proffered his hand.

Mex had completely failed to prepare himself for the subsequent burst of emotions. There was plenty of anger, but it felt artificial, almost second-hand. Sardon had assaulted, drugged and attempted to scrape-out the contents of Mex's mind. With no memory of the attack, it was easier to hate Sardon for forcing Julienne to chose between saving Mex and her own mind.

Then there was guilt. Guilt that Mex needed to blame someone for his mind not being entirely his own. Guilt because Mex felt he was something less than he had been.

Sardon seemed to be studying Mex's internal conflict. Eventually, he withdrew his empty hand without comment, using it instead to guide his guest's attention towards a pair of approaching chairs.

Mex and Yakini exchanged glances of mutual reassurance. After taking their weight, the chairs shuffled slightly, settling directly in front of Sardon. Mex noticed Sardon's chair was preconfigured to lift its occupant higher and more upright. The petty and obvious mind-game felt strangely reassuring to Mex; this was his territory. Sardon might not be the mind of a building, but such a blatant and text-book power-play made Sardon predictable. That is, unless the act was designed to create an unjustified sense of security in Mex's mind. Or may be, Sardon was just trying to make Mex second guess himself.

"I used to be good at this," Mex muttered.

"Can I offer you a beverage? Beer for you Mister Tyrian, or maybe kava for Flight Lieutenant Akida."

"The role of gracious host doesn't really suit you, Sardon."

"Well I suppose it only reasonable to be on first name terms after our shared history. I hope you don't mind if I have a coffee?" Sardon raised a finger. There was a faint ping of acknowledgement from all around.

Yakini broke her silence. "It's just Yakini. My MynCorp days are over."

Sardon raised an eyebrow. "Did you get a discharge? I must have missed that."

"Not necessary." Yakini matched Sardon's ironic tone. "My employer left the world-domination market."

"Really?"

"By the way, congratulations," Mex joined in. "I understand you have been promoted. Or at least everyone senior to you turned out to be imaginary. I guess that makes you captain of the sinking ship."

A young woman with a distracted smile entered the room and placed an espresso cup next to Sardon's hand. There were no words exchanged.

She left.

Sardon reached for the cup as if it has always been there.

Sardon sipped the drink with obvious satisfaction, and said, "I could happily play this game all day, but we do have business to discuss."

Mex let exasperation creep into his voice. "Tell me MynCorp is coming out of hiding and is ready to help defend the Earth?"

"We're not hiding. MyncCorp picks battles it can win, never pointless gestures of futility."

"You think saving people's lives is pointless?"

"If you save them today, only for them to die tomorrow, then yes I'd say that's pointless."

"So, you just let them die?"

"Mex you sound like a petulant child. I know you have a better understanding of strategy than this."

"It's hard to be objective when people are screaming all around you."

"I don't hear any screaming."

"So, what do you want to tell us?" Yakini interrupted.

"Tell you? No, nothing like that. You're here as a consultant."

Mex's tone was clipped with frustration. "So, you're not going to help. You're going to carry on playing your little power games."

"We are about to enter negotiations with the Eidolons," Sardon said calmly.

"You're mad," Mex stated. He looked at Yakini to check she agreed. She was already getting to her feet.

"Let's go," she said.

Sardon was smiling with satisfaction. "At the risk of sounding Machiavellian," he said, "you're not going anywhere."

A shiver passed through the wall behind Sardon, washing the pigment to the floor and leaving a crystal-clean window. Beyond was a laboratory equipped like a surgically-sterile torture chamber. Superconducting cuffs held a girl in a crucifixion pose a meter off the ground. Her naked flesh amongst so much dull metal seemed somehow subhuman. She was physically underdeveloped for the years written in her face; simultaneously a young woman and an emaciated child.

"It's one of Nomia's nymphs," Mex stated, annoyed with himself for not remembering the girl's name.

"Her name is Teledice," Yakini spat through gritted teeth. "Sardon, one day I'm going to kill you."

Sardon accepted her wrath face-on. "Maybe, but today you will help to save a Node's life."

Mex shook his head, struggling to understand what he was seeing. "You have no idea what you've done," he said sadly.

"I've reclaimed MynCorp property. Property you, and your collaborators, stole."

"The Nodes are people, not property."

"The two have been equivalent in the eye's of the law for almost one hundred years."

Mex shook his head. "Anyway, that's not what I was talking about. You've kidnapped a member of the best fighting unit we have. Teledice is one of Nomia's team. Heaven knows how many people will die because of this one act, and then again when Nomia comes knocking."

"You're still thinking too small."

Yakini stepped forward and rested her hands on the window between the observing lounge and laboratory. Tension ran up and down the bones of her fingers. Her hands clasped into fists when two technicians entered the laboratory and approached Teledice. They were naked under their gelatinous environment suits, but almost entirely sexless; one had hints of femininity about the shoulders and hips. Their androgyny extenuated the bestial cruelty of the Node's incarceration.

Using an innocuous looking atomizer, the technicians sprayed a silver mist into the Teledice's face. The magnification of the laboratory window increased until Mex and Yakini could see silver globules coalescing on Teledice's skull. They danced across her skin like racing balls of mercury.

As each arrived at a programmed position it flattened against the skin and faded beneath the surface.

Mex was dimly aware of his human arm rising to his own head. Finger tips traced the subtle contours of his skull, tracing imagined circuits in his brain. Paradoxically, his artificial arm stayed motionless at his side; obedient to only his conscious mind.

He wanted to plead the case again to free Teledice, but Sardon's perspective was so perverse, Mex could not construct any argument. The man possessed a will strong enough to steer MynCorp through a catastrophic degradation in capability, but existed in the parallel logic-construct of the paranoid or intoxicated. If Sardon has been one of Mex's buildings, he would have declared it irredeemable and discard the entire project to the attic of his code repository.

So, Mex watched and tried to free the Node with the power of his will.

Nothing happened and continued to not happen for several minutes; Teledice remained apparently free from expected torment and agony. Tension eventually loosened Mex's mouth, but he did not relax his vigil.

"You said we could save her life. How?"

Sardon was closer than Mex had realised. His voice was a physical sensation on Mex's skin.

"Help the negotiations to succeed," Sardon said.

"Or you kill her?"

"Or we unleash her."

Yakini was staring at the MynCorp executive with the intensity of a hunter. If Sardon noticed, he made no effort to move out of striking range.

"If José and Nomia could not talk the Eidolon's around, what makes you think you can?"

The detachment in Yakini's voice was more terrifying than the previous venom.

"Please," Sardon scolded. "I'm a professional. I understand the importance of negotiating from a position of power."

"You're completely mad!"

"That's one thing I am not. Besides, the life of the Node very much depends on my sanity."

Sardon acknowledged an incoming message with a slight inclination of his head. The two technicians left the laboratory. They turned towards the observing lounge and their expressions brushed across Mex's focus. Intelligence glistened in their eyes, but no emotion disturbed the thin line of their lips.

Sardon raised his hands as if they were a rowdy meeting to bring to order.

"Shall we?" he asked rhetorically.

Teledice opened her eyes.

*

"Bergur, you're very calm about this," Sera complained.

"Not calm. Give me another minute to metabolise the toxins from the algae spores, and I'll show you a good dose of livid."

"Stop playing with your skin flora, and turn this thing around."

"Oh, okay. Let me see. Where did I see a rudder? Or, maybe, this thing has a reverse gear."

"Sarcasm! They've taken Ben. We have to do something."

"If the endless tedium of the outward trip wasn't enough of a clue, we are passengers on this inter-planetary missile."

Sera sagged back into her couch, letting the incessant tug of g-force steal her anger. "But it's Ben. He's defenceless without us."

"You've seen Nomia when she's really angry. These Nodes are the least defenceless group of people I've ever met, and I was a pirate for years."

"You were a pirate? A real pirate?" Sera gave Bergur a sceptical glower.

"What? All the weird shit you've seen, but you don't believe in space pirates?"

Sera shook her head to clear the image of Bergur wearing a cocked hat and a hearty grin.

"But Ben's an innocent," Sera pleaded. "He's not equipped to deal with the cruelty of people."

"He must be heavily sedated."

"Why do you think that?"

"Otherwise he'd just will himself back to us."

"You think he could do that? Find our little pocket of air amongst so much space?"

Bergur sucked air twice before losing some conviction. "To be honest, I've no idea what he can do."

"Right. So, it's down to us. We have to rescue him," Sera instructed. "Start talking to ship's A.I.. Find a way to reverse our course."

Flecks of laser light reflected from imperfections on his cornea. "This is weird," he muttered.

"Could it possibly get any worse?"

"This isn't our shuttle."

Bergur's tone was matter of fact, and it took Sera several seconds to process the statement. She considered the shuttle's interior.

"You're right. It's similar, but the textures are all wrong. It's far too aesthetic for ⬚ Corp."

"Typical."

"I cannot believe Durga are playing at the old corporate espionage game. Would they really stoop to stealing a Node from MynCorp and an experimental shuttle from ⬚ Corp? What am I saying? Of course they would."

Sera growled in frustration. Bergur wrinkled the skin above his eyes. He focused on the ship interface for a full minute, before pushing the terminal away with a grunt.

"The thing's personality must be based on Alyona's; it's as cantankerous as an ice-drill with a missing tooth. We haven't achieved escape velocity yet. So, there's some hope."

"So, what's the plan."

"There is one thing we can do. But we don't have much time to chose."

"Well get on with it."

"It's pretty drastic and we need to think about our other responsibility."

She followed his gaze to the stack of algae derived ammunition. "One thing at a time. How do we get back to Mars?"

"We cut the power to propulsion, and fall back to Mars."

"You know how to do that?"

"I know one way."

"Right. And the other problem? What do we do about the cargo?"

"It tumbles back to Mars and burns up in the atmosphere, along with us."

"Not acceptable. We need to achieve two diametrically opposite goals. What do we have to work with?"

Sera took stock.

Every inexplicable knobble and widget of the compartment was etched into her long-term memory like the ceiling of a convalescent's bedroom. The Durga-built duplicate was a lazy approximation; from the dimensions of the alcoves, to the bulbous protuberance above her head. Even the texture of the bulkheads was too slick, too modern.

"The ship!" Sera exclaimed. She turned in her acceleration couch and rubbed at a bulkhead. The metal shimmered under her fingers. The metal turned from grey to silver and then glassy-black. The pale-pink glow of Mars leaked between her fingers. "The glory of modernity!"

Bergur held his hands aloft in a mock jubilation. "Sjitturinn! Now we can wave goodbye to Ben."

"Shame those muscles don't extend inside your skull."

Bergur stood immutable, showing no sign her insult had penetrated his purple skin. His inner eyelids blinked once. Sera suspected he did this just to disconcert her. Before Sera could collect her thoughts, Bergur sucked in air and spook without intonation."You're thinking, we can use the intelligent metal to fashion an escape capsule, and let the cargo fly onto Earth. While we jettison ourselves into Mars orbit."

It was Sera's turn to blink. She covered her surprise with a question."Can you do it?"

95

"Probably."

He waved the terminal back to life, and resumed his suspended splice session. Sera watched stray photons paint his face. The green and blue lasers formed mud coloured flecks around his eyes.

As Sera watched, Bergur started to grow.

Her mind shifted perspective. The distance between them was shrinking. Sera instinctively pulled her feet under her knees. There was a twisting sensation. Bergur's feet came to rest a breath away from Sera's head.

"This is cosy," she grimaced.

Bergur's voice filtered up from between her knees. "We have a problem."

"I never doubted it for a moment."

"I convinced the ship to make an escape capsule, but it won't launch; too many safety protocols getting in the way."

"I assume this is the part of the plan, I'm not going to like. What's that sound."

"I'm just drinking a few litres of water. I'm going to need it soon. Right, I'm ready."

Sera tried to look through her legs, hoping to read something in Bergur's face. "Ready for what?" she asked.

"You might want to hold your breath for the next few minutes."

"What the hell are you up to?"

"I've been brewing up a little chemistry experiment, based on the soporific algae spores."

"Is that gurgling noise coming from inside you?" Sera tried to fight an urge to be sick.

A rumbling, like the prelude to a geyser eruption, filled the tiny space. It echoed back from the main shuttle through the linking aperture. Sera hyperventilated for a few seconds, then clamped both hands over her mouth and nose. The noises became more organic; the slurping and gurgling of biology in action.

The sound reached a crescendo. Sera tensed for the explosion, eruption or whatever disgusting thing Bergur's body was doing. There was an anticlimactic moment of tranquillity and then the politest of belches. Sera caught a glimpse of a globule fly through the aperture and into the main compartment of the shuttle.

A klaxon started to pound the small space with acoustic panic. An alarmingly-calm female voice fought through the din. "Warning! Biological contamination detected. Unable to contain. Prepare for evacuation."

The metal walls shimmered and flowed across the opening, isolating Bergur and Sera into an impossibly small space. There was a crack of separation and a pulse of acceleration. Sera flapped at the wall, surprised by the unfamiliar feeling of claustrophobia. The stars were slowly tumbling. The exterior of the shuttle drifted into view. The motors glowed pink against the black backdrop. A wound in one side was slowly healing. Half a turn later, the dazzling disc of Mars left a green streak across her vision. She felt half a dozen pulses of thrust and then nothing.

"Bergur?"

"Ja."

"What have we done?"

"We've offered ourselves up to Durga in a ready-made coffin."

"We can't let them catch us."

"That's the part of the plan you're not going to like."

"I thought we'd already done that bit."

Sera drifted against the extent of her constraints. Her nose brushed the tip of Bergur's boot. Before she pulled back, she caught a faint smell of stressed metal and oxygenation bacillus. Weightlessness added to her sense of confinement, as two irrational fears battled for control of her creeping panic. Oxygen seemed to take an eternity to get from her nose to her skin. She closed her eyes. Her father's face appeared through the gloom. Above the faint green glow of an algae-rebreather, his eyes were brimming with devoted encouragement. For the first time in years, she remembered the training sessions; days underground in the remotest oxygen-starved caves, stripping down mining tools to find the missing component her dad has slipped in his pocket. Being one mistake from death had never reduced her joy at being the centre of his world for a few days.

Sera found a nugget of tranquillity left from those childhood days. She followed their current actions through to their natural end and isolated the highest priority action. "We have to disable the identification transponder, so Durga can't track us."

"Do you know how to do that?" Bergur asked.

"No," she admitted, "and it probably has as internal energy source, so we can't just shut it down."

"It's worse than that. The capsule will do it's best to maintain orbit, until we're picked up. Its primary concern will be to prevent us entering the atmosphere, burning up or crashing."

Sera's calm reserves were already running low again. "Isn't that good? Crashing sounds bad."

"Ben is almost certainly on the surface of Mars."

"Are you suggesting we have to deliberately crash into Mars?"

"I said you weren't going to like it."

*

"This is ridiculous," Mex muttered for the dozenth time.

He swam in the data-sea of the lash-up Nexus. In the real world the stand-off continued. He knew this because he still existed to contemplate his own demise.

"Absolutely ridiculous," he said again.

"Please stop saying that."

Mex flinched with the proximity of Yakini's virtual voice.

"I concur," Sardon added.

Carrying passengers into the Drop was new to Mex. Frankly, he felt his human-rights were being violated. It was an invasion of his person, even if he had to admit that less of his body and mind were his own anyway.

"What are we looking at?" Sardon interrupted.

"Probably your feet, or a wall. The occasional flash of scintillation when the splice lasers hit an impurity in your cornea."

"You know what I mean. What are we seeing?"

"The compact glowing blob is Teledice. The tendrilled hyper-beast is the Oikake or Eidolon attack-sphere. The surrounding storm is reality breaking down."

Mex was starting to recognise the sensation when one of his passengers was about to talk; a distinct burst of protocol negotiation like an intake of breath. Yakini wanted to ask something.

"Can you tell how Teledice is doing? Is she in pain?"

"She still exists, which is surprising in itself." Mex searched for something more reassuring to say. "She's still here," was all he could manage.

Sardon felt like a devil, whispering in Mex's other ear. "Will the Eidolons hear me if I speak?" he hissed.

"How should I know?"

"By suppressing your natural petulance, drawing on your experience and making an educated guess."

"Possibly."

Yakini spoke across Mex. "José and Nomia managed a vaguely linear conversation with the sphere that attacked Mars."

"This is a little different," Mex qualified. "We do not naturally have a conscious presence in Verity Space. We exist here inside an artificial construct, an avatar. We interact with other constructs using protocols created long ago by standards committees. I seriously doubt the Eidolons speak RFC1149."

"Ready?" Sardon asked.

"Ready for what?"

"I wasn't talking to you."

Mex was vaguely aware of some data traffic on the edge of his perception. Then the glowing manifestation of the Node began to undulate, and a voice that was not Teledice's radiated into Verity Space.

"Hear me. My name is Sardon Lucas. I speak on behalf of MynCorp and the Cartel which represents the interests of human-kind and associated subspecies. I wish to open negotiations with the alien presence in this region of space."

Mex single-cast a message to Yakini. "Seriously?"

The Oikake continued to grow thick tentacles that flailed and lashed at the Node. Teledice made no visible effort to defend herself. Her presence remained impassive in the face of the onslaught, but somehow immutable. The Eidolon sphere failed to get any purchase on the Node's surface. Each attack slid away from a point of frictionless causality.

Undaunted and tireless, the Oikake continued to attack.

The violence was purely visual, and Sardon's voice drifted across the battlefield with disconcerting ease.

"Are you able to speak on behalf of your creators?" he asked.

"No."

It took several seconds for Mex to realise the sphere had spoken. If felt like the memory of its words had leached from his temporal lobe, back along the auditory nerve to the cochlea and vibrated the basilar membrane. Whatever the confusion of cause and effect, the Oikake had definitely said the word no.

"I speak only to express my creator's decisions," the sphere continued.

"But your creators hear what you hear?"

"They are aware of realities in which this conversation takes place."

"Okay. I would like to discuss mutually beneficial arrangements; an exchange of information and a sharing of resources."

"These concepts are meaningless. You will cease to have existed. The Earth is being restored to a state in which humans never evolved. Your offer will not exist."

Sardon seemed undeterred by the Oikake's declaration. "Let's not get ahead of ourselves," he continued. "First we should discuss a structure for this conversation, and establish points of commonality."

Later Yakini did the virtual equivalent of a fidget.

"I think Sardon is trying to kill the Eidolons by a thousand acts of tedium?" she suggested.

"Sorry, I wasn't paying attention," Mex admitted. "Has he given up trying to get an agreement on sparkling versus still water?"

"He's moved onto the number of delegates at the proposed summit. For most of the basic stuff Sardon decided no response was an implicit yes."

"It's not even clear if the Eidolon understand the concept of discrete individuals, let alone have any body parts to pin a name badge to."

"Hence my frustration. I hate being a passenger. Where have you been?"

"Here, mostly."

Mex was baffled by Sardon's strategy. Despite the audacity of entering unilateral negotiations with beings beyond human understanding, Mex could not believe Sardon was so naive as to believe a simple treaty could be achieved. What possible leverage could Sardon possess?

Mex thought he understood Sardon, probably not well enough to predict his future actions, but certainly well enough to rationalise his behaviour. Mex's mammalian brain would have struggled, particularly after their history; thinking like Sardon required detachment and an absence of compassion or sentiment. Every action was born from complex weighing of goals, probability of success and effort expended. Given the intelligence to conceive of every permutation available to Sardon, and sufficient knowledge of the prevailing conditions, his actions were ruthlessly predictable.

Unfortunately, Mex experienced more than the usual number of emotions when he thought of Sardon. Truth be told, he hated Sardon more than the Eidolons; at least Sardon was a tangible enemy. Mex was not limited to a mammalian brain. He had bits of Julienne's, acting as a glue to the cerebral mush Sardon had left in his head.

So, Mex turned off his emotions. It was so simple, it would have turned his stomach if hadn't just disabled disgust. His glasses were running the submersion programme and Sardon was fully occupied by whatever nonsense he was engineering. With his new detachment, Mex found himself mostly free to look around.

Mex had entire suites of semi-intelligent hackware, but these universally relied on the relatively primitive design of the Nexus. The original architects had kept things simple, designing the Nexus as a grid of interconnecting nodes. All the built-in security was based on the premise that there was no way in or out other than via this grid. Mex had conceived of an extra degree of freedom, a further dimension. To the Nexus, Mex's intrusions had been as intangible as the Eidolons were to the physical universe.

With all due humility, he had been a god-like presence in the Nexus. No longer. The temple walls had been torn down, his priests defrocked and his omnipotence reduced to the tap-tap-tap of a blind man's cane. Of course, there was also the slightly deflating realisation that Julienne had been tracking his activities and had chosen not to intervene until he became useful.

More of a tolerated gremlin than a god, Mex admitted to himself.

Maybe that was his real skill; a whining mosquito not quite worthy of the effort to swat. MynCorp had always been blind to anything endothermic; if the benefit did not out way the energy expense, it did not happen.

Mex felt no resentment at his new position in the order of things, and would not until his emotions were back up and running. Somewhere he could feel a thought suggesting his current detachment should become permanent.

Teledice was still inert. The Oikake had stopped the usual tendril attach and was pushing itself bodily against the Node. The sphere deformed and recoiled as Verity Space rejected their co-location.

Mex deployed a line-tapper. In a previous lifetime this piece of code had found loved-ones sentenced to the Drop. Now it was sniffing around the battle scene and transmitting the chaos to Mex. The data was valid, the chaos was real. Even without the Nexus, Mex was able to navigate and interpret the data. A layer of his ignorance revealed itself and peeled away. There were no photons of light bouncing around Verity Space bringing a visual impression to his eyes. The three dimensional virtual reality he had constructed was built on routines stolen or reverse engineered from MynCorp. Ultimately, at the lowest level, the MyncCorp hardware must be interacting with Verity Space in a fundamental fashion. The telemetry Mex used to build his virtual world, was described by vibrations not in an electromagnetic field but in the Downey field. He had always been manipulating the fabric of reality, just through layers of obfuscating delegation.

Somewhere in the back of his mind Mex acknowledged the magnitude and recklessness of his adult life, while the rest of his brain set to work unravelling Sardon duplicity.

"So, what's going on?" Yakini asked again.

"I don't think Teledice is conscious," Mex started.

"That much is obvious."

"I mean at any level. Causality is bouncing off her. Apart from Sardon's voice, she's not generating any disturbance in Verity Space. It's almost as if she's paused."

"A causal coma?" Yakini pondered.

"Did you make that up?"

"Of course I made it up. What use would the universe have for such a phrase until now?"

"Hm. The Oikake is trying to swallow her whole. Somewhat like an immune response."

"Mex, you sound remarkably calm. Have you worked out how to get us all out of here?"

"Is that better?" The fear and anger was back in Mex's voice.

"What just happened?" Yakini started to ask. "Never mind. We have to intervene. Can you get me closer to Teledice?"

"What does closer even mean?"

"Cut the philosophy and get me nearer Teledice?"

"I could embed your avatar into the line-tapper. With a bit of jiggery-pokery Sardon might not even notice."

"As long as I can pilot it; I hate being a passenger."

"Okay. Use simple vocal commands. Just make it your inside-voice."

"Forward."

Yakini's voice no longer felt like it was coming from inside his own consciousness. Mex staggered against a wave of abandonment as it sloshed out from his newly returning pool of emotions. Yakini had left him alone in his virtual head with Sardon. Mex busied himself masking Yakini's silhouette from the pseudo visual construct being fed to Sardon.

"Do the Eidolons prefer to meet in physical or Verity space?" Sardon persisted.

"Your question is irrelevant," the Oikake repeated.

There was a pause in the meter of Sardon's digest.

"Right." Sardon acknowledged some unseen cue. "I think it is time to demonstrate MynCorp credentials. We are not to be dismissed so lightly."

The Oikake continued to dislocate its virtual jaw in an attempt to engulf Teledice.

Sardon was undaunted. "Flight Lieutenant Yakini Akida please prepare yourself. There will be very little time once we begin."

Verity Space exploded. A nova of pure entropy erupted from Teledice, obliterating all probability structure in its wake. The shock-wave propagated at the speed of reality, consuming the Oikake in an instant. Mex's code experienced numerous buffer overruns, leaving him snow-blind.

Mex tore the code-glasses from his real face and turned on Sardon. "What have you done?" Not waiting for an answer Mex checked the couch on his other side. Yakini sat impassive, her jaw mouthing soundless words. Through the laboratory window he could see Teledice straining against her bonds. Sinewy muscles threatened to tear through skin as delicate as rose petals, but her efforts made no impact on the immutability of her containment.

"What have you done?" Mex demanded for a second time.

Sardon was blinking his eyes back into focus. "That's a bit disorientating isn't it?"

"Answer me."

"Right now you should focus on Yakini. A good chunk of our existence depends on her ability to talk the Node down from self-destruction."

There was a palpable hiccup in the world around Mex. It felt like his mind took a step outside his head.

Teledice went limp in her constraints.

Yakini gulped a lungful of air. She was swearing before her eyes were even back in focus.

"I'm going to kill him," Yakini screamed as she vaulted Mex's couch. Overly long arms wound backwards ready to release a torrent of punches.

Sardon smiled in the face of her rage.

The growl in Yakini's throat turned to a whimper. Her arms and legs lost coordination and she pitched forward face-first. Mex managed to catch her head before her skull cracked on the floor. She stared up and him, blinking tears.

"He's turned Teledice into a bomb. MynCorp have weaponised the Nodes."

Chapter 5

Three times in rapid succession, Bergur's pounded his fist into the bulkhead behind Sera. The shear ferocity filled the tiny life-raft with violent echoes.

On the third blow the metal split, and his hand vanished inside the working of the craft. The sides of the tear instantly started to mend. Ripples formed away from the wound and converged on the damage, bringing fresh material to plug the hole. With a guttural grunt, Bergur withdrew his fist along with a tangle of fibrous control systems.

For a few seconds the ship continued to function. The hole closed, pausing briefly to massage the dangling innards back inside the wall. Bergur dropped the fist full he had torn lose.

"Let's hope that's enough," he started to say.

The lights went out.

The internal noises of Sera's body became overpoweringly loud. Her pulse thumped like an anti-matter drive. Each inhalation roared like an approaching sandstorm. Choking on an involuntary scream, made her gag. Her breath bounced back to her cheek from the impenetrable darkness.

The plan was insane. In preparation she had managed to rationalise away the risk, but in action, it was clearly deranged.

The oxygen levels started to fall almost instantly. All Martians know the early signs of oxygen starvation. Every child is prepared for the elevated pulse, the panting yawn and instant headache.

"If we're going to do this, we need to start now," she whispered.

"Ja," he said from somewhere beyond her knees.

There was a rustling of harness straps and something hard hit her in the side of the skull. Bergur muttered an apology. Sera barely heard him through the flashing lights behind her eyes. By the time her head cleared the first chill shiver was taking hold of her body.

"This is such a bad idea," she said.

"Ja," he said again. "Get us some light will you?"

Sera turned in her harness and awkwardly started to rub at the nearest wall. The metal was getting sluggish, either preserving its reserves, or already reliant on ambient energy. Eventually, the patch under her palm began to clear. Martian light poured through her fingers and drenched the inside of the capsule. Sera started on several patches simultaneously, using both hands and a booted foot. The activity kept the cold away, but her head was starting to pound in a familiar manner.

"I'm going to be out of it soon," she said.

"I'm coming," he muttered from a ball of muscle trying to flip direction with no room. As if to emphasise his efforts, he clipped her in the ribs with an elbow. She didn't bother complaining. How he had proposed to sustain them during the crash landing made no sense, and the little she did understand, was repugnant. She was fairly certain an unpleasant death was approaching, from one direction or another.

Bergur's face contorted into view. He had wriggled out of his tunic revealing a cylindrical chest. Each rib was the size of Sera's neck and overlaid with muscles where biology would normally suggest smooth skin should dominate. His skin was so close the fingers of Martian light seemed to shimmer just above the surface. His mouth flaps were clamped tightly closed making his face literally blank. The only expression came from his eyes, which managed to look suitably apologetic. Or at least, that was how Sera chose to translate the crease of skin above the vertical inner eyelid.

Bergur started to scratch at his skin. A transparent layer pulled clear like an elastic snake skin. It surrendered and ripped into long strips.

Rising nausea brought Sera back from the edge of stupor.

"Please stop. I can't take any more of this." She half swallowed the last words with the acrid taste in her mouth.

"I'm going to need every photon." Bergur borrowed air to speak. His breath on Sera's face was cold and stagnant. "The polymer layer keeps me safe from excessive oxygen, but just now its more important my skin flora can photosynthesis."

Sera didn't bother muddling through the nonsense. She stubbornly stuck to the last task that made any sense. She had to coax every piece of the bulkhead into transparency. She could not remember why, but somehow her life depended on light. She tried to breath inside the patches of reflected light, but the air was still empty of something essential. Her vision narrowed into a tunnel surrounded by an impenetrable conduit of darkness. Once every minute, Mars would burst through the tunnel from the top left corner. Its light rushed towards her face, but a backwash of vacuum undercut the wave, making it crash into the walls of the tunnel. Then the beam passed from her sight, leaving only the stars to wrestle with the afterglow. Sera desperately wanted to heed the warning from the Martian lighthouse; they should re-energise the tumbling capsule, pull away from the treacherous rocks of the planet and head back out into the safer waters of a stable orbit.

The Martian beam stopped.

Sera knew she must be dead. The periodic beam was not just a warning, it had become her pulse; a beacon of her life energy.

Some light still existed. The residue painted a purple shadow above her face. The purple fiend opened gaping jaws and clamped them to her face.

The purple creature of death sucked at the last of her life. The light spluttered once and was extinguished.

*

The battle loomed in front of Yakini.

There was no other points of reference to gauge distance and parallax was seriously screwed. Yakini assumed she was getting closer, but it could just as easily be Teledice and the Oikake were growing. Or maybe her view was magnified. Was there any meaningful distinction, in this crappy virtual representation of whatever Verity Space was really all about?

Trust Mex to write something ingenious but half-baked. Even a basic flight sim induces inner-ear feedback. Then at least I'd know I was moving, Yakini thought or muttered or screamed.

Mex had said the glowing blob was Teledice. It pulsed as Sardon droned on about agendas and subcommittees, but was otherwise devoid of anything Yakini might recognise as a young woman. In contrast, the Oikake struck and slashed with a primordial blood-frenzy.

Yakini refused to read anything into her recognition of violence over tranquillity. Instead, Yakini fixed her attention on the space between Teledice and the Oikake, looking for anything that might indicate damage. Layer after layer of detail opened up to Yakini. The very structure of reality was revealed as polygonal textures in the frothing soup of probabilities. Interlaced hexagons and squares ran fractal-like throughout Verity Space, as a universe of sentient minds forced the quantum superposition into certitude. The patterns, like snowflakes drawn by an early digital computer, coalesced and melted in endless cycles of chaos and order. The trashing limbs of the Oikake navigated this terrain with dislocating jolts of redirection, seeking paths of probability that impacted on Teledice's surface.

As Yakini grew closer, or the details just became clearer, she could see why the battle was so one-sided; none of the paths or pattern lead to Teledice. She was present in Verity Space, like an island in an ocean, but no waves lapped against her shores.

As they had all suspected, MynCorp had technology they were keeping to themselves. Yakini was angry, but also relieved. This way there was at least some hope, but first she needed to help Teledice.

Yakini had no idea what it signified, but her avatar had a single virtual arm. She used it now to reach out to Teledice.

The universe paused. The continuous creation of certainty from potential hesitated. Even the Oikake froze mid-lunge. Yakini could feel Teledice, but caught in a moment, a flash of recognition and fear seared into the static mind.

"Teledice, can you hear me?" Yakini called.

Yakini became aware of Sardon's voice radiating away from her. Out of Teledice and into Verity Space. He was no longer talking to the Eidolons. He was talking to her.

"Prepare yourself," he finished.

Teledice woke with a scream fully formed inside.

The space outside Teledice turned white then ceased to register at all. Yakini had a momentary impression of the Oikake flailing against a searing energy, then it was gone. Not the soft sigh of a Verity Space jump. More like the total annihilation of an anti-matter explosion.

Teledice's scream modulated into the plea of a frightened girl. "Stop. I can't hold it back. Please stop."

"Teledice, it's me. Yakini. I'm here."

"Yakini? Get away. I can't hold it in."

Teledice was there. Created by something amongst the layered constructs or Mex's code, the Nexus, Verity Space and her own extraordinary mind. She screamed again and her body splayed like wild horses were about to rip her limb from limb. Yakini did not question why she was also there in body. She took the young woman in her arms, folding her limbs back towards her body and the protection of a foetal ball.

"It's okay. We're going to take you home. It's okay," Yakini murmured.

"I can't hold it back. It hurts too much. They put it in my head. I'm going to destroy everything."

Sardon's voice returned, washing around them like a winter squall. "That's enough. Time to calm her down, before she goes nova."

Another scream tore through Yakini and pulsed out towards the reality beyond.

"Yakini, I can't hold it back," Teledice pleaded. "Help me."

"I'm here." Yakini soothed. "I'm not going anywhere. Just fight whatever it is. Nobody is stronger than you. Then I'll take you back to Nomia. How does that sound?"

"I'm not going to leave you," Yakini said again to herself.

Teledice was no longer in her arms, in fact Yakini no longer had a body. The Nexus was being dismantled, one overlay at a time. Yakini fought against the drag back to the real world, seeking a route back to Mex. Fear rushed through her as she thought of Mex exposed to whatever pulse Teledice had emitted. Was he vulnerable, or his avatar? The virtual space deconstructed itself to nothing while Yakini was still trying to connect the dots.

She was back in the control room with Mex and Sardon. In the laboratory

Teledice was hanging limply from her constraints.

The hard way it is then, Yakini thought as she launched herself across the room with as much ferocity as the ridiculous gravity allowed.

She could tell from Sardon's response that there was no chance of landing a blow, but she persisted anyway. A few inches from contact, the muscles in her arms lost rigour. Nerves all over her body started firing randomly. The floor approached her face with a completely un-martian rapidity. She screwed up her nose in a vain attempt to save a few bones in her face.

Mex arrived slightly later than she would have liked, but he saved her from most of the impact. She brought her cheek in contact with his.

"He's turned Teledice into a bomb," Yakini cried aloud. "MynCorp have weaponised the Nodes."

In the inevitable pause that followed, Yakini used the physical contact of their faces to subvocalised instructions. "Run. Get help. I'm staying for Teledice."

To his credit, Mex looked no more stunned after the subvocal message than he did at the news of nuclear Nodes. For a moment she wondered if the technique worked as well on Earth as it did in low pressure caves back home, but then he flicked his eyes vertically in acknowledgement.

Yakini was up and at Sardon again.

"Electrostatic fields can't protect you from a slow strangulation," she threatened.

"Ms Akida, control yourself for Teledice's sake," Sardon implored.

Then her fingers were on his throat. It felt wonderful to feel his windpipe convulse and collapse under the garotting strength of her slender fingers. Sardon's personal security would be here in a few seconds, and Sardon was surprisingly strong on his own. It felt like he was going to break her little finger. She pressed harder and was rewarded with a spluttering cry.

Two pairs of appallingly white hands were dragging her away and down to the floor. A knee was in her back, grinding vertebrate and cracking ribs. Maybe they did not realise how delicate her physiology was compared to Terrans. More likely they did.

Yakini stole a glance towards the exit, but Mex was already gone. There was nothing more she could do for now.

Yakini went limp.

*

There was a tingling on Mex's shoulder where the gloved hand should land. He risked a glance back towards the laboratory. Yakini was whaling and thrashing like a demonic giraffe. Her limbs whipped around with incredible force, creating a loud crack each time they made contact with a security guard. She was being progressively overcome by the mass of body and armour. Her frame buckled and caved in ways that looked permanently debilitating.

For the tenth time in as many steps Mex started to turn back to help Yakini. He was at risk of being paralysed by indecision. His humanity refused to believe he could be leaving her alone. Rationality listed the importance of getting word to Nomia, his pitiful lack of skill in a fist fight and the importance of someone staying for Teledice. Fatalism told him his capture was inevitable so he might as well take a seat and save some pain. Instinct simply screamed run.

Instinct won.

Panic had erased his memory of the inbound journey from the roof. He took a couple of random turns before slowing to think. The left side of the corridor sloped from floor to ceiling and showed no indication of openings.

He was at the outer wall.

When they landed Mex had asked Yakini if she had ever seen a building like this during her time working for MynCorp. She had grizzled something about four walls, inability to fly and an absence of interest, but to Mex this building was uniquely intriguing. Brutally simple and suggestively unimposing, it hinted at serious design effort.

Most buildings were designed to move a few metres a day, at most. Sufficient to provide a gradually evolving view or to minimise seasonal variations in weather. Persuading a city to up-root and run from the Reset, had been like demanding a parched man pour drinking water into the sea; at some point he'll go mad, jump overboard and drown. In contrast, this building was built for speed and stealth. Only a single story protruded above ground level, but to maintain its current pace there must be a much larger volume underground, pulling its way through the soil and rock. The surrounding landscape flowed up its steep sides and across the narrow roof. Stationary it would have looked like a small hillock. Mex could only imagine the complex network of roots drawing energy, minerals and all its resources from the ground beneath. He had no idea how MynCorp had solved the problem of laying down roots while moving. If they had shared the technology, tens of thousands of lives could have been saved, for at least a few more weeks.

As much as Mex admired the architecture, he was just a little concerned at the lack of windows or doors through which he could make a dramatic escape. He would need to get creative.

Necessity may be the mother of invention, he thought, but life threatening terror is a poor father.

The fact the walls were not coming alive to contain him told Mex the A.I. was extremely compromised by the lack of Nexus; things would be running on internal hard-coded logic.

He should head to the roof, the waiting flight pod and the inevitable posse of violence-addicted MynCorp thugs.

He had a different idea.

Mex used a finger to draw a downward pointing arrow on the inner wall. A moment later an opening appeared and Mex stepped out of the corridor and into a cocoon of uniformly illuminated polycrete. The texture of the walls strobed gently as he dropped into the lower reaches of the building.

After a minute, he was gently deposited into a vaguely cylindrical space, forty metres in diameter.

He had arrived at the nadir of the building.

The air tasted metallic with leaking energy. The walls were not walls, but a perfect slice through the surrounding bedrock. Strata waved and buckled across the perimeter like a stormy sea.

Mex looked in the direction the building was heading. Irregularities and graduations in the rock were drawn to the hole made by the building. A pale pebble impacted on the leading point and was refracted. Mex spun round, watching the stone form a circle of cream around the room, before reforming as a pebble sized point in the building's wake. The building dislocating the material in its path, analogous to dragging along a hole by its edge.

A ring of field generators stood in a large circle, like bristling guards. They hummed quantum incantations as they pushed the edges of physical possibility. Until recently Mex would have believed this room contained the pinnacle of probability manipulation technology. Now it looked like a kid's toy, in a newly grown-up world.

In the very centre of the space, running from floor to ceiling, was a translucent tube.

"Straight for the jugular," Mex chuckled.

There were no hard-form controls for the building's energy distribution system, but, once physically coaxed, the artery provided a simple interface. Mex pulled out his code-glasses, which configured themselves to an industrial steel-grey. He was prepared to probe for vulnerabilities in the interface, but on an impulse he hid behind biometrics borrowed from a low-grade MynCorp technician.

The identity was sufficient.

"Too easy," Mex tutted, as he shutdown the main energy artery for the entire building.

The building's systems would run on for some time with slowly diminishing capability. Like a body's circulatory system, it could take time for the extremities to notice a lack of blood flow.

Mex coaxed an opening in the freshly evacuated artery and started to climb. The inside surface was made from the same intelligent material as the rest of the building. Despite no human having entered the tube since construction, it readily offered help, first by allowing hand and foot holds to form. Then, once it had established the humans intent, the tube simply carried the man to the roof.

Mex was thrust from the womb-like confines of the artery into the maelstrom of the roof. Acoustic nullifiers struggled to dampen the deafening noise as thousands of tonnes of soil and vegetation flowed over his head. The building continued to make good speed towards whatever clandestine intent Sardon had targeted next.

The flight-pod was a few metres away. Mex sent a burst of RF to awaken the pod. It was already pulling off the ground when Mex awkwardly climbed aboard.

The flow of soil parted momentarily to let the pod escape. Within a few thousand feet the building was invisible to the eye.

Mex let a single sob of pity take control, before he turned away. Yakini and Teledice's best hope was back in the refugee city.

*

Sera knew true silence.

She had been deeper and further into subterranean Mars than even her father. The caves were so far removed from humanity her heartbeat felt like an unforgivable intrusion. Sera had always imagined death was like the silence of a cave, when she held her breath and strained to hear the planet's core.

She had never imagined there would be so much noise. Death was a roar in her bones. It bypassed her ears and directly assaulted her skull and brain. Sera seemed to have discomfort in her body and a headache; both things she had assumed absent in death. Eyelids also seemed an unnecessary distraction.

Confusion crept across her face and levered her eyes open.

A giant eye filled the sky.

The horizon was a glowing mist of purple clouds.

Sera's face felt frozen in a death mask. Her lips and nose were clamped. Her breathing was not totally her own.

Breath. That was the last thing she expected. There was little doubt she had not died. She felt relief, but it was tainted by the memories piling up to alarm her.

The sky blinked and raised an enquiring ridge of bone.

Sera tried to pull her head back. Her face resisted. Her cheeks pulled free of her teeth and stung, as if she had inflated a dozen party balloons. Something grunted a protest directly into her mouth. She relented and scanned her peripheral vision; eyes fidgeting like a caged animal. Pink light leaked around the edges of the purple clouds. The light strobed and pulsed, as it orbited her head.

Sera tried to speak, timing her throat and tongue to match the ebb and flow of air in her throat.

"Am I dead?"

The question sounded a lifetime away, dimmed by the weight of decades. The answer, when it came, was intimate, appearing in her throat and worming its way to her ears via her jawbones.

"No," it said. "Not yet."

"Bergur?"

"Yes, Sera."

"Did we crash on Mars?"

"We've just entered the upper atmosphere."

"I remember disabling the capsule and suffocating. How am I breathing and why does the air taste of lichen?"

"I am breathing for you."

"Can I be sick now?"

"Please don't."

Sera's toes and fingers started to sting with the ferocity of wind-swept sand. The sensation spread across her whole skin. She tried to thrash her limbs to fend off the attack. Her arms and legs were numb and full of an immensely heavy liquid.

"What's wrong?" Bergur said in her mouth.

"Something is stinging me. It's all over my skin."

"It's just blood."

"Whose blood?"

The shivering returned before he could answer. It was violent, but seconds later she fell limp and started to sweat.

"Hypothermia," she murmured.

"It got pretty cold."

"I feel hot."

"The joys of space-flight."

As the panic settled down, Sera began to see more. Crossing her eyes, she made out the flaps of Bergur's lips stretching out and clamping against her face. The connection was softer than she might have imagined, but the suction was inescapable. It felt like a giant fish sucking on her face. A random thought from weeks before floated back into her mind; a moment's daydream about Yakini and Bergur kissing. She had imagined more crab than fish. Maybe a minor improvement, but it still made her feel queasy.

Every part of the capsule she could see was transparent. The capsule had stopped tumbling. Beneath her fingers of fire spread across the surface. Beyond the flames, the familiar textures of the Martian surface rushed up towards them. The heat was becoming intense, drying the moisture on her eyeballs as fast as she could blink. For a moment Sera thought her vision was dimming again. The flaming planet became harder to make out. Then she was staring at a silver wall.

"Seems like the capsule is going to do its best to save us, despite our best efforts," Bergur grunted.

"So, we slow-cook before impact. Perfect."

"The atmosphere will slow us to subsonic speeds, but the impact is still going to smart."

"Is that supposed to be funny?"

"Not really."

The bulkhead above remained clear. Sera could still see one or two stars, but the atmosphere was starting to tinge the view pale pink. She could almost convince herself the capsule was stationary, hanging in the air through the power of wishful thinking. The roaring sound still rattled the unbreathable air of the capsule; the sound of reality laughing at her futile wishes.

Sera waved a hand distractedly at the mouth connection between her and Bergur. "Remind me again why this is necessary."

"I'm breathing for you."

"You're breathing out oxygen."

"I was. It's getting harder now we're in the atmosphere. Not enough UV for my skin to photosynthesis."

"So, it's a race between death by suffocation, heat or impact."

"You're the one who insisted we rescue Ben."

"And how are we doing on that front."

"Not so good."

Sera listened to the roar of superheated air impacting on their bow-shock. It was getting quieter. Sera imaged when it became inaudible they would crash. She strained to hear the noise, hoping to extend their life by a few seconds.

"How long have we got?" she asked.

She felt him shrug.

Sera rubbed on the wall, encouraging the metal to show the view. The metal was rippling and straining away from her. The shape of the capsule's interior was slowly becoming more oblate. The spare metal was flowing sideways forming a structure she couldn't see.

"What's happening?" she started to ask.

Something near her head hit the ground and gravity went mad. The acceleration couch tensed and held her tight, but every organ was somersaulting inside her skin. Bones wrenched in conflicting directions. Her own scream smacked her in the face. Bergur's lips were plucked from her face and she was gasping for air. A violent shudder split the hull. Rock punched her in the abdomen.

Sera screamed for it to end. She welcomed unconsciousness as it gripped her mind. Blackness was preferable to this chaos of rock and metal.

Her own ragged breath cajoled Sera awake.

She was being carried through an icy darkness in the jaws of a giant beast. She could feel a soggy pain where its teeth tore at her flesh, and a grating where they pressed against bone. The beast seemed to be limping, swinging her like a rag doll each time it dropped onto the lame leg.

Sera's pain was dulled by the ineptitude of her lungs. They clumsily sucked at the air. She could feel her chest rise and fall, but her body insisted nothing useful was being inhaled. She barely had time to spit out one lot of air, before her body desperately dragged in another useless load of gas.

A familiar taste brought clarity. Dust mingled with the blood in her mouth to create a metallic sludge. The sound of grit under foot was immediate, but muffled by an echo. Only the basalt caves on Mars could be so familiar, but there were no Martian animals larger than a bacterium. Which meant she was being carried, and the pain was entirely her own.

"Can't breathe," she gasped.

The swaying footsteps halted. She felt herself being lowered to the ground.

"No," she begged. "Take me back to the surface."

"It's mad out there," Bergur's familiar voice barked. "We need shelter."

"There's no air down here. Only enough oxygen on the surface."

Each word ate into her oxygen reserves. One more word and she knew she would die.

The lumbering beast groaned and lifted her off the ground. Her boot snagged on the jagged wall, then they were climbing back towards the surface.

They were one grotesque symbiotic being. Bergur was the limbs, and she was the lungs. He lurched along, dragging one leg, while she wheezed and panted. Her body felt bloodied and broken. They had been so close to each other when the capsule crashed, their bones might have splintered and impaled each others body. Maybe she really was breathing for both of them; oxygenating both lots of blood as it sloshed around their mangled flesh.

Sera's head was starting to clear. The air was still thin and bitterly cold, but her lungs were used to scarce concentrations of oxygen.

A breeze carried the sound of sand-blasted rock. Sera recognised the ringing echo of a basalt tunnel. A sand-storm was knocking at the entrance. It clawed at the walls, desperate to render what remained of their flesh.

"How did we get in here?" she asked reality in general.

Bergur stopped limping. Sera felt her body sag towards the ground. She tensed as their bodies separated, but there was no tearing of mingled flesh. All she felt was the cold of blood congealing in the breeze, and the nail-like bed of basalt gravel.

"The crash caused a cave-in," Bergur said.

"Cave-in?" Sera turned her head and winced as rock-crystals pricked her cheek. What she had assumed was the tunnel entrance was actually a gaping wound in the roof of the tunnel, a pile of rubble and the twisted silver of the crashed ship. "We survived that?"

"The capsule did everything it could. Even without internal power, it managed to grow aerofoils. I don't think we managed much of a glide, but it slowed us down a lot. Finally, it absorbed most of the impact energy. Otherwise, we'd be in much worse state."

Sera looked at Bergur. The tunnel was deep in shadow, but she could see the dark stain coating his left leg. He held a defensive hand over the wound. She turned her attention to her own body.

"How badly am I hurt?" she asked.

"Considering your body is better designed for dancing than crashing, you got off lightly."

"Am I going to live?"

"Long enough to die of thirst."

"This is my planet. I'll find water. Just get me back on my feet."

Sera closed her eyes and let the sounds of her home wash her clean. She could hear Bergur shifting rocks. The next thing she felt was the dislocation of waking. It might have been a few seconds later, or maybe hours. It didn't really matter.

Sera remembered the hiss that had woken her. "What was that noise?"

Bergur limped back into view. "I found a canister lodged in the tunnel wall. The capsule must have jettisoned it as we crashed."

"What's in it."

"Some sort of medical balm. Food concentrates. Two litres of water and a change of underwear."

"It's a start. Let me see the balm."

Bergur helped Sera sit up with her back resting against one wall of the tunnel. She wriggled her shoulder blades, searching for a dull edge amongst the jagged rock. Overall, the pain wasn't as bad as she expected. Blood had seeped through the left hand side of her jacket, but when she investigated the damage was mostly abrasive; despite her imagination's insistence, her insides were not dangling on a thread.

As soon as Sera popped the cap, the contents started to writhe like an overeager jellyfish. She beckoned Bergur to sit down, and poured the translucent puddle of cells onto the centre of the hole in his thigh. Bergur seemed completely unperturbed as the blob slurped on his blood and nibbled the damaged flesh. The internal complexity of the thing became obvious as the fluids bubbled and pulsed inside.

This was new tech to Sera, and her curiosity insisted she ask, "What does it feel like?"

"Warm," he grunted.

"Very enlightening."

The flow of blood stopped, and the thing became transparent. It was laying a sheaf of slime over the cleaned wound. After a few minutes, the blob released its grip of Bergur's leg and lay inert. Sera tentatively picked it up and transplanted it onto her own abdomen. She flinched as it reanimated and suction gripped her flesh. There was a moment of pain as her wound started to ooze fresh blood, then a numbing warmth blanketed the whole area. She watched in fascination as small fragments of grit were plucked from her flesh, passed into the jellyfish and dissolved.

"This thing is amazing," she said.

When it was done, Sera returned the thing – she was not sure if it was animal, algae or pure chemistry – to its pot and gently applied the cap. She tested her stomach by dragging herself upright. The wound throbbed in the background; a reminder she was still injured.

Sera remembered a question she had been distracted from asking. "Bergur, did you say underwear?"

Bergur handed her the supply canister. Next to a flask of water was a roll of dull silver fabric. Sera blessed the gods of her ancestors.

"It's a survival-suit! Only one, but it wouldn't fit you anyway."

Sera pulled off her ripped jumpsuit. She turned her back on Bergur before removing her undergarments. The survival-suit felt like an old friend as it adjusted to her contours. Within seconds the cold was gone and blood started to return to her extremities. The suit gripped and held the supply canister as she held it to her good side.

Sera felt complete. Fresh energy flowed from her relief. She looked towards the Martian sky. "Right, let's go find Ben."

Chapter 6

The centipedal transporter jolted as Fez pushed it beyond a safe speed for rough ground. Several of the legs had crashed into their neighbour, and now limped or just dragged along the ground.

Lesana flopped limply against her constraints, the horror of the meat factory still alive in her mind.

"What the hell was that?" Fez asked again and again without exorcising the image.

"I suppose the sphere was trying to reset the meat to its original state," Lesana muttered through a soar taste in her mouth.

"What does that even mean?"

Lesana's mind swam with the taught distinctions between cultured cells and animal husbandry, but it all sounded too hollow to be given air and words.

For her own benefit she said, "In-vitro meat has no nervous system, it's no more alive than the algae we eat."

"The algae is alive?" Fez asked with alarm.

"Any sign of spheres?" Lesana asked, craning her neck to look back along the length of the vehicle.

Fez checked the instruments and gauges. "Not that I can see, but this thing is mostly blind."

"You still sound worried."

Fez tinkered with the controls for a while before answering. "I thought I was following the tracks of the rest of the convoy, but now I'm not so sure."

"You mean we might be lost?"

"I was waiting for you, when they left," he whined.

Lesana ignored his petulance. "Maybe we should retrace our steps," Lesana suggested.

Fez ignored her suggestion but his knuckles whitened on the controls. "There's a shimmering on the horizon," he claimed. "It must be the city."

"It could be anything."

"Like what?"

"I don't know. Maybe the Reset."

The vehicle lurched to a halt and listed to one side.

Lesana braced herself against the frame of the door. "It might not be the Reset," she said with alarm. "I was only speculating."

Fez started thumbing the controls. "It's not me," he stammered. "The thing just stopped. Why would it just stop?"

"Can you fix it?"

Fez looked at her like she was speaking pure ⬚

Lesana climbed down from the cab. The rough ride left the horizon swaying for a few seconds. The ground was an insipid grey and cut by irregular furrows. She prodded a small clump of dirt with a toe. It evaporated on the breeze. As she watched the dust dance away, her gaze rose to consider the full extent of the wilderness.

Fez kicked one of the vehicle's legs and grumbled an obscenity Lesana could only guess at.

"I've never seen anything so barren." Lesana's eyes were still straining to see the edge of anything.

"Mine." Fez was back into his adolescent monosyllabic dictionary.

"Mine?"

"Open-cast mine. We've passed loads since the start. MynCorp microbe-things, stripping the soil and rock of useful stuff."

"But it's huge."

"This is nothing. There was one. It took a week to get through. The buildings almost starved. Nothing left for them to suck out of the ground, except heat."

Lesana swallowed a mouthful of the dry wind, stripping the remaining wisp of moisture from her throat and dragging a convulsive cough from her lungs. Puffs of dust stirred around her feet with each spasm. Her hands were heavy on her knees, the muscles around her spine tense but useless.

Gulping air she rasped. "What are we going to do?" She looked up and blinked at the place Fez had been standing. "Fez?" she called.

He reappeared from the back of the vehicle with a smile of false bravado. His clothes bulged in a dozen places. "Load up," he said, tossing an apple.

Lesana blinked. "We can't abandon the food."

"Not much good out here."

"They'll come back for us."

"Maybe. I'm not going to sit here and hope. You coming?"

Lesana was certain she was not going to be left alone. She had always spent a lot of time on her own, but always with the hubbub of society all around her: real and virtual.

The arid plane looked like the dusty remains of desiccated bodies. The only feature was the shimmer on the horizon. Fez gave the centipede leg one more kick for good measure, and set off in that direction. Lesana grabbed all the fruit her clothes could accommodate, stuffed a handful of soft berries into her mouth and trotted to catch Fez.

The conversation between them soon dried up as shared doubt took over their minds. The doubt became trepidation and finally outright fear. Lesana stopped walking.

"It's not the city," she declared.

Fez stopped and rocked between Lesana's frown and the unearthly storm rising into the sky ahead.

"You think it's the Reset?" he whispered below the audible range of the fates.

"I'm certain."

"Shit! What do we do?"

Lesana turned and started to walk back the way they had come. She could hear Fez groan and then the uneven scratching of his shoes racing to catch-up. Lesana found herself breaking into a canter until her pace matched the thudding of her heart.

As soon as her breath deepened to accommodate the blood demanded by cramping legs, the desire for water became overwhelming. She was forced to slow to a fast walk. When they eventually got back to the broken-down vehicle, frustration and thirst was threatening to cripple her with tears.

Fez busied himself reloading with more fruit, but his shaking hands betrayed the desperation they shared.

Lesana pointed towards the setting sun and one of the cardinal points they had not explored. Fez nodded and they dragged tired feet in the new direction.

Night fell and still they walked. The sky turned charcoal and then slowly the stars ignited; first in ones and twos but then in swathes.

They walked in silence. At dusk they argued about how fast the Reset was catching them. The only reference was the height of the shimmering in the sky, but neither of them could convert the altitude into a distance.

A hundred questions plagued Lesana's mind. What would be the first thing they knew? Would they hear it or feel it get near? Or, would they just pop out of existence without even knowing it was happening? Was that what she hoped? Would they die of thirst before then?

She did not speak the questions aloud. Doing so seemed likely to tempt fate. They barely talked at all.

The stars behind them started to dim. Each time she risked a look behind, there were less, until even the stars directly above started to wither until extinguished.

Each step she expected to feel her trailing foot seared out of existence. She grew more and more exhausted and her throat cracked, until fruit juice stung rather than soothed. In the darkest moment of the night she almost imagined she wanted the Reset to catch her and bring the night to a final conclusion; better the certainty than endless fearful footfall.

Just as the sky behind started to fade from black to cerulean, the stars straight ahead flickered a couple of times and vanished. Lesana stopped walking. She had been following each constellation as they sank into the west, now she felt dizzy and disorientated.

She could feel Fez's laboured breath nearby. He croaked a couple of times and then managed to speak.

"What is it?"

"It's all around us. Can't you feel it? The air is heavy, almost moist."

"We can't be inside it. Not unless, we survived."

"Is that even possible?"

"Not according to Julienne and the rest of the council."

"Could they be wrong?"

A grey light permeated the air, revealing a Fez shaped shrug. Lesana could see her feet now. She crouched down and dragged her fingernails through the dirt.

"The soil is still barren. I thought the Reset was supposed to undo human tampering."

"Maybe this is just weather."

"Morning fog. That means the Reset is still coming."

Lesana turned on the spot, hunting for any sign of approaching danger.

Fez touched her shoulder. "We should keep moving," he said.

Lesana resigned herself to still being alive and picked up her leading foot. It remained hovering in mid-air. A chill crept over her skin despite the perfect insulation of her clothes. She turned twice on the spot.

"What?" Fez asked.

"Which way is west?"

*

Julienne waited for Mex to land on the roof of the Mickelson building. She forced herself to stand perfectly still. She chose to interpret the eagerness with which he had left as war fatigue. It was a simple matter of will. Uncertainty was contagious and the entire city was on the cusp of an epidemic. Most of those around her were technicians or pilots, mostly MynCorp defectors. As far as they were concerned, Julienne was the best MynCorp had to offer, brimming with high-tech implants and tactical training. She was the calm authority amongst the bustle of the flight base.

She was trained to lead, but at some point she had stopped doing so out of a sense of duty or necessity. It was only when she paused to watch any one individual, she knew she continuously put herself forward for all of them. The shift in her motivation was even more dramatic than her abandonment of MynCorp, but Nomia and José seemed to have that effect. Julienne might lead men and women, but Nomia and José were the inspiration behind everything.

Nobody could know Julienne's mind limped like a three legged dog, physically and mentally, more scar tissue than grey matter. Except Mex, he knew. She had no secrets from him any more, but that was okay; Mex was the exception to all her rules.

His pod made the slow descent of a cautious auto-pilot. Mex dropped free and dragged his tired body towards her. She could see signs of shock in the trembling of his finger tips and the grey-white of his skin.

Julienne forced herself to stay still, letting him take the few steps to her. He tried to smile, but other emotions bustled for control of his face. Then he fell into her arms. The moment they touched lips and foreheads, they started to share minds. Mex gave her everything. In an instant she knew all that had happened since his departure and exactly how it made him feel. She gave him tactical confirmation about his decisions, wonder at his ingenuity and empathy for his emotions. Together they quelled doubt, explored permutation and reinforced conviction.

"Go and get some rest," Julienne said aloud.

Mex started to object, but Julienne intervened with another kiss. "The council is already in session, I can tell them anything they need to know. You're a wreck. Get some rest," she insisted.

"Julienne," he paused. "I wish you'd been there. We would have been stronger together."

Julienne decided that was enough.

"Teledice is alive," Julienne announced.

José looked as if he might contradict her, then his features went slack. Julienne wondered if she looked the same when communing with Mex.

Communing, she thought. I like the sound of that. She imagined what she and Mex shared was a poor simulation of the connection between José and Nomia, but communing was a good word.

The council was watching her expectantly. Julienne tried to muster some of the focus she had formerly enjoyed.

"MynCorp have found a way to weaponise the former Nodes, rendering them inert beforehand. Sardon Lucas has Teledice in a subterranean building. Mex has supplied a recent trajectory."

"Inert?" Nomia asked.

"Something deeper than unconscious. Detectable but invulnerable to the Eidolon spheres."

José seemed to have recovered from his initial scepticism. "To what end?" he asked.

"MynCorp are attempting to threaten the Eidolons into a negotiated settlement. If Sardon is being candid, in death, a single Node is capable of permanently damaging a significant volume of Verity Space."

Mr Gaverson, the erstwhile administrator of the Jefferson-A, seemed to have aged another couple of years since Julienne had seen him this morning. The wrinkles on his forehead were starting to overhang his eyebrows, casting a shadow that exaggerated the dark rings around his eyes. He held up his hand before speaking.

"What does that even mean?" he asked with a temerity that made Julienne feel guilty for her answer.

"Mutually assured destruction," she stated.

Alyona stood to one side. Despite her essential skills, no one had found the time to formally invite her onto the council. Rather than explicitly test her loyalty it seemed to be expedient simply to keep her position unofficial. The Jefferson community leaders had a natural distrust of Alyona, but Julienne was probably the only person in the room capable of conceiving how badly Alyona could harm them if she was not sincere.

"And Yakini," Alyona asked.

"She's remained with Sardon Lucas to help Teledice."

"There are many more people in the city. Some will die without Yakini's leadership. Mex should have remained, and Yakini should have returned," the former ☐ delegate stated.

"It was Yakini's decision to stay." Julienne could hear the defensiveness in her own voice. Some of Mex's guilt had bled into her own copy of the memories.

"Teledice is alive," Nomia reminded everybody. "We need to rescue her."

"We can't possibly fight a war on two fronts." Julienne thought she detected an edge of despondency in José's voice. She instinctively reached for a processing node to replay and analyse his words. Nothing happened.

Well you wanted to be a real girl, she thought with a satisfying level of irony.

"We'll go," Julienne announced.

"You and Mex? You are the best chaperones my Nymphs have, and aren't you both working to stabilise the Jefferson minds?"

Alyona whirred gently before speaking. "Julienne and Mex have the skill-set best suited to a rescue mission. Also, their absence will have the least impact on the city's viability."

Julienne enjoyed Alyona's frank manner, but her overtly mechanical body was a reminder of why Julienne continually struggled to absorb inter-personal skills. There was a certain cosmic irony in the fact Julienne was trying to develop an ability her implants used to simulated perfectly for the purposes of social engineering.

José roused himself. "I don't think we should risk sending any of the Satyagrahi. Not until we know how MynCorp abducted Teledice."

Julienne made a mental note to emulate José's use of the name initially given to Nomia's nymphs by the refugees of the Reset. José was much more careful than most to avoid identifying the Nodes as formally part of Nexus. Julienne identified heavily with helping them develop an identity beyond their former function. Secondly, it was not entirely clear how the citizens of this destroyed world might feel about their part in demolishing MynCorp's capabilities.

"So, it's agreed."

Nomia bit her lower lip. She nodded but her eyes were on José.

*

138

Sera rubbed the cowl of her survival-suit clear of her ears.

"Hear that?" she asked Bergur.

"Thunder?" Bergur grunted. He had been monosyllabic since they started their trek. Sera suspected he was finding the pace challenging. His legs were significantly shorter than Sera's, and his muscle bulk made him too heavy for the red-green crust of lichen and rust. Each time he stepped forward, the crust held until his trailing foot lifted, then he sank to his shin. He didn't complain or ask her to slow down, but she could tell he was tiring fast. With meagre supplies of water neither of them was going to survive long. At least Bergur did not appear to sweat. A Terran would have already surrendered all their water to the parched atmosphere.

"It's not thunder," Sera corrected. "Watch."

A few seconds later a fireball erupted to their left and scorched a path across the sky. When it was almost directly overhead, the roar became the scream of tortured air. The fireball grew bulbous louvres and decelerated rapidly. Its path became more erratic, until it dipped behind the skyline of rocky outcrops.

Sera chewed her lip as her mind performed ballistic calculations. "How far away do you think it came down?" she asked.

"Not far. What was it?"

"Shipment from ammonia mines inside Phobos."

"Inside?"

"Phobos is primordial. An icy core wrapped in accumulated rubble," Sera explained.

Sera turned and started to walk parallel to the smoke trail left by the fireball. Bergur groaned and followed. He was limping again.

They crossed an open plane of featureless sand, before starting to climb the remnants of a crater wall. As the ground became firmer Bergur caught and passed Sera. The gradient was making her feel the lack of oxygen. She instinctively reached for the space in front of her face where the breather should have been. The survival suit became more porous, letting her shed some heat.

Bergur turned to check Sera's progress. "That suit doesn't leave much to the imagination," he commented.

"I don't want to know what's going on in your imagination," Sera answered gruffly.

"I was just wondering if Yakini has one."

Sera let out a growl of frustration.

After a couple of false peaks, they crested the crater wall. Beyond was another plane of rippling sand. Black dust streaked the crust of ferrous-red and lichen added a tinged of green. Even during Sera's lifetime, the bold-red of Mars had become a memory. Organic material was starting to stabilise the itinerant sand. Although a long way from a useful topsoil, new biosphere cycles were sluggishly starting, or maybe, restarting.

A broad streak of virgin-rock ran artificially straight across the plane. Far to their left it diverted towards a column of black smoke, rising from a fresh crater. Bearing down on the crater was a black structure of funnels, pipes, towers and irregular protuberances. It seemed to be creating the streak in its wake, like a nightmare-mutated snail. The thing itself was more like a spiny crab, encrusted with extra barnacles. At the heart of the crater, and the source of the smoke column, was the intact meteorite. It glowed slightly with excess heat.

"What is going on?" Bergur waved a hand vaguely at the valley.

When Sera turned away from the glowing meteorite, she realised how fast daylight was failing. "We need to get down there fast," she said.

"But where is there?"

"It's an atmospheric conditioning platform. Can I explain on the move?"

Sera didn't wait for Bergur to answer. She shifted her weight for the descent, ignoring needle-complaints from both shins. Mostly the surface was firm enough to take her weight. Occasionally, a crusty cracking-sound came from beneath her heal. Each crunch bought her father's voice back to her.

"Like a spoon through a fresh-baked meringue," he would mutter cryptically.

When the crust broke there was a disconcerting lurch and Sera's back was thrust upright. The rest of the time she weaved her way across the surface with bent legs and a slalom-rotation of the hips. Even after the trauma of the crash landing and the precarious survivability of their situation, she felt the thrill of being in her natural environment.

Her father had been the one to teach her the importance of dune-floating. She understood her survival depended twice on her ability to cross the sand without breaking the surface. "Don't waste your energy digging in the sand," he used to preach. "Think of your grandchildren playing in planes of grass. The future top-soil depends on you floating without a trail." To a young Martian girl, years of hefting mining equipment, had made him impossibly large and ungainly, but he could climb a dune without dislodging an algae-tinged grain. His gait had seemed magical compared to her gangly and uncooperative legs.

About halfway down to the valley bottom, Sera turned back to check Bergur's progress. He was at the head of a jagged wound running from the crest of the hill. Here and there, red sand bled from deep puncture holes.

Sera sighed and tried not to blame Bergur for being a big purple lump with all the grace of a rockfall.

Bergur's mouth flaps hung open in the glare of her frown. "What?" he demanded.

"We need to make it to the platform before it gets dark."

Sera turned her face and expression away from Bergur, and concentrated on the length of her stride.

As they approached the platform jutted higher into the sky. The profile was convoluted and aesthetically corrupt, but the surface lacked detail; like a conceptual design, it was still waiting for practical concerns to constrain its specifics. Bulbous-topped chimneys burped green-grey fumes into the sky. The plumes dispersed rapidly, tendrils reaching for the atmosphere like the talons of some insidious spirit.

The sun flattened itself against the horizon, bathing the platform in a red light reflected from the rocks behind them.

Bergur and Sera halted in unison. His mouth flapped appreciatively. She grimaced as if an old wound was weeping fresh blood.

The structure loomed above them. Its base emerged from the bed-rock like an extrusion of basalt. The surface gradually morphed from stone to black-metal in the first couple of metres. As it shed the granularity of rock, it gained the textures of technology. Pipes breached the surface, twisted and sank back into depths. Inspection hatches protected the modesty of the internal workings. Mechanistic vibrations leaked through the surface, making grit dance endlessly in gasket groves and manifold junctions. The structure tapered outwards as it ascended, engines and machines grafted onto those below, as if the designers had underestimated the size of the project. The overall effect was of a cartoon lambasting the evils of the industrial revolution.

"If ever a machine could look malicious...," Bergur muttered.

"By usual standards it is," Sera said from where ever her mind had wandered. "It's conditioning the atmosphere; deliberately polluting it with greenhouse gases and nitrogen. Anything to keep the air-pressure above the Armstrong limit. The early colonists had to wear pressure suits to survive, not just because they were poorly equipped genetically. When we arrived the air was so thin anyone exposed died quickly. My dad told me the last thing you feel is the saliva on your tongue, literally, boiling away."

Bergur gave his usual grunt of acknowledgement. "Tell me about it," he commented. "Why do you think I look like this. This face is not a fashion statement."

"Right." Strangely, Sera hadn't given any thought to the reasons behind Bergur's physiology. She tried to imagine his home planet, but realised she knew next to nothing about the Eridani system.

Bergur didn't give her much time to contemplate her ignorance. "How do we get in?" he asked.

A voice full of dust and congealed-grease accosted them from behind. "You ask very, very, nicely," it said.

*

Brent shook her head emphatically. "I've jammed with a lot of half-baked rigs, but there is no way I'd plug myself into that."

Mex surveyed the racks of minds cannibalised from aircraft, ground vehicles, maintenance bots, farms and factories. Each added a tiny extra to the combined mind and to the overall audio-visual maelstrom of whirs and blinking lights.

"You know why they call these picominds?" the technician asked.

"The Turing scale of sentience," Mex parroted.

"Exactly. Each of these if a billion billionth of a sentient mind. Plug a thousand together – hell, make it a million – and you've still a universe away from anything that can care if you live or die."

A series of responses queued in his mind for consideration. Mex sifted through the list and chose one. "This rig is pure class compared to what's already in here," he said tapping his left temple with his clay hand.

"Fare dooes," the technician conceded.

He sounded like himself, but Mex could not quite remember if conversations used to be a series of multiple choice options. Then again, doubting his own sentience might also be a simulated response. Madness, or simulated madness lay down that road.

Mex pushed his code glasses to the bridge of his nose and waved a splice session into being. He dropped, landing hard inside his Jefferson avatar. The mindscape of the Jefferson buildings made Mex think of a medieval cathedral fallen on hard times and squatted by an amateur dramatics company.

The two Jefferson brothers lay coiled around each other like discarded rubber tubes. Occasionally one brother would raise a languid head and spit shards of black hate at the other.

"Boys. My boys. I hope you haven't been fighting again," Mex's avatar shrilled.

"No Mother," the brothers chimed in unison.

"Good, I want you to focus all your energy on the journey."

"Yes Mother."

"Do either of you have something you want to tell me? No? Are you sure?"

"I couldn't help it. I was too hungry."

With a swish of virtual satin, Mex stepped towards the wayward brother. He/She raised a hand with a dramatic intake of breath. The snake like body of the building's mind recoiled and shrank to a black featureless slug.

"I'm sorry," it stammered.

Mex brought his/her hand down gently and stroked the mind's crumbling scales. "Do I not always provide for you?"

"Yes, Mother," the mind purred.

"You don't need to wander off-course or eat the buildings we pass. I provide delicious snacks on your path. You just need to keep going straight."

"Yes Mother."

"And you know why it's so important to keep moving forward?"

"Humanity is depending on us."

"That's right. You're both leaders now. All the other buildings look to you for guidance."

"But they suck us dry. The tethers, can't we let them go? We'd not be so hungry if we let them go."

"Don't you dare. I would be so disappointed in you both if anything happens. Every building lost is a failure."

"But the other minds. They are not like us. They hate us."

"Nonsense. Do not let me hear you thinking like that. You are their leaders. Where you go, all others follow."

"Yes Mother."

Mex felt something brush against his/her leg. Mex kicked backwards and something cried out in anguish.

"So hungry," the second brother complained.

Mex performed a status ping of his avatar. The Jefferson mind had corrupted half a dozen picominds with its attack, entangling its own processing potential with the meagre power of six minds ripped from the hearts of farm-bots.

"How dare you. Go and sit in the corner and think about your actions." Mex pointed at an arbitrary fissure in one wall.

"Yes Mother," the offending brother demurred.

Mex was already retreating, drawing his minds back behind layers of defence. "Don't disappoint me boys. I'm counting on you." He/she said from a safe distance.

"No Mother," they hissed.

Julienne was standing by his side when Mex pulled the glasses from his face. He felt her mind first then her hand touch the back of his neck. The two tingling sensations merged at the back of his skull. Mex reflexively conjured a mental box and pushed part of himself inside. These were fragments of doubt and guilt he needed time to process before he could let Julienne feel them.

"I thought you were resting," she said.

If Julienne noticed his lockdown, she gave no indication externally of internally.

"Jefferson-B decided to stop for a snack."

"How's it going in there? Are they still destroying each other?" she shared an image of her own encounter with the brothers, complete with straining tendons and Fez's panting breath on his neck.

"Not good. They'll keep moving for now, but my control is tenuous. I'm working on an enhanced personality to exert a stronger emotional control, but I need time and some real processing power."

"I think that will have to wait."

"We're going after Yakini and Teledice?"

"You and me."

"I'm ready."

Julienne watched him for a few moments. She was appraising something he could not quite fathom. For a moment he worried she was prizing open his mental box.

Mex leant forward and kissed her with determination. The skin contact shorted the barrier of individuality. They each maintained parts unique and particular to themselves, but it was like two perspectives of a single entity. Their relationship felt much more straightforward when they were together. They complemented each other perfectly: augmented, amplified and completed. If only he could be sure where Julienne's feelings ended and his own began.

"So, what's the plan?" Mex asked with the remains of a breath.

"Plan? Since when do we need a plan?" Julienne teased.

The flight-pod left the ground like a dandelion seed on a breeze. Mex relaxed and let the soft ball of acceleration settle into his lumber. Unlike Yakini, Julienne asserted the merest of suggestions to the flight control. The pod's brain felt the air around it and slipped between the layers and rolled over the eddies, producing a feeling of effortless flight. Mex closed his eyes and marvelled at the feeling, more like floating than flying. The military grade pod was an order of magnitude more sophisticated than the taxi-drones he was familiar with. There had been a similar feeling in the last minutes of his mad flight to the Dyson station, in a less than space-worthy drone. Then the feeling had been somewhat attenuated by simultaneous suffocation and hypothermia.

Mex touched Julienne to share the feeling. She smiled, but telemetry was already starting to leak back to Mex from her interface to the pod. He became acutely aware of the millions of corrections being made to the aerofoils every second. The pod was reconfiguring itself at a frenetic rate in order to produce a feeling of tranquillity within.

"We'll start at the extrapolated position of the MynCorp building and spiral out until we find Sardon," Julienne stated after they had reached a cruising altitude.

"Then what?"

"We form a strategy based on a real-time analysis of the tactical situation as it unfolds."

"You mean, we improvise?"

Julienne gave him on of the open-mouthed smiles they had practised together. Mex laughed, instinctively touching her hand, so they could share the experience.

They flew on. Mex let his mind wander until time passed without notice.

"This is the most probable location," Julienne announced. "I'm drawing on stereo imaging data to look for movement, but we''ll need to process the data together."

"Of course. Activating arcade mode."

Julienne grimaced without comment.

The pod banked and started to spiral clockwise. High clarity images of the ground flooded into Mex's mind. Two layers in overlay. Anything larger than a rabbit and moving leaping out of the picture as if in flight.

"Let's hope the building can't submerge completely," Mex joked distractedly.

Ten turns later they flew over an isolated silver tower.

"Is it just me or is that building leaning at an infeasible angle," Mex asked. He opened his eyes and looked through the hull to confirm the effect was not a data artefact.

"I don't think it is a building," Julienne suggested.

"You think it's a giant work of art."

"No look at the top,"

"Are those chimneys?"

"I think they're engines. I'll circle around."

On the second pass Mex realised what he was seeing. With a change in mental perspective, the tower was clearly an interplanetary cruise liner buried nose first in the ground. Rings of debris revealed the force of the impact, but the structure had survived. The surface was a perfect mirror except for patches of black like leopard's spots where the heat of re-entry had burnt away the outer skin. Cluster of nozzles jostled for space at the rear, now clear of fusion products and collecting rainwater.

Dozens of people emerged from the shadow of the building and started to wave their arms in the air. Mex and Julienne shared a look of pain.

The pod banked to resume the search pattern.

"We couldn't," Julienne asserted.

"No," Mex confirmed.

They continued to paint a spiral on the ground with their shadow. The clacking of bamboo rattling in the wind drifted up to them as they flew over a vast plantation. The monoculture became a monotonous blur until a small patch of green stems leapt into the air and floated with disturbing artificiality.

"There," Mex indicated.

"Got it," Julienne clipped.

There was a lurch. The pod's aerofoils retracted and they dropped a hundred metres in a few seconds. Mex clamped his jaw shut. He tasted blood. Julienne grunted and disconnected from the pod's mind.

"It just died," she shouted over the sound of buffeting air. Her fingers stabbed at a manual control console, repeatedly prodding a red flashing indicator.

The ground grew detail at an alarming rate. The feathery expanse of bamboo became a grid of distinct spears.

"Julienne," Mex pleaded.

"Got it," Julienne grunted.

Fixed wings grew rapidly from the cockpit. The wings bit into the air, rattling the teeth in Mex's jaw. His ears popped and the violence of descent washed through him.

The edge of the forest clattered against the underside of the pod. They glided on for another few seconds in calm air, rough grassland racing underneath. Julienne wrestled a fraction more lift from the wings, the nose lifted and the belly flopped into the ground.

Air escaped his lungs in a mixture of a grunt and a scream.

They bounced twice before the nose hit the dirt and the world flipped upside down.

Chapter 7

I'm worried, Nomia admitted.

I'd be worried if you weren't, José thought back.

I mean, I'm worried about you.

Her concern was interrupted by a grunt from the circle of Nodes; Satyagrahi, Nomia corrected. José's reactions were faster. He stooped and caught the young man before his head cracked into the bare concrete floor. There was an intake of breath as the others in the circle took-up the slack. Somewhere close behind the city, the Reset lurched forward and then stalled.

Nomia broadcast a health check to the circle, and got back nine tired affirmations.

How is he? Nomia asked.

Out cold. We should get him back to the Suparna.

Nomia felt José start to manipulate the surrounding reality, convincing the Universe that he and the boy were actually on the inner surface of a rotating sphere parked at an Earth-Moon Lagrange point. Reality flickered with a moment of confusion; two people potentially in both places, but certainly in neither.

Nomia grasped at the coattails of José's manipulation and tagged a ride through the Verity Space between the two versions of reality.

There was a brief feeling of vertigo before Nomia's body experienced the full centripetal gravity of the spinning Suparna. She stumbled, but she had learnt to keep her feet. Nomia had a better instinct for searching and visualising alternative realities, but José was still better at conceptualising a shift in non-inertial reference frames. The earth was spinning, orbiting, nutating and precessing its way through space. The Suparna was performing its own dissimilar dance. Visualising the change in location was one thing, understanding how two points were moving with respect to each other was entirely another. A few weeks ago, Nomia had looked up inertial frame on a wiki. The explanation was less satisfying than her own intuition.

Kaamil was waiting with two nurses. José tried to lift the boy onto a trolley, but his own wiriness betrayed him. He grimaced weakly as the nurses took the boy, lay him down and wheeled him away.

Nomia smiled a greeting at Kaamil. He experimented with a reciprocal expression, then discovered something on his shoes that urgently needed to be studied.

Nomia took a deep breath. "Let's see how we're doing," she said.

José and Kaamil fell into step behind her.

The outer sphere of the Suparna had been entirely turned over to logistics. Small brick-shaped shuttles manoeuvred through the hexagonal holes to open space. Scavenger missions brought back supplies or refugees from stations and lost colonies throughout the solar system.

"What's the total now?" José asked Kaamil.

"One thousand nine hundred and eighty-three, but the rate of new arrivals has dropped off significantly."

"Less than two thousand survivors from all the colonies, including the Moon?"

"That we've found. Some may have made it to the surface. There are still more than we can accommodate long term."

José grunted his acknowledgement.

They stepped onto a silver disc. Nomia looked up as they rose into the air with a hiss of high velocity ions. The outer surface of the next sphere slid across her view like a metallic cloud. Her stomach performed more somersaults as the artificial gravity faded, and then again when an opening appeared in the cloud revealing the third sphere spinning roughly in the opposite direction.

The lifting-disc vibrated slightly as the ion drives struggled to match the acceleration of the second sphere. Weight returned to Nomia's body in time for her to step off the disk and into the Suparna's main refugee camp.

Someone nearby coughed. It was more likely from dehydration than contagion, but Nomia held her breath instinctively. The shear mass of people created a background hubbub that rolled around the surface of the sphere. Neat rows of prefab huts clustered around larger medical centres or food halls. People bustled everywhere; carrying crates, bags, or each other. Mostly, they avoided eye contact. Those who did not turn away, looked too dazed and exhausted to be actively frightened; an entire community suffering from the shock of trauma.

"There's no colour," Nomia commented. "Everything and everyone is grey."

"Is that good or bad?" Kaamil asked.

José snorted something close to a laugh.

"Colour has an effect on emotions," Nomia explained. "If you have shelter, food and water, environment is next most important. We need some colour."

"Which colour?"

"Experiment. Explore your creativity."

Nomia moved back to the lifting-disc; these refugees were not her responsibility. The disk lifted them through a smaller hexagonal hole in the third sphere, and kept rising. Another refugee village was spread across the inner face of the third sphere.

The disc strained to match the trajectory of the fourth sphere. It settled on the surface with a grateful ping of cooling metal. Her team were gathered near the edge of the opening. Nomia took each of them by the hand, exchanging a mental greeting.

"You should all be asleep," she gently chided.

"Is it true?" Ethemea asked on behalf of them all.

Nomia wished what she knew about Teledice's abduction into all their heads. Oinoie started to cry. The others watched him closely, studying and learning.

"We will get her back," José said emphatically.

"Show me how things are going here." Nomia opened her arms to encompass her Nymphs.

Ethemea led the way to a bulbous blister rising from the grey surface. An opening formed as they approached. It leaked a warm breeze laden with the aroma of lavender. They entered a vestibule and waited a few seconds for their clothes and shoes to adjust to the increased temperature and smoother floor texture.

"I'll wait for you here," Kaamil stated.

Nomia felt the relief of the Satyagrahi and choked her protest. A sympathetic touch of the arm was all she could offer for now.

Inside the shelter, Nomia's senses were immediately overloaded. The communal living space was a mishmash of organic textures and colours.

There were no hard surfaces or anything obviously mechanistic, in fact, nothing remotely like the medical cells in which they had awoken from the Nexus. There were twenty or so young men and women in the space. They were loosely clustered in their tactical teams, but many sat in twos or threes, talking softly, communing in meditative posses or simply exploring each others faces with their fingers. Despite the clashes of colour and style, the overall impression was soothing and relaxing.

To her right, José took a shuddering breath. His eyes were moist. All day an emotion had been slowly corrupting his face. Now the look of devastation was complete.

What are we doing to them? José thought at Nomia.

At least now they have a choice.

But what a choice. We've turned them into child soldiers; all they know is fighting.

Nomia carefully restored the look of calm serenity to her face and moved abut the room. She touched each person who had learnt to appreciate physical contact. For the remaining few, she limited the connection to eyes and gentle words.

José stood to one side and watched like a guardian spirit.

Beyond the communal area sleeping cells lined the corridor. Many cots contained sleeping figures, as still as death. Every so often they would see a Satyagrahi staring fixedly at the ceiling, too exhausted or traumatised to sleep. One cot contained two bodies, asleep but grasping each other like their lives depended on never letting go.

Nomia gave time and attention to every Satyagrahi, awake or asleep. José watched for a while, before indicating her was going ahead to the infirmary. When Nomia joined him, he was deep in conversation with a medic dressed head to toe in sterile white.

"Twenty-six," José stated.

Nomia did not need to ask what the number signified. Twenty-six of her brothers and sisters were victims of the war. Most had neurological or psychological damage. The lucky ones had physical injuries, which might heal soon enough for them to rejoin the fight.

José spelled out the situation. "With the twenty-one who never recovered sufficiently to join us and the eleven we lost to the spheres, we are now at less than half strength."

A new emotion was building in Nomia. It seemed to want control of her tongue. José was frustrating her; pointing out the obvious, as if it were her fault. Entangled within the feeling was her own guilt.

"It's only going to get worse," José continued. "We will have to switch from three shifts a day, to two. The burn-out rate will go through the roof. Then we will have to chose between shielding the Suparna and resisting the Reset. Within a month we won't be able to maintain either. Probably less."

"Let's get back to Earth and talk it through with the council," Nomia said as calmly as she could.

José opened his mouth to say something, but all that emerged was an empty sigh.

Kaamil was standing exactly as they had left him. His head tilted to one side and his data tethers writhed in a sea of transmissions. Nomia was digging deep inside to find something supportive to tell him, when a flicker of consternation creased his forehead.

"What is it?" she asked.

"I'm not sure. Something's…"

There was no warning rumble. The air turned to rock and smacked Nomia hard enough in the chest to knock her off her feet. Then the ground buckled and threw her high in the air. As she tumbled slabs of ground and sky broke free, carving a path of destruction through the Suparna.

There was series of six thumps that ripped through the air and threatened to crush Nomia's chest. A piece of the inner sphere loomed larger each time Nomia's spin allowed her to look up. She split her fear between the returning ground and the falling sky.

Instinctively, she reached into Verity Space for a safe outcome, only to find her view of reality restricted to a single causality. Nomia had enough time to feel a little surprised. She had assumed they were being attacked by the Eidolon spheres. Not only was this not the case, but somehow her Satyagrahi were maintaining the anti-Eidolon cloak, despite the chaos.

Nomia was helpless like she had not felt since the Nexus. The ground thumped the message home with the impartiality of true gravity. Her vision narrowed to a thin tunnel, filled entirely with the falling chunk of sky.

Her sight seemed to be distorted, because the slab of sky morphed into a sphere. It landed a few metres from Nomia with concussive force of a bomb, spewing out a crater of debris. Nomia was thrown back to her feet, where she wobbled precariously.

José was on his knees and coughing. Kaamil lay blinking on his back.

Not ready to trust her feet, Nomia shouted over the ringing in her ears. "Kaamil, what happened? Are we under attack?"

José swallowed another cough and looked at Kaamil for a response. The pilot continued blinking the rhythm of an internal dialogue. José groaned and waved a hand at Kaamil's nearest foot. The leg jerked and Kaamil sat bolt upright.

"Six projectiles have penetrated the Suparna." He spoke without human inflection. "Hypersonic on entering ship's atmosphere. Significant damage from sonic shocks. Reconstructing trajectory indicates hyperbolic approach from Moon's shadow."

A spasm ran through Kaamil's body and emotion flooded back into his face. "Utter madness!" he exclaimed. "They must have literally stirred the dust on the Moon's surface as they passed."

"They?" Nomia begged. "Who are they?"

"I'm not sure."

José levered himself upright and offered Kaamil a helping hand.

"I'm guessing we are dealing with a human assailant." José stated. "So, our most immediate quandary is whether we are being shot at or invaded."

*

This time they decided to sit tight. Wandering aimlessly in the fog was more terrifying, than crouching and straining every sense into the void.

Fez bit into another apple. Lesana could hear him chew and the struggle he had swallowing without saliva. She wanted him to be quiet, so she could listen.

The fog was cold against her cheek. Lesana opened her mouth and let the moisture brush her tongue. It was getting thicker to her left. There was no breeze, but the fog was building-up like it was being pushed towards her.

Her thoughts were as vague as the grey light, but when reality dawned, it was instantly clear.

"It's coming," she cried.

Lesana rose to her feet and started running.

She could hear Fez panting behind, but he held back. He obviously was not sure of her sanity; if she was hurtling headlong to her doom, he wanted enough warning to put on the brakes.

She ran until her legs betrayed her. Fez tried to scoop her up, but they both ended up on the ground. There was a brief tangle of frantic limbs, and then they were climbing up each other hand over hand.

Fez held a sound-quenching finger to his lips, but Lesana was squinting at the grey above their heads.

"I think it's clearing."

"I can hear something that way."

They swapped postures.

"Sounds like transport drones."

"You're right. I can see much further."

A rejuvenating breeze rushed past them, taking the fog and throwing it high into the sky. A tight cluster of spires and towers celebrated with a shower of sparkly reflections. This regimental order of this city was instantly distinguishable from desperate exodus that shaped the refugee city. A cloud of taxi-drones attended the towers like honey bees around a blossoming tree; cross-pollinating the people from building to building in endless cycles of toil.

Lesana was transfixed by the banality of it.

"It's like they don't even know there's a war on," Lesana said with wonder.

A strangled groan leaked from Fez. He was facing away from the city, looking at something that captivated him totally; the Reset loomed like an approaching storm-front. It was close enough for Lesana to see the ground being consumed at its base. It advanced over the denuded ground like flood-water over parched mudflats.

With mounting alarm, Lesana traced the imminent path of the Reset to the city; the buildings had to be aware of the approaching threat, even if the people had collectively decided to avoid looking out the window.

Lesana started to run again. "We have to warn them!"

Fez followed without reply.

The ground became smoother and a more urban shade of grey. Running became easier, but Lesana flagged anyway. As she entered the gap between the first low-prestige buildings, Lesana slowed to an urgent trot. There was nobody visible at ground level. She tried to approach a primary entrance of one building but it refused to acknowledge her request to enter.

Stepping back and looking up, Lesana caught sight of a dozen taxi-drones accelerating hard, away from the city. They climbed towards a clear flight path and vanished behind the accumulated skyline of the main city.

"Good luck," she whispered after them.

The drones reappeared, rewinding their path like they were on elastic threads. As each was swallowed back inside the host building, Lesana swore she could see passengers screaming through the shell of holographic advertising.

The next building was also in lock-down, and the next. Lesana ran towards the heart of the city, smashing her fist against sealed doorways and shouting for anyone's attention.

"The Reset is coming!" she cried, but the only answer was the grumble of a mass transit vehicle deep under her feet.

A diabolical noise pursued her: stone on metal, diamond on glass and tinged by something organic, half scream and part brutalised flesh. The Reset was tearing through the city, one building at a time and heading straight for Lesana on the central plaza.

She had not managed to save a single person.

Slumped on her knees with the Reset close enough for the reality-deforming surface to twist a sickening knot in her stomach, the guilt was crippling; as if she had personally guided the Reset towards this point.

The skin either side of her spine started to tingle. Defunct follicles raised phantom hairs on her arms. The air in her ears rang-out with harmonics rising up from primordial atomic modulations; the noise of the big-bang rallying for one final flourish.

Memories started to unwind before her eyes. She mentally flailed as each flashed past, unsure if fear of death was playing with her mind or if the Reset was unpicking her very existence: the shame of being caught messaging a friend during a college test, the vulnerability of finally meeting a virtual lover, the fear of the Drop when redundancy loomed.

Lesana waited for a more significant memory to appear, something she would fight to preserve. This could not be the sum of her existence. A fatalistic sense of cosmic-irony flickered at the corner of her mouth; an advanced alien race tearing holes in reality to eradicate pure banality.

"Bring it on," somebody said using her voice.

Lesana exposed herself to the Reset, arm and legs limp on the ground, head slumped to one side. The Reset finished with the buildings on the far side of the plaza. It sprinted across the open space with a jolt of acceleration that brought Lesana flinching back to her feet. The prospect of running made her legs shake. She groaned in disappointment, both that she was not ready to surrender and at her lack of courage when facing death.

Even as she was turning to run, the Reset covered half the dividing space. She bullied her legs into a canter, making a futile dash for the line of building façades overlooking the plaza.

Her senses probed the space behind her heels, desperate to detect and avoid the pounce of a pursuing predator. The Reset played with her perception, tinkering with the speed of sound and parallax. One moment she was convinced it was on her heel, the next it was a million heartbeats to her left or right, then it sounded ahead and her stride would falter.

A new sound emerged. The reassuringly-human whirr of a dozen electric wheels accelerating hard. A bullet-shaped transport vehicle with blue livery careered into the plaza, gyroscopes screeching in anguish at their mistreatment. Within the transparent tip of the vehicle Fez grinned manically as his fists hammered overridden controls.

The vehicle spun on its front axle, the remaining wheels locked and sliding across the plaza surface. For a moment it teetered on the verge of turning over, then, with a hiss of emergency coolant, it collapsed back onto all its wheels.

The front screen melted away and Lesana clambered into the second seat.

Lesana attempted a grin. "What took you so long?"

"I was looking for one in blue. You ready to get out of here?"

Fez stabbed at the console. It flashed red and blurted a beep.

Lesana risked a glance at the tsunami of silver about to crash over their heads. Fez tied his fingers in knots as they danced over the console, creating a dozen different bleeps and interrupting a series of calm voices offering automated advice.

"What did you do before to get it going?"

"It didn't make any sense, so I thumped it."

Lesana reached across and brought his base of her fist down hard on the console. For a moment the material cracked, before melding itself whole again.

The vehicle lurched back into motion. Collision avoidance systems completed the aborted turn and, with a cacophony of klaxon effects, pulled the vehicle clear of the Reset.

Doomed building blurred into anonymity as they picked up speed. Lesana shuddered as a couple of tears escaped onto her cheek. The acceleration stopped and Lesana lost any sense of motion. The city rushed past in stilted formation, like a funeral precession marching towards oblivion.

"Why is nobody trying to escape?" Fez whispered.

"They might not even know what's coming. The buildings have gone into lock-down like its some bad weather."

"What weather is so bad you have to hide?"

"Have you never seen the history shows? All those mega storms at the end of the industrial age."

"The only history I know is what my mother told me; the enslavement of the people by the corporations."

"It was the corporations who saved us from the global catastrophe. They ushered in the post-industrial age."

"I don't know anything about that, but if the corporations put an end to all the bad stuff, who was it they stopped?"

"I don't know. I never thought to ask."

They passed the last building and emerged onto a plane of matt-green grasses. Fez widened the angle on the rear-view projection and they watched in reverence as the Reset consumed the last of the city. When the last tower flickered from view, Lesana let out an age-old breath. There was nothing more she could or should do. Her guilt was about the past and could settle in amongst a lifetime of petty regrets and shames.

Normal thoughts and concerns emerged by degree.

"So, what're we carrying?" Lesana asked.

"Take a look."

Lesana brought up a manifest on the console.

"Executive mineral water," she read. "Perfect. Can we go home now?"

"I think so. This thing has a decent navigation system. We should be fine."

Lesana let the flowing landscape and the drone of the motors lull her towards sleep.

"I couldn't save a single person," she muttered at an approaching dream.

Her head slipped to the side and was caught and held by the seat. As her eyes flickered closed she thought she saw a body amongst the grass. Her eyes fully closed, then flashed open with a glimmer of hope.

"I saw someone," she declared.

"We're not stopping to pick-up bodies," Fez complained. He caught Lesana's expression and did not object a second time. The vehicle turned as he guided it towards the point Lesana indicated.

She jumped down to the ground and moved towards the man. He was crouching on all fours staring fixedly at something indistinctly black. He was completely naked. His body sagged slightly with a mixture of accumulated years and more recent hardship.

Lesana slowed.

"Are you okay?" she said softly.

He looked up with soft, sad eyes. "What's this?" he asked.

"It looks like fur or hair."

"Oh." He stroked his scalp and looked at her expectantly.

Lesana reached out a hand. "Come with us."

*

There was a fizzle of consciousness. A disorderly reality approached at breakneck pace, bringing a crackling sound like burning wood, and there was pain.

Mex flinched upright and cried, "fire!"

His legs were stuck out in front of his body. The fabric was charred beyond its ability to heal but there was no flaming flesh. Pale skin poked through the ashen remains of his tunic.

Mex tried to isolate the source of the throbbing at the base of his skull. He let out a whimper of disgust when his focus made it to his right arm, more clay-coloured pulp than limb. As if embarrassed by its own sloppy state, the arm congealed into something more human. The transformation only added to Mex's sense of nausea.

I really need to get an arm graft, he thought.

You're awake, a second mind said in his head.

"Julienne," Mex said out loud. "What happened?"

"We crashed. The pod set fire to a couple of trees. You were rendered unconscious. I carried you to a safe distance. Eventually you woke up."

His eyes uncrossed enough to take in his surroundings. Julienne squatted a couple of metres in front of him. A line of regimented trees formed a coarse backdrop to her cat-like figure. Her clothes were in a lot better state than his. A few areas of heat damage but largely it had returned to pristine white. Soot and worry smudged her face. A faint trail of steam leaked from her mouth with each breath.

"You don't look like you were in a crash," he commented.

"I didn't take a nap in a forest fire. Your suit saved you."

He patted an area of damaged fabric. "Thank you," he said.

"Then I saved you," Julienne added.

"Thank you both."

Julienne grunted.

"What now?" he asked, clambering to his feet. The ground was hard, cold and covered in an artificially turquoise lichen. Mex was tentatively relieved when the pain remained the same. His body was complaining in general rather than about a specific injury.

Julienne shared a mind-map of their surroundings based on a memory recorded during the flight. The gliding crash had carried them a dozen kilometres from the MynCorp building. At the speed it was moving they would never catch it on foot. Without debate, they started walking north towards the only viable strategy: the crashed cruise liner.

After a few minutes of walking across gently rolling hills Julienne relaxed. She kept up a pace Mex found demanding, but her arms started to swing rather than pump. "It's nice having you to myself for a little while," she said, reaching out and slipping her hand into his.

The familiar flash of guilt bolted for its mental box, but not fast enough to prevent Mex from flinching.

He tried to cover his reaction. "I'd prefer slightly more romantic conditions than this."

"Have you been avoiding me?" The tension was back in her voice.

"What? No. Why would you say that," he stammered, but she was there, inside his head, her thoughts right next to his.

"You have doubts about us," she stated.

"This really is not the time or place."

"These are the only times we have. If we don't live now we probably never will."

"I can't argue with that," he said glibly.

"Do you know what I think?" There was a ferocity in her question that prevented Mex from answering. "Either, I disgust you even more now we are the same, or you found it much easier to love me when I didn't love you back."

Julienne had stopped walking. Mex turned to face her. He put a hand and a facsimile of a hand on her cheeks. "Nothing about you disgusts me; amaze, intrigue and astonish, but never disgust."

She was too close for him to fight the second accusation. Julienne studied him for a moment and then withdrew into her own head.

She marched on without another word.

"Merde!" Mex muttered in her wake.

A kilometre out from the crash site a man and woman came panting into view.

"Over here," they shouted as if Mex and Julienne had not heard their laboured progress up the hill. "Are you from the crashed pod we saw?"

Mex nodded. "We lost attitude control. You know how it is with these old-fashioned minds when they get over-hungry."

The pair just stared in confusion. They were both painfully thin. Expensive clothes tried desperately to maintain a fashionable flair on their emaciated bodies. The woman coughed dry air through chapped lips. "You can't imagine how good it is to see you. We were starting to think we were the only ones left on Earth. This is Earth isn't it?"

"Yes this is Earth," Mex confirmed.

"Good. But nobody came for us. No traffic at all. Nobody answered our distress call. The moon is dark, no sign of life. Mercul even suggested we had gone back in time. We haven't gone back in time have we?"

"Not as far as I know. The corporations are in meltdown and what with the war, there's nobody left to mount rescue missions."

Again Mex was met with blank stares.

The man put a suppressing hand on the woman's arm. "Let's get our guests back to the ship. They can tell everyone what's been going on. I'm Cnaeus and this is Aemilianus."

The woman called Aemilianus looked crestfallen. "Yes. Yes. Of course. Do you have any water, or food, but mostly water?"

"No, sorry," Mex admitted.

The crashed cruise liner looked even more unlikely from the ground. The nose had crumpled and melted to absorb most of the kinetic energy of the impact. The resultant pool of super-heated metal had solidified to create rigid foundations for the leaning tower. The rest of the ship was remarkably intact. A cylinder of silver pointing towards the southern cross, crowned by rings of giant egg cups.

Thirty people were waiting for their return. Some were too weak to stand and slumped against empty cargo pods. Those strong enough bombarded Mex and Julienne with a hundred overlapping questions. Mostly they wanted to know if they had water or food. Mex just held out his empty hands. Next they wanted to know about the rest of a supposed rescue party. Frustrations mounted. They became increasingly agitated and pressed into a tight circle.

Julienne's fingers crept towards the weapon concealed at her hip.

Mex flexed his larynx and demanded silence.

The crowd became instantly mute and stood blinking in confusion at their own compliance.

"The Earth has been invaded. Humanity is on the brink of annihilation. Nobody is coming from anywhere to rescue you. There is no place safer than here."

There was a minute of silence.

"Where are the crew?" Julienne asked the Cnaeus.

"Most died in the crash or soon after. A few left to search for help. They didn't come back. The last officer died in an unfortunate incident last week; when the water system failed things got a bit fraught."

"Are there any pods or ground vehicles left on board?" Julienne asked in a flat tone.

"One, but we don't have the authorisation to use it."

Julienne brushed shoulders with Mex. Think you can get past the lock-out?

Please, he thought back dismissively.

We need to tread carefully, these people are beyond behaving predictably.

Are we going to leave them?

You want to stay and lead them?

We could tell them we're on a mission to save humanity.

Do you think they'll care?

Mex applied his most reassuring smile. "Aemilianus, if you give us a tour, we'll see what we can do to help. Julienne here is quite skilled."

"Skilled at what?" the older woman asked expectantly.

"Mostly everything."

From inside it was immediately clear the ship was top-end luxury. They entered through a rough cut doorway and into a cabin that occupied an entire floor. Designed for periods of zero gravity, the décor was unaffected by the twenty degree slope of the floor. As they entered each room the furniture bobbed excitedly and slithered towards them, as if the floor was perfectly level. The rapid breakdown in civil society was evident by the debris accumulating in the lowest corner of each room, and the beds that resembled animal dens more than the satin purity of their conception. The walls were drab grey without the usual projected view. Low-level emergency lighting completed the cave-like feel.

Mex tried to imagine the suite in full glory: mood-matching lighting, full open-space immersion playing on the walls and truffles on the pillow. He could not get beyond the feeling this was a cell for the condemned.

They left the cabin and entered an emergency stairwell.

"I'm told the waste-processing plant is four floors up." Aemilianus pointed towards a transport tube. "If you don't mind, I'm going to have a lie down. I feel quite weak. And cold. Why is it always so cold?"

"We're a long way south," Mex commented.

"South of where?"

"South of everywhere."

Mex and Julienne started to climb, a dozen grumbling voices following close behind.

The services had not been arranged with the serious intent of human maintenance, but the designers had at least acknowledged the possibility the ship's mind might be incapacitated. A warren of narrow passages joined the pieces of embedded kit, and intricate schematic maps were embossed in the wall at each junction like the genealogy of a family with flexible morality. Julienne led the bedraggled party in a stooped dance to the water recycling plant.

"The crew said it won't work without power," someone said from the back of the pack.

Julienne rubbed at the dull surface until she had generated enough charge to power up the status indicators. "Even without the engines it should find enough ambient energy to keep the purification process going," she explained, drawing the group closer by pointing at blinking red fuel bars. "It's the silvering of the hull. The ship tried to minimise energy absorption during re-entry. Probably saved all your lives, but now you're stuck with no reactor power, diminishing quiescent power reserves and no way of drawing energy from the environment. We need to persuade the hull to pellucidate."

People started to nod in agreement and restate Julienne's words to those who looked confused. Mex drifted to the rear of the group before heading back three junctions to a passageway Julienne had mind-flashed to him.

Directly under the skin of the hull Mex found a rack of pods for space burials and a spherical all-terrain vehicle. He formed a hatch in the side of the sphere to reveal a fluid-like layer and then another curved surface. The inner sphere was aligned to local gravity but swung round easily to let him slip inside. The surface glowed in his presence obscuring the dully lit compartment outside. There was a unidirectional pilot seat at the centre of the sphere and four simpler seats around the equatorial perimeter.

Mex slipped into the pilot seat and was immediately punished with a squawk of complaint from the instrumentation.

"Pretty please with cherries on top," Mex said as he slipped his code glasses from their pouch.

Five minutes later Mex rejoined the tour group to help pass armfuls of gossamer thin fabric down to ground level.

"Spare solar sail," Julienne murmured cryptically as she passed. "We good?"

"All good."

Outside Julienne supervised the unfurling of the sail on a north-facing slope. Once the corners were pinned against the wind, she ran a tether to the ships skin and rubbed the end into the surface.

"Keep an eye on it," Julienne instructed her helpers, before slipping back inside the ship with Mex.

Just outside the chamber holding the spherical vehicle, Julienne held up a finger first to her lips and then to Mex's forehead.

Three people inside, she thought.

Mex had heard nothing, but nodded.

"We're armed," a man's voice shouted from inside. "We just want you to take us with you."

Julienne reached towards her own weapon. Mex touched her wrist. You don't need that, he thought.

Julienne sighed. Raised her hands to chest height, palms forward and walked into the chamber. Mex followed smiling cheerily.

A man with gold flecks embedded in his cheeks like freckles, aimed a ceremonial gun at Mex. "You," he said. "Not a word."

Mex nodded and smiled his most harmless smile. Julienne stepped closer and the gun swung to point at her chest.

Another man and woman stood behind the gunman, their shoulders hunched defensively. They seemed content to let the first man speak for them all.

"I know you're leaving and I know we'll all die if we stay," the gunman said.

"You won't last any longer where we're going," Mex chimed.

The gun flicked back towards Mex. "I told you..." the gunman started.

Julienne was already moving.

She ducked low and stepped forward. Her head popped back up in front of the gunman's chest. Her left arm curled over his gun arm pushing the gun under her armpit and out to the side. Her other hand thrust up and through the jaw of the man. There was a crack of bone, followed immediately by the discharge of the gun. The gun was not intended for battle. Plasma detonated from the muzzle like an erupting volcano, making the subsequent silence ear splitting.

The gunman collapsed to the ground holding the bottom of his mouth and gurgled obscenities. The other two assailants tried to bury themselves in the wall and became motionless with fear.

"Go," Julienne demanded through gritted teeth. "And take him."

"Nicely done," Mex commented after the three had dragged themselves away.

"Too slow."

Concerned by the tension in her voice, Mex reached out and touched Julienne. His armpit exploded in virtual flames. He withdrew his hand and the symbiotic pain faded to an echo.

"You're hit."

"Just muzzle flash," Julienne grimaced. "Let's get out of here."

*

The Chief Engineer leant in close, pursed his lips and blew at Sera's face. Leaning back and taking in the cabin with his hands, he spoke with shaman-solemnity.

"Our air is your air."

Sera opened her mouth wide and expanded her chest theatrically.

"My strength is your strength," she replied.

The cluster of miners and engineers relaxed into babbles of conversation, and bustled to touch Sera's arm. She smiled and accepted the attention graciously.

The Chief watched from nearby. He was chuckling to himself.

"Well, well. Little Sera Tamakautoga. All grown up."

"Uncle Ne'igalomeatiga, it is good to see you again," she replied through the throng.

"Uncle? I haven't been called that since you were a frenzy of noise around your father's legs. In those days, I bet you called every miner Uncle."

"It really is good to see you. I just wish it was under more leisurely circumstances."

"Personal trouble?"

"Personal in as much as I've got wrapped up in bigger troubles."

"Just like your father."

Sera smiled weakly.

Ne'igalomeatiga allowed some of his bravado to slip away. A new face emerged from behind the smile. Sera was brutally aware of the elapsed years in the deep chasms of his eroded face, as if he had been blighted by glaciers; forming in his eyes, gouging a path from the corners, before scouring the skin of his cheeks.

He spoke more softly now, contemplating each phrase for subtext. "The invasion seems too far away from here. Whatever human fate may hold, we keep working. Is it as bad out there as it sounds?"

"It's pretty desperate, but MynCorp and Durga seem to be going out of their way to make things worse."

"Nothing's new under the sun." He glanced in Bergur's direction. The words faltered on his tongue. "Let me give you the grand tour, and you can tell me who's chasing you."

"Chasing us?"

"You arrive on foot, at dusk. Bruised, battered and accompanied by..." For a moment Ne'igalomeatiga hesitated as he searched for an appropriate pronoun. "...by whatever that is."

Bergur chose that moment to casually open his mouth flaps, revealing rings of pointy teeth. He seemed content to play the dumb alien. Sera noted the way the miners avoided looking directly at the purple anomaly. Bergur wandered through the cabin, causing subtle ripples in the path of those around him. For his part, Bergur kept his movements slow and predictable. He had one pair of eyelids closed, obscuring the rapid eye movement of his calculating mind.

"Fair point," Sera conceded.

"Let me guess. MBT or Durga Corporation?" Ne'igalomeatiga speculated.

"As if there's a difference any more. Does that cause you a problem?"

"Only if we get caught helping you. Even then, it's a brave new planet. MynCorp has gone and Durga is struggling to take its place. The economy is on a war-footing. If they were masochistic enough to take away my mining rights, I'd probably enjoy the rest."

Sera looked sceptic, but said nothing to contradict him.

"Any which way, you're going nowhere till dawn. Let's walk and talk. I'll show you the highlights of my little city."

Sera made eye contact with Bergur, and nodded towards the exit. He bowed his version of a nod, and closed the polite gap he had awarded Sera and Ne'igalomeatiga. Many of the miners gave furtive glances at Bergur's back, more able to accept his existence now they did not have to confront him directly. Sera realised how much faith Bergur was putting in her decisions. At no point did he question the trust she placed in these miners. He was evidentially not a natural follower, but he seemed to have a rare understanding of his limits; taking control when his expertise allowed, but slipping into subordination when he was unable to offer insight. Sera was surprised how respect had crept into her opinion of Bergur. She clearly remembered thinking he was a pointless lump of purple machismo. Now she envied his serenity, compared to her own self-doubt and continuous sense of inadequacy.

He's just like Yakini. That's why she loves him.

The thought took Sera by surprise. She was not even aware she had been hunting for an explanation. Once or twice, she had caught herself blaming Bergur for Yakini's betrayal, as if he had polluted the time-stream back to before Yakini had left Mars. She was brutally aware such blatant irrationality was a manifestation of her own feelings of culpability.

It is exactly these untimely periods of introspection that paralyse you when you should be projecting conviction and determination.

"The perflurocarbon minerals are cracked in these canisters. The fluorine is diluted with Nitrogen in the space above, before being vented from the top spire-funnel."

The passage through which they had walked was rough-hewn into the bed-metal of the structure. The floor was polished to an onyx-shine by a continuous flow of boots. No conduits or ducting spoiled the natural feel. Light seeped from patches of almost white moss, which clung to the roof in two irregular strips.

Bergur asked another question. "How many platforms like this are operating on Mars?"

"Six or seven. Now the settlers can get around without pressure suits, the urgency has dropped off somewhat. We're still terraforming the atmosphere with green-house and buffer gases, but our efforts have slipped off the political agenda in recent decades. There used to be over a hundred platforms frantically trying to get the air pressure over six kilo pascals. They even encouraged dust storms, just to hold onto a little more sunlight. Once the carbon dioxide began to sublimate from the polar-caps, nature started working with, rather than against, us."

"And the meteorite?" Bergur sounded politely curious, but his eyes sucked knowledge from their surroundings.

"We've known the core of Phobos was largely ammonia ice since the first probe, in the middle of the twenty-first century. It's a perfect source for an atmospheric buffer gas; passively, adding pressure without any complicated geo-cycles, at least, until we get some top-soil."

"What about the oxygen levels?"

"Not our department. Pressure and temperature are all we care about. Oxygen is the responsibility of all those biological types. Too mucky for us diggers."

If there was any irony in Ne'igalomeatiga's voice, Sera could not detect it.

They started to climb a solid staircase. It spiralled and morphed into a skeletal structure of black metal. The spider-web seemed impossibly fragile, yet even Bergur passed without a spasm of distortion. They continued to climb into an atrium of industrial noises; blasts of steam-saturated air, crunching of metal teeth on rocky food and the satanic-roar of molten metal.

The skin above Bergur's eyes lifted quizzically.

"This space is largely involved in maintaining the structure and working of the platform. It's pretty old school: Refining, smelting and casting. We have limited supplies of nu-metal, and generally, when pushed to the limit, these intelligent materials tire too quickly. We generate more metal ore than we need as a bi-product of the fluorine extraction. We put it to good use, then grind it back into the ground when we're done."

"Makes sense," Bergur shrugged. "We still use dumb-metals for ship building. It's more predictable."

Ne'igalomeatiga looked impressed. "Rather you than me. All that hard vacuum around you. I'd want a metal intelligent enough to notice and seal any holes."

"Bit of vacuum never did anybody any harm."

Ne'igalomeatiga looked dubious and slightly deflated. The rest of the tour was more predictable: passages of cell-like dormitories, complicated mazes of humming pipes and towering condensers. They had climbed higher, trapped inside the skin of the primary fluorine-chimneys. At the top was a small cylindrical space edged by a pressure seal. Ne'igalomeatiga handed

Sera and Bergur a rebreather mask, before fitting his own. Sera graciously let him check her mask was in place over her mouth. Bergur contemplated the sack of algae and oblong mouthpiece for a moment, before putting it back in the storage rack.

Ne'igalomeatiga rotated the room using a hand-winch protruding from one wall. There was a hiss of escaping air and an inrush of noise. Sera's ears and nose equalised pressure reflexively. Her survival-suit instantly stiffened and grew a cowl to encase her head.

A small railed balcony jutted from the side of the chimney and overlooked the jagged spires of the platform. Despite the savage cold Sera was drawn to the edge.

Although the sun had set several hours before, the sky still contained large, dusty, swathes of shimmering violet. Few stars were visible, but Phobos was a dull lump rising in the West. Compared to Earth's Moon, Phobos seemed battered and defeated; grossly irregular in shape and dirty with poorly reflected sunlight. Sera watched it for a few minutes, gauging its movement and growth against the relatively static point of Deimos.

Sera turned to the bright doublet of the Earth and Moon. She became aware of Bergur standing nearby.

"It's still there," he commented.

It took her a moment to realise he was not being flippant. It was entirely possible the Earth or Moon could vanish from reality and history at any moment. Somehow, the realisation seemed even more shocking when seen against the cosmic background.

Her lips moved in a silent prayer for Yakini, Nomia, José and even Mex and Julienne.

Chapter 8

"I'll see to the Satyagrahi," Nomia stated, already starting to pick her way through the debris strewn deck.

"Right, Kaamil. You and me." José asserted. "Let's see what we're dealing with."

Kaamil hesitated, his eyes tracking Nomia's back, then he turned and followed José towards the nearest inter-sphere portal. The smaller pieces of wreckage were already starting to pool and flow back into their original configuration. José nudged a large lump that had pinned the transport disc to the deck. The grey-white material took the hint and slumped to the deck.

"Where to?" Kaamil asked as they stepped aboard.

"Are you and the Suparna feeling up to inspecting the nearest impact site?"

Kaamil gave no acknowledgement of the question, but the disc rose briefly before plummeting steeply towards the outer spheres.

They arced over the sprawling remains of a hospital camp. The orderly rows of prefab buildings and treatment centres had been jumbled beyond the eye's ability to discern shape. In chaotic scenes medics and patients fought side by side to rescue those trapped inside collapsed buildings. The walking wounded milled like worried sheep.

The camp was behind them before the destruction could eat into José's determination, but he tensed as another camp spun towards them. From a distance the scene looked just as devastating, but the few extra seconds were enough for the Suparna to have started reacting. The same collapsed buildings were disgorging the humans protectively cocooned inside. Prone bodies were rising from the debris and flowing clear. They formed regimented rows, amongst which, gowned medics were triaging the injured and re-injured.

The refugee spheres were a mess. In places the fabric of the deck had buckled throwing entire camps into the air. Most of the damage had been caused by the shockwave; circling the closed space, picking up things and people and dumping them back down on the next revolution.

José and Kaamil glided over the damage, the crying of frightened people drifting in their wake. A quarter revolution on, the ground started to show signs of heat damage; charred edges to storage containers, structures melted and fused into deformed shapes of monstrous proportions.

They were flying parallel to a black streak gouged from the deck. As the sphere rotated beneath them, the channel cut deeper, until it ended in a plume of concentric black rings. At the epicentre was a blunt bullet of glowing metal.

José looked at Kaamil for redundant confirmation.

"The Suparna can detect no radiation other than thermal. The object appears to be safe to approach," Kaamil volunteered.

"I suppose if it hasn't exploded by now..." José let the statement die before the fates could hear.

José stood nearby as the deck slowly expelled the invading splinter of metal. The thing was about ten metres long and wide enough to reach to José's chest. It looked unerringly like a flying coffin, apart from the umbrella shaped air-brake at one end that added a slightly phallic overtone to the impression.

"Isn't an air-brake an unusual addition to a missile?" José asked.

"Usually it implies the cargo of the craft should reach the destination with minimal damage," Kaamil confirmed.

"If there's a food parcel inside this thing, someone is going to pay."

With a few minutes of exploration, Kaamil discovered a seal welded shut by the energy of the crash. The metal was brittle from heat damage and surrendered after a few blows. Steam rushed from the opening and escaped into the air.

The inside of the craft was entirely filled with thick webs of acceleration-absorbing filaments, like an army of spiders laying siege. Cocooned at the web's heart was a human shaped shadow. Kaamil strangled a whimper, but José was too transfixed to notice.

The figure was absolutely motionless but held to attention by the tension in the threads. José reached into the cavity, instinctively avoiding the touch of the webs. He hesitated just short of contact causing his thumb to brush against a thread.

What happened next took a few seconds to reconstruct. The only discernible motion was the slow wither of the acceleration web. José noted the capsule was designed for a single use, but most of his brain was trying to decode what had changed.

"José," Kaamil ventured.

José looked at Kaamil with a mixture of confusion and impatience. He found himself directed by Kaamil's gaze. A figure lay on the ground ten metres from the capsule, identically dressed in seamless black gloss. Identical to the figure in the depths of the missile. José spun back and directed his indignation at the empty capsule.

"How in hell?" he implored.

The outline of the figure on the ground was shimmering. José and Kaamil edged closer. There was an eerie buzz nagging at the edge of perception.

Kaamil cocked his head inquisitively, "I think she is having a fit of convulsions."

"She?" José took in the overall shape of the suit; close to two metres long and well defined muscles but the ratios were undeniably female. José touched the nearest leg. His wrist instantly started to ache. The slick surface was shaking violently but too fast to see clearly. He withdrew his hand and nursed the protesting joint.

"I would guess she is in shock," Kaamil continued. "Probably due to the trauma of the landing."

José started to investigate the cowl and face-plate of the suit. He tried and failed to grip the fabric around the neck, so probed at the edge of the face with his finger nails.

From nowhere, a blow landed on José's shoulder, bowling him to the ground.

"Hold her down," José bellowed.

Kaamil placed hesitant hands on the nearest arm, but as soon as he leant in with his weight, pain invaded his face and he recoiled. José growled in frustration and stepped across her chest. He landed hard on her chest, a knee pinning each shoulder. The suit barely deformed, but the buzz of vibration sank out of audible range. José clamped down on his bladder muscles as his bowels threatened to shake themselves free.

Turning his attention back to the face José found the four pressure points required to pop the seal.

The woman's face was a blur of pain. Her brow creased and uncreased so fast the wrinkles strobed from nose to crown. Her eyelids flickered like the wings of a humming bird, and the corners of her mouth drew Lissajous curves across her cheeks. The average impression was of slender elegance.

"She looks DogStar," José said.

"Aren't they famous for their decelerated metabolisms and extreme longevity?"

The woman's features suddenly became perfectly defined, pores and minor blemishes materialising like an image coming into focus. Her eyes sprung open and locked onto José's.

"Why are you here?" he demanded.

She frowned briefly and them became still. Something switched off behind her eyes.

"Is she..." Kaamil started to ask.

José got to his feet and tried to draw something meaningful from the perfect stillness of the invader. "We need to find the other five before they do whatever they intend to do."

The second capsule was lying at the centre of its own circle of devastation. An entire refugee village in preparation had been raised to piles of grey rubble and then smelted into amorphous homogeneity.

José shook his head and wondered how anything human could survive such an impact, but the capsule lay with the internal cavity exposed and empty. Kaamil started to spiral out from the impact point while they both looked for some sign of the occupant.

"This is futile. We need help. What can Suparna see?"

"Space," Kaamil shrugged. "Primarily, space. We do not spy on our residents."

"Don't be facetious. You can't run a community this size without a million internal sensors: temperature, barometric pressure, partial pressures, chemical composition. Come on. You must be able to track half a dozen hyper-accelerated intruders."

"Against a background of explosions, destruction and panic? How careless of me."

José gave Kaamil an appraising stare. "Well you picked a hell of a time to develop an obstinate streak."

Kaamil flinched. His defiance melted instantly into nervous contrition. "I'll do everything I can," he said meekly.

José shook his head. "It wasn't a criticism," he said.

Kaamil's data tethers thrashed excitedly. "Somebody just hijacked a shuttle," he said excitedly.

"It doesn't make sense for them to leave, unless they've already completed their mission."

"The shuttle is not heading for space. It is heading inwards to the next sphere."

"Stop them."

"I've already overridden the control. I'll bring the shuttle to us."

José looked worried. "We need some backup. Who do we have that can fight?"

Kaamil did not answer.

"Well?" José prompted.

"Sorry, I assumed the question was rhetorical. This is a refugee and medical camp. The only ones here who we know can fight are the Satyagrahi."

The statement echoed from a universe in opposition to José's expectations. He was frozen by the pure wrongness of the Nodes being classed as combatants.

A suggestion of motion distracted José. They were flying over a camp that looked largely intact. People had gathered at one end to welcome those arriving from less fortunate camps on the same sphere. Something was flitting between the cabins. Each time it changed direction along its zigzagging course, there was a momentary flicker of black.

"There!" José pointed to Kaamil. "Weaving through the buildings. Do you see it?"

In answer, the flying disc banked hard and drew parallel to the weaving blur. Kaamil pointed ahead to huddle of parked shuttles. José grunted an acknowledgement. The disc accelerated way beyond what felt safe for an open platform. José sank to his knees and grimaced.

The running figure broke free of the buildings and into an area of open deck. The disc flew near the shoulder of the running figure. It became clear this one was male, but had the same tall slender figure characteristic of DogStar genetic tendencies, and was clad in the same hard and black bodysuit. He was starting to slow to a speed traceable by the human eye. His arms were still pumping with shimmering determination, but his feet slipped and slid on the deck.

José noted the high gloss on the deck surface and raised an eyebrow at Kaamil, who smiled proudly. "The Suparna," he confirmed.

The disc rotated slowly and moved into the invader's path. The figure started to weave, his finger tips touching the ground as he leaned into each turn.

"Stay with him," José coached.

Crouching at the edge of the disc, José's face was close enough to shout over the buffeting wind. José drew on reserves of conviction. "This is a refugee vessel," he declared. "We are not a legitimate military target. Stand down and declare your intentions."

The figure ducked and vanished under the disc.

"Where did he go?"

José whipped his head round to direct Kaamil. The black clad figure was just rising to his feet behind the unsuspecting Kaamil. José's facial muscles were faster to react than his voice. Kaamil started to turn. Then he was airborne, his limbs and tethers flailing like a crane fly. José tracked Kaamil's trajectory to see how he landed.

Without guidance, the disc pitched dramatically, throwing José overboard. For a stretched moment he was treading air, and then the breath was crushed from his lungs and he was spinning from bruise to bruise. For the last dozen metres he was skidding and spinning on his stomach.

José glided to stop just as the flying disc pitched edge-first into the ground. José saw the black-clad figure step gracefully from the crashing disc and accelerate to a blur without breaking stride.

"Are you okay?"

Kaamil was standing over José, holding his disabled arm to his chest by the elbow. José tried to filter through the pain signals flying in from every part of his body. Finding nothing conclusive, he sat up. The world lurched and dimmed for a moment, before finding a degree of focus.

"We are not equipped to deal with this."

Kaamil agreed and added, "I think even Julienne might have her hands full."

"Which begs the question, why invest such high-end biotech on a refugee camp?"

An identical look of revelatory horror deformed both their faces.

"The Satyagrahi!"

The sphere rumbled over the tundra, air whistling across the surface dimples. From outside the vehicle was the dull grey of something designed purely for emergency use. At the heart a lithe woman operated a series of gyroscopic controls with her right hand. From within, the sphere offered a panoramic view of the monotonous terrain, but she starred ahead with unwavering focus. A man crouched by her left side. He wore mostly tattered rags. Tufts of his hair was singed to a brittle black. She talked and grimaced while he applied a salve to the exposed skin under her arm pit.

"Do you understand the plan?" Julienne checked.

"I'm not sure it has the required sophistication to be called a plan."

"That's so you can understand it."

"Touché!" Mex dabbed a little more salve on the plasma burn. "Does it hurt?"

Mex felt Julienne open a little more of the mental link between them. An avalanche of searing pain burst through the connection. A fraction of a second later it was gone. He did not ask again.

"Mex, the conversation we were having before the cruise liner."

"Yes?"

"I'm sorry if I'm putting too much pressure on you."

"You're not. So much has changed." Mex held up his clay hand and used it to tap the area of his forehead he imaged most of her nanotech was lodged. "I just need some time to digest it all."

"Compared to finding out a psychotic pilot suffocated me, before my employer unilaterally decided to resurrect me in a body that's not my own? The same employer who thinks they can wipe my memory and personality arbitrarily?"

191

"Maybe some truths are too disturbing to be revealed," Mex pondered.

"Really? After everything, you're having second thoughts?"

"No. I don't know. Can we talk about it after we rescue Yakini and Teledice?"

"Don't worry. We'll talk."

Mex retreated to a seat on the equator of the sphere and tried to look inconspicuous.

"There it is." Julienne pointed at an undulating hillock moving across their path. "I'll get ahead of it." The sphere banked to the left and accelerated.

"How sure are you about this tech?" Mex nodded at the modified weapon on her lap.

"As long as the building hits us head-on, all will be well."

"Otherwise?"

"The transition will be rough and painful."

"I never did get around to teaching you how to deliver bad news."

Mex and Julienne abandoned the sphere. It trundled off, programmed to retrace its path to the crashed cruise liner.

"Ready?" Julienne asked.

"No," Mex admitted.

Julienne shifted her grip on the weapon and fired at the ground. A two metre patch of earth started to shudder and froth. Julienne adjusted the weapon and a shaft began to excavate itself, the soil overflowing the hole and forming a ring of moraine. The walls of the hole sizzled and solidified.

Julienne holstered the weapon and stepped into the hole. She dropped from sight without a noise. Mex crouched on the edge, stared into the shadowy depth and jumped. He landed on soft soil. A pair of graceful hands caught and held him firm.

Julienne's suit was glowing with a soft orange light, turning the wall of the shaft to a dirty sandstone colour. One side was vibrating and emitting a shrill whine. Pebbles and fragments of soil started to rain down on them.

"Get closer," Julienne instructed.

Mex did not need telling twice. He hugged her tight, as if their survival depended on the strength of his embrace. He felt her lift her weapon once more. The noise of the approaching building shifted. It seemed to spiral around Mex, making him feel dizzy and nauseas.

A light burst through the wall. A distorted view of a hall grazed the hole. It moved clockwise across an arc of the shaft, while the view of the room spun anticlockwise. Mex understood the building was not hitting them head on, but the refracted reality was too contorted for him to know what way to jump.

Julienne pushed hard towards him and they were tumbling. Mex braced for an impact with the ground that never came. Up and down switched with left and right. They were in the hall, under the ground, then back in the hall.

Mex coughed soil onto a polycrete floor and blinked at the artificial light.

"We made it," he said.

There was no answer. Mex thrashed around, searching for Julienne with his hands and scrambled vision. He called out in horror.

"Quiet," came the demand from a distant point of the hall.

Julienne stalked through the forest of field generators and helped Mex to his feet. "What happened to stealth?" she chastised.

"I thought I'd lost you!" Mex exhaled.

"If you had, shouting wouldn't help. Focus. Can you tap into the building from here?"

Mex allowed himself a quick pout while he reconstructed a mental map of the building and then discarded the panic-stained mess. Shaking his head, Mex strode towards a malleable internal wall. He felt rather than heard Julienne follow. A bubble in the wall transported them up to the human usable parts of the building. Mex pointed at an innocuous door and Julienne burst into the empty office, tendons braced for combat.

Mex took a seat and pushed the ivory-white code glasses up to the bridge of his nose. He saw the office door close and Julienne take up a guard position, before the splice lasers took his full concentration.

Prowling around the posted areas of the network, Mex gleaned morsels of information from all-staff messages and poorly constructed responses. He trod as softly as possible, mimicking the behaviour of a bored executive filling his time with idle chit chat.

"So stupid," Mex muttered.

"Don't be so harsh on yourself," Julienne murmured from somewhere beyond the projected universe of data.

"I mean this building. All buildings. The Nexus put back the development of artificial intelligence by at least a century. Why bother building minds when you simulate an A.I. in the Nexus for the cost of a few dozen Drop victims? Post Nexus we're cast back to the dark ages of digital computing."

"Can we talk history later? Have you found Yakini and Teledice?"

Something was climbing towards a climax. A collective tension permeated the virtual representation of the building's inhabitants. Executive orders were becoming more urgent, less concerned with preserving morale, staff responses more guarded. Mex extracted the emotions between the presentation of information to build a personality; a persona for the MynCorp collective. If it was a single human it would be excited to a state of nihilistic determination; crash and burn or sore into the heavens.

Mex scraped the code glasses from his face."It's happening now!"

"We need a new plan," Julienne started,

"No time."

The door opened under Mex's control, distracting Julienne for long enough for him to slip past her and into the corridor.

"What are you doing?" she demanded.

"Improvising," Mex said as the door slid back into place and locked.

If her eyes were lasers Julienne would have melted a hole straight through the door and his skull. Mex shuddered.

"I hope Sardon kills me," Mex prayed to the gods of cosmic irony.

It took almost five minutes for Mex to attract enough attention to be captured and dragged into a holding cell. Sardon Lucas marched into the cell soon after. He looked on the edge of exhaustion, skin almost grey from neglect. A manic energy animated and inhabited his devastated body.

"Mex Tyrian, welcome back," Sardon proclaimed.

"Back? I haven't been anywhere, but you look as if you could do with a holiday."

Sardon waived aside Mex's mock concern. "You expect me to believe you have been hiding in the building for days?"

"I faked my escape so I could stay and tinker."

"And the pod we shot out of the sky earlier today?"

"I suppose that was a rescue mission. Shame, I would have liked to watch them blow this place into the bedrock."

"But you found time to find a change of clothes since I last saw you."

"I work better in clean clothes. Helps me to focus."

"Focus on what?"

"You know. This and that. Strategically placed trojans. The odd worm or two. You'll find out if you go ahead with your plan."

Sardon stared at Mex's face for a long time. Heat prickled the skin in his arm pits. Mex clamped his jaw shut, determined not to crack.

"You're bluffing," Sardon decided.

"If you say so. I must have given myself up because your security systems defeated me. That's the only explanation."

Sardon blinked.

Mex knew he had bought Yakini and Teledice a period of grace and precious time for Julienne to mount some kind of dramatic rescue.

*

The combined whirr and whine of the dozen independent drive pods was like a badly trained orchestra. One pair of wheels was at least half a beat behind the rest, forever reaching a crescendo just as the bulk were dipping to a new plateau.

The inconsistency irritated the man. His eyes flickered over irregularities in the ground they were travelling over, searching for anything to explain how twelve wheels could spin at different rates.

The man had no name. Even in his head he thought of himself only as me.

He sat in the cab of the water-transporter. He felt naked. The boy named Fez had reluctantly donated his trousers. They adapted to the man's larger waist but his shins poked from the legs. His torso was bare except from his arms, wrapped tight across his ribs. He shivered as cold leached from his vacant mind.

The woman named Lesana adjusted a control and the air in the cab warmed another couple of degrees.

Fez rearranged his makeshift shorts for the hundredth time, in yet another attempt to cover pale matchstick legs.

"Look. I'm sorry I stared," Lesana repeated.

"Perfectly good legs," Fez muttered.

"It's not that," Lesana explained. "It's just I've never seen anyone without epidermis tone control; should they really be so pale and blotchy?"

Petulance creased his face. "We didn't all grow up in some pampered corporate slave-house."

"Pampered slave? It sounds so terrible."

Lesana laughed. The anonymous man detected an edge of desperation in the giggle. The boy joined in.

Fez jeered. "Forced to rest in a comfortable bed without worrying if the room might eat you while you sleep. I don't know how you survived."

"Lunch with girlfriends. Nights sim-visiting distant planets. It was hell."

The man was not aware he had an opinion, but found himself speaking anyway. "Soulless, thankless existence. Aimless monotony. Indentured labour reinforced by the threat of the Drop."

The woman and boy stopped laughing. "Thanks," Lesana said with bitter irony. "I think I deserve a little romantic nostalgia for a time when I didn't fear for my life every moment."

He wanted to apologise, but did not trust his own mind to find the words. He turned to look at the passing landscape, trying to remember where he had been and what he was running from.

From a distance the city looked static but oddly strung out. As the vehicle drew closer, the towers could be seen to gently sway and move disconcertingly against the horizon. The precession was lead by a pair of black shard-like towers. The man turned his head slightly to the side. He imagined the two towers as one, broken in two jagged halves.

Tethers ran from building to building, like vines in jungle. They writhed and stretching with the collective motion of the city organism. The tethers pulsated as something viscous slithered between the buildings. The surface of each tether was crusty and flacking. Chinks of light danced through the cracks as information burst around the city.

"I know this place," the man said.

"You're a Jefferson town refugee?" Lesana sounded hopeful. "Maybe we can find someone who knows you. Help you get your memory back."

"Maybe." The man felt oddly disconcerted by the prospect.

"I wonder how you ended up in the middle of nowhere." The man was curiously reassured by the edge of distrust in the boy's voice.

The two black towers lurched to the left and detoured towards a hamlet of low buildings and cherry trees heaving with white and pink blossom. The rest of the rag-tagged city stumbled to a halt. Tethers tightened and strained, forcing the rest of the buildings to heave to the side and follow. Fez steered the water carrier in a wide arc, giving the towers a significant berth. Lesana and the man watched through the window as people streamed from the hamlet. They were met by a small armoured vehicle that darted out from the shadow of the towers. The inhabitants seemed agitated, waving and shouting as the two towers converged on the first cottage.

A tall woman stood on the roof of the armoured vehicle and gesticulated decisively, but the inhabitants continued to run at the advancing towers, until they stalled. The crowd instantly became subdued and started to retreat.

The towers had not collided with the cottage. There was no eruption of masonry or polycrete. The base of the towers distended and slowly but inexorably they began to swallow the cottage whole.

"That's disturbing," the man understated.

Lesana pointed to their right. "Have you seen what's coming? The Reset is only a few hours away. Better to be fuel than erased."

The man offered no comment.

"I'll swing round to Osiris IV," Fez said. "It's pretty well behaved; the water tanks should still be reliable."

The man continued to watch the building-on-building cannibalism in a rear-screen. The black towers were feasting on one cottage after another. Mid-meal they shuddered in unison, like a pair of dogs being brought to heel. They obstinately finished devouring their current mouthfuls and then moved off, leaving the inhabitants in a dazed huddle amongst the debris.

As the anonymous man lost sight of the hamlet in the shadow of the city's mass, some of the survivors were joining the stream of refugees converging on the city. The others turned their back on the Reset and retreated inside the remaining cottages.

The man sighed at both the stupidity of denial and the futility of fighting; better to stand and face the Reset on your own terms.

*

Nomia rubbed her shoulder. "Well, we're not getting out that way."

Oinoie managed a half-hearted giggle. Nomia gave him an appraising arch of the eyebrow.

The collapse of the entrance had been triggered by Nomia bursting her way in. What had started as a rescue had resulted in all the Satyagrahi being trapped together.

"Chania, try the wall," Nomia pointed.

Chania blinked with alarm, as if surprised to find he was physically present rather than watching from a distant, safe perspective. He unfolded his cross legs and carefully followed Nomia's direction to the piece of wall he calculated she had intended. He looked back at Nomia and frowned when he saw how unstable her arm and finger really were, but he dutifully pulled aside a wall-hanging of purple and orange, and started to rub the wall instructively.

Nomia was not surprised when after a minute Chania gave her an apologetic shrug; intelligent materials seemed to de-evolve rather rapidly when exposed to multiple Satyagrahi for any length of time.

The nymphs fell into step behind Nomia as she moved through the common-room. Dozens of pairs of eyes followed her intently. She knew they were looking to her for some indication to how they should react.

They had experienced battle on Earth, but here and the caves of Mars were a sanctuary. The two situations had never overlapped before, and they lacked the experience to adapt.

Nomia picked up a couple of domestic items and righted a table. The spell was broken. Other started straightening the living space. The building was basically intact apart from the collapsed vestibule. They were probably safer trapped in here than outside.

She moved through to the anti-chamber from where the Suparna determinism shield was generated. The half dozen Satyagrahi were still sat in a tight circle. The commotion had not penetrated their immersed state; the contradiction of manipulating reality to remove uncertainty required a particularly detached state of mind.

Nomia used her flowing sleeve to gently brush debris from the naked scalp of a male Satyagrahi. This group had not taken names and were collectively known as the Incognito. She gave the freshly cleaned head a gentle kiss of gratitude.

"One disaster at a time," she whispered. "The last thing we need just now is the Eidolon's or their Oikake turning up."

Nomia moved back into the corridor. She marched past the empty sleeping cells and into the medical area. A couple of bedridden Satyagrahi propped themselves up on their elbows to watch Nomia lead her procession through the ward.

Nomia paused at each bed to offer a smile of reassurance. At the very rear of the building was a pair of small rooms for performing medical procedures and storing supplies. Beyond these, Nomia found what she was looking for.

A transparent blister made up most of the rear wall. The material was super pliable so that a shuttle could nestle up against it and essentially dock. Supplies, or more often injured Satyagrahi, could be moved directly to a treatment room with minimal contact with the other occupants of the Suparna.

The heavily inverted horizon made it look like the building was tipping forwards. Nomia instinctively braced herself against falling towards the window. The terrain was significantly more irregular than it should be. Lumps of the ship's fabric had been torn free, but were now melting back into the deck and being redistributed. There were no other buildings on the inside surface of the innermost sphere. Ambiguous lumps signified parts of the original ship, the Suparna had decided not to cannibalise. Somewhere amongst them would be her engines, anti-matter containment bottles and energy-exchange units; baffling to Nomia in all respects other than their potential to annihilate everyone and everything on board. She drew minimal comfort from the fact that being able to ask if these were intact meant they very probably were.

The blister was configured to detect an approaching vehicle and adapt to whatever door, hatch or opening it came up against. For a fully soft-form shuttle the entire wall could melt away, fully integrating the two spaces. José had insisted on interfering with Kaamil and the Suparna's natural open nature, by configuring a permissibility panel into the wall. It was a rare moment when Nomia found herself double guessing his motives.

Nomia raised her hand toward the lock panel, when something made her hesitate. Her Satyagrahi were staring as one out of the transparent aperture.

"What do you see?" Nomia asked.

"Nothing," Chania said as if he meant just the opposite.

Nomia joined them; six pairs of eyes scrutinising the static landscape.

They saw nothing, but flinched simultaneously.

"Back inside," Nomia hissed.

The Nymphs alarm had already spread through the Satyagrahi collective. In the infirmary, Nomia assigned an able-body to each walking wounded. Three conscious but unmovable Satyagrahi pleaded with their eyes, but remained mute. Nomia gestured at the five unconscious bodies lying in a neat row against one wall. The three nodded their understanding and lay back as still as manikins.

An impatient tapping echoed through from the rear. The bedridden three opened panic-stained eyes. Nomia gave them a matronly frown and made a calming gesture. One by one they settled back into their pillows. Nomia waited until their eyes were closed and the rise and fall of the tapping was generating no discernible flicker of awareness.

Nomia dragged herself away from her invalid brethren.

Silent, expectant faces greeted them in the communal space. Nomia raised a redundant finger to her lips. The tapping noise was barely discernible from here, but they all noticed when it stopped.

Nomia's senses flowed back from the doorway and spread all around, as an inquisitive cloud of uncertainty. The building came alive with barely perceptible clicks and pops, each too short for its existence to be confirmed and too subtle to be definitively new.

Even Nomia whimpered when a frantic scrabbling sound started up in the vestibule. The Satyagrahi started to back into the recess where the Incognito remained entranced and unaware.

The scrabbling sound became a destructive noise. Something was digging its way into the building, like a thousand manic insects crunching on metal leaves.

"Wake the Incognito," somebody whispered.

"The Eidolon will find us," somebody replied.

"We need access to Verity space," the first voice retorted.

Nomia cowered with the others, her mind scrambled for purchase on an indistinct threat. "Lowering the determinism shield is a last resort," she asserted. "Without it everyone on the Suparna will die."

Magnified by fear and proximity, the Satyagrahi emotions started to bleed and permeate throughout the collective. Even with the shield such a concentration of potential was tugging at the fabric of reality. A point of eruption was fast approaching. Nomia had no idea what would happen when it arrived, but she was certain the damage would be irrevocable.

Different light slashed through the room. The last few pieces of debris disappeared in a frenetic blur, leaving a gaping wound in the side of the building. The light dipped briefly as something entered the room.

The air adjusted and then became perfectly still. Even Nomia's breath was frozen in her lungs.

Abruptly, a wall of black blocked the view of the doorway. Nomia's eyes struggled to shift focus. A figure clad entirely in black had materialised in front of the cowering Satyagrahi.

Nomia found herself rising to confront the invader. Her head was level with the black chest as it heaved through the taunt fabric. Nomia strained her neck to confront a face rendered inscrutable by a rigid and featureless mask.

"Which of you is a Nexus Node?"

The voice was clipped and scraped its way from ear to brain.

Nomia ignored the question. "Who are you?" she demanded.

The figure cocked its head, but not in response to Nomia's question. After a moment in which Nomia got the distinct impression the figure completed a protracted conversation with a third party, the figure managed to speak again.

"I require one male and one female."

Nobody moved, but now the figure had a Satyagrahi dangling from each arm. A foam was spreading and solidifying over their bodies, making motion impossible and holding their joints and neck rigid. Nomia got the immediate impression they were being packaged for transportation like pieces of cargo.

The light changed again.

"Nomia," José shouted from the entrance. "Release the shield. We can't fight them like this."

The black figure started to move. Even hampered by a body in each hand his motion was hard to follow. Nomia saw José and Kaamil being jostled by rapid concussions as they braced a beam across the building entrance. The next moment the blur was heading back towards the cowering Satyagrahi. Nomia reached out an arm in an attempt to snag a foam covered body, but the blur skirted her reach, and vanished towards the infirmary.

"Please, no," Nomia pleaded.

José was running after the invader. "Wake them up. Get the shield down," he repeated, then he was darted into the corridor.

Nomia gave herself no time to process the danger of the action. Pure faith drove her on. She turned her crouch, whispered an apology and slapped the nearest Incognito across the cheek.

The noise of palm on flesh reverberated through the group. The Satyagrahi's eyes flashed open but without focus. The remaining Incognito grunted under the increased stress of maintaining the determinism shield.

Five more slaps rang-out like gunshots.

The entire Incognito sat dazed but awake.

The outside universe gnawed at the edge of Nomia's perception. Reality seeped through the fissures in the shield and spread uncertainty throughout the cowering Satyagrahi.

"We don't have long."

Nomia was already moving. Her waking senses rushed ahead in Verity Space. She could feel a potential reality coalescing in the near future. The last remnants of the shield obscured the details like frosted glass, but she could discern several invaders converging on the Suparna's inner sphere. One was near, glowing in the projected luminescence of two half-conscious Satyagrahi. Even wrapped in packing foam and heavily sedated, their reluctance to leave their home was dragging at their captor, slowing his progress to human proportions.

José was growing. His anger and determination subconsciously plucked at minor threads of probability, boasting his pursuit. Nomia did the same. She flashed through the rear wall of the building without worrying about its solidity.

The invader paused at the aperture to the next sphere. Nomia arrived to see José approach the figure with his palms outstretched.

"Just give us back our friends and you can leave without interference."

The figure cocked his head, then took one step back. Three other figures appeared, blocking José's advance.

Nomia came to full-certainty at José's side. How do you want to handle this?

We don't have time for subtlety.

The air behind the invaders started to sizzle and hiss, as a sphere of air either escaped or was forced out of existence.

"Behind you!" Nomia's warning merged with a screech of frenetic panic.

The invader dropped its human load and thrashed desperately at the Eidolon attack sphere. His limbs strobed in and out of existence, generating a whine that pulsed with the inhuman screech.

The sphere consumed the reality that had been the black clad figure and moved on without pausing. It ignored the cocooned Satyagrahi and advanced on the nearest invader. The three figures moved in unison. One started a series of harry runs on the sphere. The other two looped behind and retrieved their illicit cargo.

Two more sphere's materialised either side of a laden invader, forcing her to drop the Satyagrahi and dart away.

José broadcast a thought to everyone nearby. You cannot win against the Eidolons. This is your last chance to stop this insanity.

The thought was chisel perfect in Nomia's mind, but the invaders ignored him totally. They continued to strafe, feint and generally pester the Eidolon spheres. Nomia could feel more spheres forming all over the Suparna. Panic was already starting to spread like a virus through the population.

Nomia wanted to react, but her mind was not entirely her own. A change in state was reconfiguring her memory. It was the nearest the sphere's masters came to a direct contact, like discovering a forgotten conversation from the past.

Nomia was still trying to unravel the new memory, when the Suparna was erased from reality.

Chapter 9

The question had been hidden amongst her memories of Sera. Yakini came across it while staring at the ceiling of her cell. Exploring her regrets helped to stretch the tedium and distract from the inevitability of the next torture session. Sardon seemed determined to push Teledice to breaking point regardless of all the reality destroying consequences. His search for hair-trigger control of Teledice's ability was reckless to the point of self-destructive. Each time Sardon brought Teledice to the brink it was down to Yakini to talk her down. These were the only moments Teledice seemed lucid, a short period of panic before the next stupor began.

Yakini was emotionally exhausted. The perfect state for long periods of retrospection with nothing to distract her from nostalgia, grief and heartbreak.

There, in mid flow. The future according to Sera, interrupted by a voice – more a thought – which did not belong on Mars.

Why?

The question was loaded with nuance no human voice could achieve. Or perhaps her brain was simplifying a complex catechism into single word. Either way, she knew the Verity Space aliens, the Eidolons, were baffled by the principle of mutually assured destruction, and they had come to Yakini in search of answers.

"How the hell should I know?" Yakini shouted at the impassive ceiling, but she knew she could do better.

She struggled with the question for two more of Sardon's experiments before realising the difficulty she was experiencing was the source of an answer. Not to the direct question, but the assumption that lay beneath.

Diversity. The collective of human races are so diverse it is often impossible for one individual to understand the motivation or perspective of another. We cannot be understood and should not be judged by the actions of one or a few.

Yakini replayed the memory of Sera over and over, adding and refining her answer each time.

The next time Sardon brought Teledice to the edge of detonation, Yakini tried to steady part of her mind. While Teledice was wailing straining at her physical and mental bonds, Yakini was looking for some recognition the Eidolon's were picking through her memories for their answer. Then she was back in the isolation of her cell, none the wiser but twice as despondent.

A muffled voice blew in with the processed air. "Yakini, is that you?"

"Mex? You're back." Hope tiptoed into her voice.

"Yes. Like I've never been away."

"Where are you? What's the plan?"

"I think I'm in the cell next door to you."

Yakini's voice cracked and broke twice before she found something her mouth could manage. "You call that a rescue?"

"Sorry. How's Teledice?"

Yakini could feel the reticence in Mex's voice, even through the attenuation of convected air. She held tight to what Mex could not say; anything he was keeping from Sardon could only be good.

The front and dividing walls thinned and were absorbed into the floor and ceiling. Mex and Yakini were standing side by side, face pressed to air permeable patches of wall. Sardon stood behind them, crumpled and twitching from exhausted neural-transmitters.

"Teledice is perfect, and is ready for deployment." The triumphalism made his eyelid flicker manically.

"Sardon, you're really losing it," Mex sympathised, then his voice switched to something beyond compunction. "Have a lie down. Rest. Sleep."

Yakini found herself sinking to her knees.

"Nice try." Sardon grinned and the spell was broken.

"Everything you say is filtered before I let it near my brain," Sardon said.

"Yeah, I get that a lot," Mex sighed.

"It's time." Sardon turned and led the way to the laboratory where Teledice was constrained. Four security guards, concealed behind black armour, flanked them every step of the way.

Teledice looked just as frail and deathly as ever, but Mex's reaction highlighted her deterioration. He coughed away a tear, then his face hardened and he turned away.

Sardon ushered them all into the observation lounge and offered Mex his former seat at the head of a bank of modified splice terminals.

Sardon spread himself across his seat like a monarch testing a new throne. "I have to say Mr Tyrian, that this is all going to be a lot easier with you here."

"I sincerely hope not."

"We snaffled your code during your visit, but it seems there is more skill in the operation than is apparent from first viewing."

Mex grunted away the unwelcome compliment. He was still arranging his code glasses when Sardon gave a nod to the technicians in the laboratory.

Reality took a sharp intake of breath and the laboratory space was packed to degeneracy with Eidolon spheres.

Mex hesitated and looked ready to run.

"We're really having an impact. The aliens have learnt they cannot dismiss MynCorp so lightly."

Mex bustled to get the sessions started. He dropped into Sardon's mock Nexus with little concern for his passengers. Yakini's head swam as she ricochetted between virtual and physical worlds.

The Oikakes packed and thrashed the local Verity Space to a lather. They fell on Teledice like waves against a sea wall; an avalanche of excited violence diffused and repelled back into the next attack. Teledice's presence was impassive. Her sphere of influence seemed sacrosanct, the only constant in a universe of flux. Yakini knew the immutability was an illusion. Teledice was simply paused, ready to be unleashed at Sardon's whim.

"This is Sardon Lucas speaking on behalf of MynCorp, the Cartel, humankind and related subspecies. Alien presence, do you hear me?"

The man who would be king, Yakini thought. The title was part of a memory Yakini could not trace, but it was related to an argument with Sera about the relevance of Earth culture. There were dozens of parts to the memory that did not sound like her or Sera; answers to questions unasked.

Even with the disjointed sensory panorama of Mex's Drop client, Yakini could feel Sardon fidgeting. "Why are they not answering?" he demanded.

"Maybe they're tired of your petty warmongering," Mex goaded.

"I think the Eidolons might be talking through me today," Yakini interrupted.

"That is unacceptable," Sardon blustered. "They cannot change the rules of negotiation unilaterally. Especially not in this manner. No offence Ms Akida, but you are not an impartial mediator."

"Absolutely no offence taken. I think I have an answer for your objection." Yakini sorted through the collection of responses she remembered and chose the most appropriate. "They say, my mind is better suited for explaining their perspective than the spheres."

Mex chimed in. "Can we continue this conversation in the real world?"

"No," Yakini and Sardon declared together.

Yakini would have preferred leaving the Nexus, if only to get away from the feeling Sardon was breathing in her ear, but here and now the Eidolon words felt immediate and accessible.

"Have the Eidolons considered my offer of a mutually beneficial alliance?"

"They have no interest in such an alliance. They are only interested in advancing the viability of this reality."

"They realise the consequences of rejecting my offer?"

Yakini was still trying to frame her response when she was dumped back into a juddering reality. The floor vibrated cold into her cheek. Her eyes came back into focus and she found herself lying face to face with a bewildered Mex. She mouthed the obvious question and he mouthed back Julienne's name with the slightest flicker of a smile.

The movement of the building became apparent in its absence. A second later the uniform glow of the walls stuttered once and then ceased. The darkness was total. Human noises drew on the absence of light and became absurdly amplified. Yakini heard lips part, the skin made sticky by apprehension. An intake of breath then an unhinged chuckle.

"Your doing, Mr Tyrian?"

"Maybe," Mex said slightly too readily.

"Or maybe someone else. Someone with an insiders understanding of MynCorp facilities and a natural propensity for sabotage?"

"I've no idea what you are talking about."

"I'm talking about Ms Julienne Garland."

"Never heard of her," Mex professed.

The walls quivered back into luminescence revealing a grinning Sardon. "Quite," he said. His head tilted a fraction as if Sardon was listening to his very own shoulder-devil. "There she is. How disappointing."

Yakini noticed Mex's eyes lose their edge of focus. She gave him a quizzical look, but he simply shook his head a fraction of a turn and resumed studying Sardon, as if looking for a moment to strike. Yakini was struggling to decipher what was going on. Her mind was full of answers waiting impatiently for a question to confound. Like the punchline to a joke, they floated on the edge of meaning, in a contextual limbo. Two phrases refused to be subdued. They pushed at reality, desperate for an opportunity to be spoken. Yakini let them roam around her tongue, on the edge of elucidation.

This is the why.

All out actions against humanity converge on this moment.

*

For several exquisite moments the pounding of fist on metal absorbed itself into dreamy memories of childhood; curled up amongst deflated mine-heads in the bow storage-hold of her father's truck, listening to the reassuring thud-thud-thud of the drill-head below.

The banging stopped. Sera frowned in her sleep.

"Sjitturinn! Sera, you in there?" The Kraken-bark did not belong in her childhood.

"I'm up, Bergur. I'm up." Sera reluctantly acknowledged the grown-up world. She rolled out of the low cot, and landed on her discarded survival suit. Despite the mineral smell of the air, the downward drag on her body made her think they were on Earth. Sera unfurled her limbs and climbed to her feet. She discarded the heavy-fatigue in her legs with a slap to each thigh.

Before Sera finished sliding into the survival suit, Bergur's fist resumed its heavy pounding on the door. As soon as the first couple of seams had started to heal, she thumped the door open.

"Where's the fire?" Sera struggled through sleep-haze for reserves of sarcasm.

"Raining from the sky," Bergur replied. "Sorry to wake you, princess, but they're here."

"Who's here?"

"I don't know. MynCorp, Durga. Take your pick."

"It's nice to be wanted," Sera said weakly.

Sera let Bergur lead her back towards the reception area, while her brain made the jump from dreams of childhood. He took each twist and turn with the conviction of casual familiarity, or of someone who had chosen to exchange sleep for tactical exploration.

A clatter of metal on rock brought them to a halt at the last turn. The final pressure door hung partially open on heavy mechanical hinges. Precious breathable air leached through the crack towards the entrance membranes. Through the crack, Sera and Bergur watched a pair of Durga officials march up the entrance ramp. They stopped oppressively close to

Ne'igalomeatiga, who greeted them with ritual and an easy smile. Both of the new men wore standard business fatigues, but the shorter of the two had a corporate-opportunism engram emblazoned on his lapel.

"Please indicate that you accept the cost of this security check," the shorter official declared.

Ne'igalomeatiga nodded marginally, his smile immutable.

Yakini placed her lips where she guessed Bergur's auricular organ might be. "They mustn't see us. We can't bring that kind of grief down on Ne'igalomeatiga's crew."

"So, stealing one of the corporate jump-jets is out of the question?"

Sera answered with her silence.

Eight more officials entered the atria. Two unfolded a tripod and mounted a fist-sized device at the apex. The device started to hum.

"No, no, no!" Sera complained.

She turned and ran, trusting Bergur to follow. Sera was half way down the corridor when the first pulse passed through her. Like the beat of a bass drum, the sonic wave made her organs spasm.

"They're probing the place, looking for us," Sera cried. "We need to find somewhere noisier."

Sera headed down the first stairwell, towards the drilling room. A droning sound grew from her subconscious hearing, and into audibility. It was the background sound of a mining platform; the noise that made new recruits irritable and distracted.

Bergur's mouth flaps quivered. He pointed towards the next junction, held up two fingers, then one in front of where his lips should be. Pipes and conduits defined the shape of the corridor. Sera started to weave herself

216

into the fabric of the factory, blending into the shadows and grime. Bergur lifted himself up by a cable tray and vanished into a cavity in the ceiling.

Sera quietened her breathing and waited.

A pair of torso stepped into view, guns held charged and ready. Sera felt another sonic pulse rattle her stomach. There was no way she could untangle her limbs from the cat's cradle of pipes to launch any kind of defence. She was trapped and helpless.

A second sonic thump passed through her.

One of the men grumbled something unintelligible, then stomped out of sight.

Sera waited as long as she could before spitting stale air from her lungs.

She crept back into the light. Bergur lowered himself by one arm and followed her towards the drone of the drilling room.

When Sera opened the bulkhead the volume remained the same, as if the sound avoided air in favour of the metal as a medium, The taste of minerals and ore was a blanket on her tongue. She glanced at Bergur. His face flaps were firmly closed. Apart from two ovals of discolouration around the middle, his head was a featureless mask. A completely unbidden and inappropriate image of Yakini and Bergur popped into Sera's mind. A thousand emotions were pouring across Yakini's face. Every thought and feeling rippling out from her eyes, across her cheeks, and playing with the corners of her mouth. Bergur lay beneath her, totally inscrutable.

"What now?" Bergur asked.

Sera shook her mind clear. The main drill protruded from the ceiling and vanished into a rock-lined hole in the floor. The whine was welling up in the hole and spilling out onto the rocky floor of the room. Small pebbles danced in a layer of liquid grit that sloshed out towards the edge of the room. A few metres out the grid solidified and returned to dusting of hard dirt. A dozen pipes, as thick as a Martian's chest, snaked over the edge of the hole and vanished from sight. The walls of the pipe undulated like a swallowing snake.

Sera identified the alcove she was looking for. She climbed a ramp, and opened a hinged hatch in the side of a bullet-shaped capsule.

"Don't touch the shell. Just the hand rail," Sera instructed.

Bergur followed her up the ramp, and stared at the dull-grey surface. Somehow, Sera read suspicion and curiosity in his demeanour. Ignoring his reticence, she slid inside, feet-first, and started to power up the escape vehicle.

Bergur kicked her once in the back as he struggled into his own recumbent harness. He grunted an apology in the middle of a string of guttural expletives.

Even strapped into a prone position, Sera's face was a hand's width from the inner surface of the pod. A simple control console hung on a spider-web of shock absorbing threads. Physical switches were arranged around a ruggedised display. A green bar indicated the pod was powering up. A second whine slowly eclipsed the main mining drill.

Even in the confined space, Sera had to shout to hear her own voice. "Close the hatch. Keep your extremities away from the hull, and say goodbye to your hearing."

The whine climbed to a shriek. The cowl of Sera's survival suit climbed over her ears and solidified. The whine simply bypassed her ears and used her skull as a drum. She felt as if the noise was drilling into her bones and threatened to liquefy her body. A scream started to grow in her stomach; her body's attempt to fight fire with fire.

The green bar finally reached maximum and Sera punched the launch switch. The nose of the capsule dropped and buried itself into the Martian bedrock. The noise either dropped to something bearable or the hearing centre of her brain had melted.

"You okay?" she tried to ask Bergur. She could feel her voice in her jaw bone but nothing from her ears. Sera tried to twist in her harness to see Bergur's face. In the turning, a finger tip brushed against the capsule hull. The epidermis instantly liquefied and fell as a drop of fluid cells.

Sera yelped and swung back into position. Sucking one finger, she took her frustration out on the control console. She left the satellite positioning system active for long enough to take a bearing, then she shut-down all external transponders, except the magnetometer. They would have to navigate using dead reckoning, a task made trickier by the annoying lack of planetary magnetic field.

Sera tinkered with the relative viscosity of the liquid rock around the capsule, bringing their bearing to point towards Vanuatu City. She directed the magnetometer to sample the local magnetic field; piecing together a global direction from fragments of an ancient field frozen into the bedrock.

Rubbing away her ear protection she tried to talk to Bergur again.

"Are you still with me?"

"We seem to spend a lot of time trapped in small spaces together." His voice was almost directly behind her head. The recumbent harnesses were staggered, but he was shorter than any Martian. Sera wriggled uncomfortably.

"I think this is my least favourite so far," he continued. "Are we underground?"

"Yes, it's the only way I know to get clear of the platform without being spotted."

"Are we planing to tunnel our way to Vanuatu?"

"Hopefully."

"Isn't that going to take rather a long time?"

"A few hours. Assuming we don't miss."

"Judging by the way my teeth are slowly coming loose, this is a sonic drill."

"Yes, a combination of resonant vibration and tuned electrostatic field is momentarily liquefying the surrounding rock. Be thankful for the layer of hydraulic oil between the hulls. Without it we would be a garish puddle."

"I find our run of luck almost overwhelming."

They lay in silence at the heart of an acoustic storm. The bedrock of Mars turned to liquid as it touched the nose of the capsule, flowed past the bullet shape, before instantly solidifying in their wake. The only evidence of their passing was a trail of impossible eddies forever frozen into the planet's strata.

*

Chimalsi Okonjo considered the Martian technician for a moment, weighing up which tactic would ensure maximum productivity.

"That is simply not good enough," he said. "Keep trying as if your very life depended on a successful result."

Chimalsi let a grimace crease his carefully designed face. He nodded ostensibly to dismiss the technician, but internally he was acknowledging having achieved an optimal approach with this particular subordinate.

Tabansi was a different story; an unstable tight-rope of a story. When MynCorp had been the dominant force on Mars, it had been easy to keep the MBT leader on-board. My enemy's enemy is my friend might be a cliché, but like all tired expressions, contained elements of truth. There were aspects of the current operation Chimalsi had to keep from Tabansi, but, like many former revolutionaries, the man was prone to paranoia. Chimalsi trod the narrow path between obviously excluding Tabansi, and revealing the true nature of Durga Corporation's plans.

A cloud crossed behind Chimalsi's eyes as his usually well tethered imagination flashed up an image. There would be serious repercussions, if Tabansi knew the Node was not only still on Mars, but also being held against whatever it used as a will. Chimalsi experienced a premonition of just how dramatic years of suppressed guilt could manifest, given the right trigger.

The secret to managing Tabansi was keeping the body busy and the ego caressed. The MBT leader was heading up the operation to supply bio-technology to the Earth resistance fighters, and even act as the public face of Mars during the war. Conveniently, this suited Chimalsi well. The war was a distraction, a smoke screen behind which Durga was rearranging the pieces on the corporate game board.

The Node twitched a finger.

Chimalsi flinched.

"Do we need to increase the rate of sedation?"

The technician looked up from scrolling telemetry. Anxiety twitched the corning of his eye. Even unconscious the Node instilled more fear than Chimalsi could induce face to face. This emaciated husk of a body, with skin barely thick enough to hold back blue veins of insipid looking blood. Even awake the Node had barely seemed capable of holding onto its name. Chimalsi clearly remembered the Node stating his name as Ben with an unnecessary question mark on the end. He had stored away the uncertainty, along with other tell-tails ripe for manipulation.

"It's hard to be sure," the technician admitted.

"You can't even tell if its conscious or not?" The derision was calibrated to reinforce the fear with self-doubt.

"He's brain image bears no relation to anything I've seen before. Maybe if the patient had been conscious when he arrived I would have been able to establish a baseline."

Chimalsi let his fingers brush against the black velvet texture of the Nodes restraints. "These bonds would be of little use if it should wake."

The technician looked sceptical, but did not question his superior. Chimalsi picked up a needle sharp instrument from a workbench and stabbed the end into the Nodes thigh.

"Now you have a baseline measure of its consciousness."

The technician seemed transfixed by the single drop of blood forming on the Node's leg.

"Show me the latest model," Chimalsi barked.

A three dimensional graphic fizzed into existence in the air above the Node's body. At first glance it looked like a map of the stars in a galaxy. So, many points of light, the brain was forced to simplify the image into clusters, patterns and structures. The technician reconfigured the image from a map of neurons to a representation of connections, quantum states and entanglements. Chimalsi cast an expert eye over the simplified map of a mind.

"It's incomplete," he accused.

"The scan is complete, but the map is not." The technician couldn't help but correct the inaccuracy.

"The subject is a little short of personality, but the gaps in this map would render it able to do little more than regulate bodily functions."

"It's not just the gaps. Look at this."

The image was replaced by another with completely different structure.

"What's that?"

"The previous attempt. We have ten of these, all different."

"This is not the same person, probably not even the same species," Chimalsi stated.

"It is the same scanner and the same subject. Just ten minutes apart."

Chimalsi resisted the urge to question the accuracy of the result. It would make him look weak to pursue avenues that were second nature to the technician. He had to keep hold of the initiative and global perspective.

"Speculate. What could produce this effect," he demanded. "What kind of mind could appear to be incomplete at any one moment, but change drastically in the next?"

"If I was to draw an analogy, it's like the shadow cast on a screen by a spinning shape. You see a simplified but changing image of the more complicated shape."

"Okay. So how many snapshots do we need before we have a complete model?"

"We'd have to create a data-cube with an extra dimension, then stack the scans?"

Chimalsi nodded. The technician hesitated in the way Chimalsi recognised as a reluctance to deliver bad news. "Don't tell me you can't do it."

"We'll find a way."

The Node twitched the same finger.

So much dust.

It swirled around the man's ankles as he walked. At one time plants must have grown in this dirt, pushing optimistic fronds between the clumps of fertile soil: fed by the dirt, being fed on and feeding the soil. Cycles of patient renewal; complexity, to simplicity, to complexity. No need for development or progress, only the pseudo-random dance of evolution's hunt for perfection.

The man knew he had once been a cauldron of complex desires, aspirations, dreams and convictions. Now they had drained away and turned to dust. He could see no reason to wish his old self back.

The man walked on.

The dust clung to his exposed feet and ankles, forming a defensive crust against hope or doubt. He faced straight ahead with blood-shot stare. There were no tears or irritant in his eyes, and yet threads of red formed a web around the iris. He had seen too much destruction to remember, too much to remain intact.

The man walked towards a wall. The wall advanced on the man. They both converged on a patch of grass speckled with expectant daisies. The wall reflected a distorted image of a city in retreat. Convulsing behind the façade were other cities of stone, glass or mud. Countless people and every type of creature echoed a single scream; a denial, a refusal to accept oblivion.

The man's feet brushed the first blade of grass but he felt no joy. Dust or grass, it was all the same, just different manifestations of a nature set to reject his existence.

Charge started to prickle his skin. What he perceived as consciousness was pushed towards the back of his skull. A flicker of inquisitiveness disturbed the man's tranquillity. An ember of his former self, pontificated and speculated from some mental cranny. It postulated a fundamental field novel to his reality, strongly interacting with the Downey field of causality, but also weakly interacting with the electromagnetic field of chemistry and electricity.

The man stopped walking. Dust drifted down from his shins and settled on blades of grass reeling in his wake.

The wall did not falter. It's advance was inexorable and relentless.

The man's face started to flush. Heat was forming and building up below the skin. Pores opened to exude sweet, but capillary forces were breaking down. The man's skin was dry like dust.

"What the fuck are you doing?" a female voice screamed in his ear.

A hand gripped his wrist with a force born of absolute terror. It spun him around and dragged him three lurching steps from the Reset.

The voice was hardly recognisable but the hand belonged to the woman called Lesana. She looked back at him, pleading for him to move faster. She tried to lock eyes with him, but her gaze was dragged to the obscenity at his back.

The man obeyed. His will was weak and fickle.

"Faster", she demanded and he obeyed.

When she could drag him no further, Lesana dropped his arm and they trotted side by side.

"What in hell's name were you thinking?"

"Almost nothing," he stated.

"You almost died and you were thinking nothing?"

"It was bliss for a moment. Then I started thinking about field theory."

Lesana looked at him with incredulity, tinged with anger. Her jaw clamped shut against whatever she wanted to say next.

"Thank you," he said, but there was no gratitude in his tone.

Lesana was panting hard. The rasping of air over trembling lips acted as a catalyst to all sound. The acoustic world crashed in on his sensory isolation: the crunching of their feet on loose grit, the thump as his bones absorbed the shock of each footfall, the collective groan of a city in flight, and the endless wind heralding a global climate in crisis.

Even at a limping trot they made good progress back towards the city. The lead maintained by the city was slender. The Reset would be pushing into the suburbs, if the city had any.

"At least I know one thing about myself; I'm no athlete," the man croaked, losing conviction mid-sentence. He was grateful when Lesana ignored the attempt at humour.

The shadow of a trailing building fell across them. Shaped like a hexagram, it ploughed a pair of precarious furrows through the ground. Its tether hummed with tension, running taunt between the heart of the star and a monolithic cube of a building ahead.

As Lesana and the man drew level with the star, the humming from the tether started to climb in pitch and volume. A few seconds later the noise was bypassing his ears and directly mining the man's skull. His gums flayed as his teeth pulled at their sockets, but before he could react to the pain, there was a crack of thunder and a sizzle of recoil. Silence replaced the fractured tether.

"Shit!" Lesana swore in contrast to his own relief.

People started to pour from the two star points even before it creaked to a halt and sank tip-deep into the ground.

"No. No. No. Not another one."

Lesana lurched to the side and broke into a stilted run. The man followed without thought.

Half a dozen antique ground vehicles were already loading essential supplies and people too frail or injured to walk. Lesana acknowledged a few people as they weaved their way through the exodus. The nod and grunt of greeting exhibited an efficient minimalism bred from infinite repetition.

A tall man stood by the building entrance. He wore black and a belt laden with security paraphernalia. He was watching people leaving the building like a wary shepherd, nodding occasionally as if ticking off a mental check-list.

"What can I do?" Lesana shouted up at him.

The man looked down, blinked once. "Lesana," he said once with no suggestion of familiarity. Then he turned his neutral expression on the anonymous man. Again the blink, but this time he gave no name.

"He's with me," Lesana said. "He won't get in the way."

The logistician turned back to Lesana. "Join epsilon team. Sweep third and fourth floor. You have fifteen minutes before we pull everyone out. Go."

The nameless man felt a flicker of annoyance at being dismissed so readily, but it was a faint and feeble thing. Lesana found a gap in the thinning stream of fleeing people and they darted through the entrance.

"What are we doing?"

"Checking for stragglers."

The entrance hall was almost clear of people. If formed an irregular atrium, rapidly widening above their heads into a space of oblique angles and toroidal protrusions. The lack of right angles messed with the man's depth perception, threatening simultaneous agoraphobia and claustrophobia. Lesana headed for a staircase that zigzagged its way up into the confusing space. She attacked the stairs at pace. After four steps one knee gave way and she fell backwards. The man reached out a steadying hand and eased Lesana back to upright.

"You're exhausted," he said.

She waited until they had climbed to the fourth floor before saying anything in response. Her breathing was convulsive, barely controlled. She pointed towards a corridor of random proportions.

"Check each room. Visual sweep. Call-out. Listen and then move on."

The man moved through each empty room. The building fabric had reverted to its base form, absorbing every piece of furniture, character or individuality. A few personal items lay scattered on the floor, clothes were roughly piled to form makeshift beds, and pieces of technology piled like firewood.

Lesana joined him on the fifth room.

"You look pale," he stated.

"I'll be all right. I'm not used to so much running. I'm not sure I ever climbed a flight of static stairs before this." Her arms swept to encompass everything. "Why did you walk off?"

The man was thrown by the change in topic. "I decided to face the Reset on my own terms." Outside his head the explanation sounded hopelessly weak.

"Your own terms? There were no terms. The Reset doesn't even know you exist. It doesn't negotiate."

"Negotiate? No, I suppose not."

"You were giving up."

"Maybe," he admitted. "If you think that, why did you come and get me?"

"Because you don't have the right."

"Surely, that is the only right I truly have."

"Not when we are being annihilated. You have a duty to fight for everyone else. Look at me."

"I am."

"No, look at me."

The man tried to see Lesana afresh. Exhaustion bent her back, exaggerating the slender frame and stick-thin limbs. Sweat and dirt defined her face, forming their own contours over the soft slopes of a mid-budget face. In contrast, her clothes were spotless, except where the cheap fabric was starting to lose its sheen. In a crowd she would be anonymous, body and dress made generic by fashion and market-driven genetics.

The man wrestled to keep inside the pity he felt.

"Exactly," was all she said.

They moved down to the third floor and renewed their search from room to room.

A voice boomed up from the ground floor. "Out! Time up," it demanded.

"We only have two more rooms," Lesana said softly.

The man nodded and they moved on. The last room was empty. It smelled faintly of vomit and urine. A pile of rags formed an undulating dune against the back wall. Lesana called out, but the man was already starting to turn back towards the staircase.

"Wait," Lesana demanded as she moved into the room.

The man watched as she peeled back the top layer of rags. Two oval smears of dirt lay beneath. Four bright eyes flickered open and blinked with apprehension.

"It's all right," Lesana purred. "Time to get up and go for a walk."

Some of the rags stirred and separated themselves from the pile. From their relative heights, there must have been a couple of years between the two girls.

"Shall I carry you," Lesana asked the smaller girl.

There was a flicker of communion with the bigger girl before she opened her arms.

"Let's go," Lesana said sweeping the girl into her arms.

The other girl looked up at the man. "What's your name?" she asked. He knelled down to bring his head level with hers. "I don't know," he said.

"That's silly," she said.

The man laughed. It felt like ice cracking under a spring sun. "Maybe you can help me find my name."

"I'm good at finding."

The man took her hand. "Yes, I believe you are."

*

Nomia allowed her consciousness to linger in the space where the Suparna had been parked. Heat leaked from four tumbling figures, black clad against a black background. Background stars flickered as they were eclipsed by the erratic spin of the contorting bodies.

Morbidity kept Nomia transfixed.

She expanded her senses further, until she could feel the vapour boiling on the tongues of the invaders. Pressure and heat loss was slow and painful inside the body armour.

A small shuttle burnt a luminous curve towards the drifting figures. Wrapped in stealth materials it crossed space with arrogant impunity. The vastness of space made its energy-profligate dash seem slow and lumbering. Vacuum crept inside the four sets of body armour. The occupants would be dead before the ship arrived.

Maybe Nomia could save them. So little of her consciousness remained in this part of space. She could not decide if she wanted to try; compassion was the mortar she had used to bind her fractured personality. To surrender compassion would be to invite psychosis, but these invaders had threatened her brothers and sisters. Surely some kind of retribution was in order.

The rhythms separating life from physics ceased in one of the suits.

A mammalian disgust shook the fragment of Nomia from its reverie. She started to search amongst the possible futures, searching for one in which the remaining three would survive until they were rescued. Open space was unyielding in its determination to reduce everything to its own level. Dramatic intervention was required to bend reality enough for humans to survive a swim in hard vacuum.

Nomia was just starting to drag enough herself back to this place, intending to muster the mental force necessary, when an Eidolon sphere popped back into existence. It hovered around the drifting bodies, sniffing Verity Space for juicier quarry.

Without hesitation, Nomia snapped back to the Suparna.

Guilt could wait its turn. Right now, she had people depending on her.

For the first time Nomia noticed Kaamil's left arm. Normally it hung useless at his side, limply contrasting with his articulating data-tethers. Now he cradled it to his chest, the hand thrust through a hole in his tunic. He looked pale and confused.

"We've moved," he stated.

Nomia nodded. "Get someone to bind that arm."

Kaamil's fingers shifted defensively and he grunted something close to agreement.

"The Nymphs," José stated with suitable awe. "While we were bogged down with the threat directly in front of our faces, they just removed us all from the fray."

"Are they okay?" Kaamil asked.

"The shield is building," Nomia said. "I need to go find them."

"I'll look after these two," José bent over the two foam wrapped Satyagrahi.

Even without their overlapping consciousness in Verity Space, there was something about José that worried Nomia deeply. He ground unspoken words between his teeth. A cruel anger deformed his sagely features.

Later, Nomia told herself.

It was a dozen hours before Nomia and José found themselves alone and together. The Satyagrahi had survived unscathed, but trauma crept into their bastille in a myriad of subtle ways: trembling fingers, distant stares, flinching at the gentlest touch. Nomia spread her calm as wide and thin as it would go without evaporating all together.

José focused on tactical matters. Finding the few Satyagrahi strong enough to fight, and organising a change of personnel. The team from Earth who had been resisting the Reset, arrived exhausted beyond normal endurance.

It would be days before they could return to duty; another team burnt-out by unreasonable demands. They briefly rallied when they found their brothers and sisters alive, but their collapse was hastened by the destroyed illusion of sanctuary on the Suparna.

"Enough."

Nomia found José holed-up in what would have been their room, had they ever found the time to be together.

"Enough what?" Nomia asked, even though she dreaded the answer.

"First MynCorp, now DogStar. When the shield went down, you must have felt the hole where Ben should be. It can only be Durga. The only member of the Cartel not to attack us is Ж, and they probably would if they still existed."

"We're not fighting for the corporations."

"They are part of humanity. The same humanity we are sacrificing all of our lives for. And yet they still treat us like objects to be owned and dissected."

"Most wars are fought on multiple fronts. You taught me that."

"We cannot possibly win like this. All the Satyagrahi are going to die, either at the hands of the Eidolons or the corporations. Either way they die for nothing."

Nomia bit her lip. She wanted to reach out and touch José. She sat next to him on the bed, their shoulders separated by a chasm of unspoken thoughts.

"What are you suggesting?" she asked.

"We both got the same message from the Eidolon."

Nomia nodded. "All the Satyagrahi have the new memory."

José looked surprised. For a moment consequences flickered across his frown, but the despair settled back into place.

"Amnesty."

"We can't accept." Nomia stated without room for doubt.

"We can. You, me and all the Satyagrahi. We walk away. Take up the offer of a fresh start somewhere else. Maybe a reality of our own construction."

"And leave all of humanity to die?"

"We cannot save them. All we've done is make things worse. Everyone on Earth is suffering a slow drawn-out death, because we interfered; convinced we knew best. Determined to prove our humanity."

"This is not your decision to make."

"Nor is it yours."

"The fight goes on. The Satyagrahi are as one on this."

"You've already talked to them?"

"We reached a consensus immediately."

"They'd do anything you ask. They are not ready to make a decision like this."

"That's patronising."

"Is it? They've experienced nothing except exploitation and fighting. They're not equipped to see they deserve better. It's partly my fault. I was so desperate to preserve the purity of your naivety. I encouraged you to be a creature of pure instinct."

"Now you're being arrogant."

"Maybe, but I'm right."

Something was wrong with reality. The fabric of the Universe was being rearranged, one fibre at a time. A slow and deliberate manipulation of fact into something equally viable, but unrelated.

"What are you doing?" Nomia asked.

Sweat was forming on José's brow. The tension in his shoulder Nomia had thought was stress, was now a trembling effort. "Do you remember explaining how you avoid giving me any opportunity to say no?" he asked.

Nomia could feel all the Satyagrahi distinct and clear, but the rest of the Suparna were frozen in a limbo. Parked in a virtual waiting-room, their reality stalled in an interval between moments.

"How are you doing this with the shield up?"

"This room. I made a little sanctuary. Modified the shield, like one way glass."

Strain clipped his sentences into individual breaths. An alien feeling tainted Nomia's spirit; the only person beyond doubt had deceived her. The complex web of modification being unfurled around her was the product of protracted deliberation.

José was crying. He did not deserve to cry. She was the one being betrayed.

"No. I won't let you!"

Nomia exploded inside José's delicate manipulation, blowing contrived probabilities out to the extremes of likelihood. Where José had delicately constructed a potential reality in which the Satyagrahi had never joined the war against the Eidolons, Nomia was a force of pure destruction.

José cried out in pain.

His very being was entwined with the reconstructed universe. Nomia was tearing holes in his construct and consciousness with the same eruptions of chaos.

When she was done, the Universe beat back to life. Nothing had happened. Nothing had changed. All that might have been was still only a possibility. The war was still a reality. A reality Nomia had to face alone.

Nomia searched ever corner of reality, stretching her senses and consciousness to the limit of her endurance. There was nothing to find.

José was gone.

Chapter 10

Bergur pulled the tiller hard, bringing the aerofoils closer to the stream. The yacht picked up speed, and started to corkscrew along the ice-tube. The blades rattled across the corrugations in the frozen wall, screeching occasionally as the lateral thrust bounced the blades out of their grove. This close to the planet's surface, sunlight made the walls of the ice-tube glow turquoise. Occasional fractures in the bed-ice formed black zigzags, fracturing the surroundings like lightening in negative.

Bergur stared hard through the translucent hull of the yacht, trying to pick out features in the ice; looking for an external reference to get a sense of speed. Dissatisfied, he let the aerofoils relax and adjusted the trim to grab more of the flow. The yacht shifted to run with the stream. His gut sensed the deceleration, even as his brain accepted his progress along the tube had probably improved. With an adrenaline seeking grunt, Bergur pulled the craft tighter to the current once more. Finally, satisfied with the burst of acceleration, Bergur fell back into the hammock, fully closed his eyes, and enjoyed the corkscrew sensation in his stomach.

Something pinged off the hull, bringing Bergur to full attention. The second impact was hard enough to scratch the outer skin, leaving a scar that floated against the blue background.

Bergur was still reaching to neutralise the aerofoils when the impacts became a continuous noise.

"Ice storm!" he shouted against the din.

His cry traversed two worlds: different planets, separate times and opposite states of consciousness.

The ice storm followed.

In front of him Sera was swearing. Her shoulder blades were twitching with tension as she thumped switches on a control panel Bergur could not see. The noise was worse than hail on a poly-resin roof. Bergur felt the capsule's forward motion falter and then completely stall.

The noise of impacts immediately stopped.

"What did we hit?" Bergur asked.

"Ice," Sera shouted back, her voice full of frustration.

"Ice?" The overlap of dream and reality added to Bergur's disorientation. "Are we okay?"

"We will be if I can get us to the surface before the drive completely fails, and we're entombed in rock."

"Entombed? That sounds permanent."

Sera didn't answer. The capsule started to bob. First the nose lifted, then the tail. Finally, the complete capsule rolled onto its starboard side.

Sera let out a long overdue breath "I think that's it," she said.

"What's what?"

"Buoyancy. We're floating. We should be on the surface."

"Did you say we hit ice?"

"Yes, quite a large deposit. I probably should have spotted it in the magnetometer readings, but it's not my expertise."

"So, this submarine is fine going through rock, but can't handle water?"

"Ice." Sera corrected. "Liquefying ice is a completely different technique to rock."

Bergur reached forward for the hatch release. He hesitated. "Where are we?" he asked.

"We should be a few kilometres from Vanuatu City."

"You don't seem to sure."

"It's not easy navigating underground. No global magnetic field, no stars and this thing is a bit noisy for sonar."

Sera sounded annoyed. Maybe she felt he was questioning her capability. Bergur tried to dial-down his curiosity; if he needed to know something Sera would tell him eventually. For the hundredth time, he noted how simultaneously different and similar Sera was to Yakini. Ultimately, the difference was one of self-confidence. Sera was just as capable as Yakini (maybe more so), but she lacked the single-minded conviction that made Yakini so compelling.

He knew better than to placate Sera with platitudes. "Shall we have a look?" he asked.

She wriggled above him and pulled something from her belt. Her survival suit grew to encase her head, as she fitted a rebreather to her face and algae pack to her shoulder. It pulsed a dull-green that clashed with the symbiotic flora of his own skin.

She raised an affirmative thumb. Bergur reached up and cracked the hull seal.

Sera stood on top of the dead capsule and surveyed their surroundings. To Bergur, one direction was indistinguishable from any other. So when, Sera pointed towards a jagged bluff, he saw no reason to question her judgement. He started to walk, knowing she would catchup easily. Sera hesitated, maybe less confident than she appeared.

Within a few strides she took the lead. Shortened her stride, she gestured downwards. Bergur understood he should reuse her footprints. Whether it was for his benefit or the planet's, he wasn't sure.

Bergur concentrated on keeping his legs moving while Sera made effortless progress across the unpredictable surface. For Bergur, each stride was uncomfortably long and his feet susceptible to crunching through the surface crust. He allowed his higher brain function to fade; lulled asleep by repetitive motion and sinking oxygen levels. It helped him to forget about the brown flecks of dead flora spreading across his skin. If anything he was surprised it had taken so long. How many alien suns and atmospheres had he foisted on his symbiont? Despite the inexorable nature of his condition, he had no doubt there would be plenty of opportunity to die in a blaze of spectacular glory, long before his skin suffocated him. A chuckle rippled through his mouth flaps. It turned into a futile yawn; pulling useless gases into vestigial lungs.

The bluff grew rapidly into a mountain range like nothing Bergur has ever seen. A chaotic row of savage teeth gnawing at the sky. A few streaks of ferrous sand ran like blood down towards the plain. Approaching the outer rim of the crater by foot felt uncomfortably like being lured into a predator's den. Of course it did not help that several factions bent on his demise resided within the crater bowl.

Sera pointed at a black dot near the base of the crater wall, and adjusted her path towards it. Bergur was too addled by oxygen starvation to acknowledge her instruction, but his feet continued to fall where hers had passed.

They cleared an electrostatic barrier and entered a dimly lit tunnel. Bergur felt the surrounding oxygen level rise; his skin almost sucked at the surrounding air. The cramps in his limbs faded as toxins were filtered and expelled. Given enough rest his body would absorb the dead skin flora. He would maintain a better colour, but it would not prevent the inevitable outcome.

"I suppose we need some kind of plan," Sera said after removing her breather.

"It's a shame Nomia didn't leave a few Nodes on Mars. We could use a little improbability-magic."

"If she hadn't evacuated to the Suparna, Ben wouldn't be the only one we'd need to rescue."

Bergur saved any more comments until his brain had more time to wake up. At the end of the tunnel they emerged into the tranquil air of the crater. The thumb-sized sun glinted through the crystal canopy over the city.

"Sera, weren't you part of a paramilitary group?"

"An independence movement." Sera said tersely.

"Either way, can you call on some fighters for support?"

"Maybe given time. Most of the people I trust are either on the Suparna, or scattered."

"So what are we left with?"

"Surprise."

"You mean Durga will be surprised when two people launch an attack on their headquarters? Maybe they'll die laughing."

"We'll find out."

They saw very few people as they made their way through the city of green cubes. Those they saw looked exhausted by the continuous tension of fear. A few acknowledged Sera with delighted cheers and touched foreheads. Nobody asked her where she had been or where she had come from. It was as if their curiosity had been eroded to nothing by streams of bad news.

Nobody seemed to notice Bergur. The same blind-spot he had witnessed on the mining station. He still was not sure if it was a form a xenophobia, or a survival instinct in a repressive society. Bergur continued to play the role of dumb alien.

"There it is." Sera was pointing at a particularly large green cube. It was maybe three stories high, but it was hard to tell through the algae continuously slurping within the skin of the building.

Sera pointed towards the top of the cube. "What was that?" she asked.

Swirling patterns were forming in the algae. Subtle changes in the flow formed shapes, like clouds he had seen on Earth. Something almost reptilian prowled across the surface. Around it, gaps in the algae revealed the complexity of the infrastructure within the building.

As they approached, a dozen Martians burst from a double doorway and ran away in stumbling panic. Half a dozen more in armoured jackets staggered out, their hands clawing at their heads. Two crawled to safety and collapsed a few metres from the building.

Sera and Bergur reached the doorway. Something continued to patrol the skin of the building, but nobody else emerged.

"Once more onto the breach?" Bergur suggested.

"What?"

"Never mind."

As he stepped inside, something ineffable began to tug at Bergur's sanity.

*

A cascade of buffer under-runs heralded Mex's abrupt dismissal from the Nexus. At some point he had fallen to the floor, or the floor had fallen on him. He was still facing Yakini but now they both had their cheeks deformed by juddering polycrete. Mex lifted his head enough to easy the jarring in his teeth. Sardon was already back in his seat. His jaw tensed in the way Mex had come to associate with an incoming message.

Building locomotion disrupted.

The message popped into his head like it had come from Julienne. Mex had thrown the piece of spyware in Sardon's direction with little hope of it sticking, now he had to hide his surprise at the unusual feeling of fortuity.

Yakini was looking at him oddly. Mex folded caution into the corners of his eyes. A question evaporated from her lips.

The walls flickered once and the room was plunged into darkness.

Sardon received a burst of telemetry that Mex had no way of interpreting, but from the resultant growl of frustration there was little doubt Julienne was making a move.

The lights came back on with a jarring brilliance. Yakini was stood with her back to the observation window. Behind her Teledice hung limply from metallic constraints. Around her green status lights throbbed like the rhythm of an artificial heart.

Mex gave Yakini a reassuring smile but she was scowling fixedly at Sardon with a new level of hatred.

"Such a shame," Sardon lamented. "Ms Garland is literally half the agent she used to be."

Mex was ready to respond with a smattering of false bravado, when a more familiar connection was opening in his head.

Mex?

Julienne. How close are you?

Not close enough, but I've spliced one of my implants into the building's grid.

You know I love it when you talk techie, but Sardon knows where you are. You have to move.

I burnt a fist sized hole in one of the main conduits but the power only cut-out for a moment.

I'll see what I can find out. Now move!

Mex sensed Julienne withdraw. A moment later Sardon received a status update from a security team.

She's not here.

Sardon did not waste breath on frustration. Continue to secondary targets, he messaged. Agent Garland will continue to attack infrastructure. Prioritise power systems.

There was location information tagged to each message showing both the current location of the sender and additional tags related to the content. Mex snagged a copy and pasted it to a scratch-pad.

Sardon directed Mex and Yakini back into their seats and retrieved the code glasses from the floor. "I don't think we need to wait for Ms Garland to be captured," he said. "Let's return to the negotiations."

Mex invented a couple of imaginary risks relating to navigating the Nexus during a power or communications glitch. Neither the threat of a brain haemorrhage nor a heart seizure had any impact on Sardon. Yakini just glowered and followed Sardon's every instruction with a fatalistic ambivalence.

Two minutes later they dropped back into the Nexus. The Oikakes were continuing their tireless assault on the static presence of Teledice. Sardon resumed his negotiations, addressing the region of Verity Space infested with the writhing spheres.

I would like to table a few example scenarios and ask our alien guests to rank them in order of preference. Number One. Earth and her colonies are subject to indefinite quarantine to be marshalled by yourselves. Number Two. All colonies are purged and humankind is restricted to the inner regions of this solar system. Number three. The human species self-culls to no more than one billion individuals and restricts annual economic output to ten thousand yotta Joules.

Sardon gave over a dozen scenarios, glibly trading genocide for economic freedoms; billions of lives equated to a few dozen percentage points of corporate profits.

Mex felt a ping in an implant he imagined to be near his ears.

Julienne?

I need help. I'm being boxed in.

There was insufficient bandwidth to include inflection but Mex could imagine the skin at the bridge of her nose forming two symmetrical creases of frustration.

I'm sending you a list of targets Sardon thinks you might hit and recent locations of his security teams. Got it?

Got it.

There was no point telling Julienne to be careful, or holding on to the link for a few more seconds of contact. Sardon was brilliant, ruthless and psychotic. Being careful would get them killed only shortly later than being reckless.

Having waited patiently for Sardon to offer up parts of the human race for MyncCorp's gain, Yakini's answer was simple and definitive. The Eidolons are unable to rank these alternative realities because none of them are this universe.

Please explain, Sardon requested.

Yakini made a few abortive attempts to form an answer. She seemed lost in multiple thoughts, like someone trying to elucidate a chaotic dream while still asleep.

Physical sentience modifies Verity Space through acts of will but is subject to the laws of nature. They are the cause and the subject of causality. The single perspective on reality is lifted when a species transcends but there is a cost.

Yakini stumbled before switching to an analogy. The Eidolons are like actors in a play that is forever changing, but they must act all the scenes simultaneously.

Yakini's voice trailed away. When she spoke again lucidity was replaced with bitterness. None of that matters. Sardon, you are not asking the right question. This is not about what MynCorp can gain or lose. This is about you.

A burst of telemetry on Sardon's feed shocked Mex back into the real world. The part of his mind in the Nexus lurched and lost control of his avatar. He struggled to make sense of the multiple streams, while part of him watched the three of them tumble in the virtual maelstrom of the Oikake battlefield.

Yakini yelped in both worlds and reached out for Teledice, further destabilising Mex's precarious control. With a grunt of frustration Mex accepted he could not do both and left the Nexus avatar to its own devices. Sardon was firing instructions to multiple security and technician teams, directing a battle both of people and infrastructure.

A third perspective jostled for Mex's attention. Shimmering between the visual world of the laboratory and the software world of the Nexus was a vision of a corridor rushing past at a sprint. There was the rhythmic undulation of pumping legs and athletic lungs. Mex almost fell off his chair and had to sit on his hands to keep his limbs under control. This was full arcade mode, but without physical contact, but Julienne was near and fighting for her life.

The vision lurched sideways and the corridor flipped into retreat as Julienne grabbed a look over her shoulder. Perfectly judged, she saw two black clad figures appeared from a side corridor and level weapons whining with charge. The perspective lurched again and Mex had to endure losing sight of those readied weapons. Julienne was sprinting for another junction. Mex could feel the tearing pain from the plasma burns under her arm and a new grinding pain that could well be a broken ankle.

There was a pair of concussive thuds from behind. Mex projected Julienne's name in panic, but she was already low against the floor using her momentum to slide the last metres to the junction. A blast of acoustics bolts tore through the air above her making the skin on her back ruck-up and wrench the muscles below.

Julienne was back on her feet and moving without hesitation. Her arms pumped, fingers slicing the air like daggers. Mex realised she was empty-handed and he could not feel a bulge where a gun usually hugged against her hip.

Mex. Update me. Now.

Two more figures in black stepped into Juliennes path. One already had a projectile weapon levelled at her head. Julienne adjusted her position in the corridor slightly. Mex could feel her calculating angles maximising the probability she intersected the line of sight from the gun muzzle to the two agents behind. The arm holding the gun tensed as he gripped the trigger, Julienne folded at the waist whipping her head to the side. There was a crack of electrostatic charge and something pierced the air next to her ear.

Julienne continued to roll at the waist. She let one leg drag so that she spun against the direction of motion. The top of her head narrowly cleared the gun arm, then she was upright again, her back to the gunman, their arms entwined.

One of the pursuing agents was already crumpling from the charge impact. The second hesitated, his weapon not yet levelled. Julienne dug two fingers into the tendons in the gunman's arm. He yelped and involuntarily pulled the trigger twice. Her head cracked back. Mex felt the back of her skull crush the gunman's visor and something more organic crunch underneath. The man was suddenly a dead weight on her shoulders. She started to drop and continue the previous spin, delivering the dazed agent into the arms of the last gunman. His hands disabled, Julienne stepped forward and stabbed two knuckles into the side of his neck.

She was running again before his unconscious body hit the floor.

Mex?

Right. Here's what Sardon knows. Mex fired a burst of data. He's rerouteing power and bringing redundant systems on-line as fast as your disable them.

I don't know what else to try. I can't see a way to get to you, but I'm having no effect out here. I can't out-think him.

Mex could feel her mounting desperation and frustration. She did not need to add a reason. Both bidden and unbidden she had sacrificed so much of what made her unique, and yet she was still expected to be a super-soldier when humanity needed her the most. She was a product of the most selfish social construct ever known to mankind, and yet all she had known through both her lives was sacrifice. Paradoxically, he believed himself part of an egalitarian alternative, and yet he frequently acted only out of self-interest. The same egocentricity that made him fight to make her something he could love, then recoil from the intimacy he helped to create.

"Mr Tyrian?" Sardon demanded. "Your attention please."

Mex was mostly back in the laboratory. He brought the Nexus avatar back under his control. Yakini had dragged them through the battlefield until they nestled up against Teledice, putting them on the front-line where reality melted under the savagery of the Oikake onslaught. Close up Mex could see something new was happening. The sphere's were no longer attacking Teledice directly. They were targeting all their efforts into the thin shell of Verity Space immediately adjacent to the catatonic node, like they were digging a protective ditch or moat.

Sardon resumed his one man crusade to civilise the Eidolons.

To continue, there are various ways in which MynCorp can facilitate your role as guardians of reality. For example, we could offer the processing potential of, say, thirty percent of human minds to help monitor Verity Space, running algorithms custom designed for your application. And when you find a race in need of eradication we can provide weapons superior to your current spheres, specifically, the high yield armament on display today. A weapon that we have demonstrated is impervious to all Verity Space attacks. Attenuated, it can destroy your targets with a single blow, at maximum yield it acts as a deterrent against pre-emptive strikes by any aggressor you might encounter.

By now Yakini was a spitting her responses. The spheres are not about destruction. Restoring reality takes times. Speed is of no concern. The rest of your offer is meaningless. You're still not asking the right question. This is about you Sardon.

Let's not get personal, Sardon lamented. It's important to keep the negotiations professional. So this demonstration of our resolve should in no way be interpreted as aggression.

Sardon's jaw tensed a fraction. Mex fired up every piece of hackware he could find however tangential to telecommunications. His entire arsenal of DOS attacks and protocol exploitations exposed in single flick of his eye.

Unaffected, Sardon's message cut through the chatter without a single retransmit. Activate Node. Minimum yield.

In the physical world Yakini lunged blindly at Sardon. One knee came up onto the desk. Her arms reached forward, fingers extended like an eagle's talons. Mex reacted a fraction of a second later, but an additional turquoise laser was already starting to strobe at the edge of his vision. Yakini fell face first onto the table, convulsed once then lay still. All the muscles in Mex's body tensed, bending his bones until splinters cracked from their surface, then he was as limp as a doll. Yakini lay motionless on the table drool leaking from her mouth but absolute hatred boiled in her eyes.

They were forced to stare unblinking into the Nexus as Teledice woke with an outpouring of violence. The shell of her sphere pulsed, not with the undulations of Sardon's messages, but with the climbing intensity of a bomb building to the point of detonation.

Even the Oikake paused their attack, as the pulsations blended into a continuum. There was a crescendo. The Nexus code interpreted the outpouring as a blinding white light. When it faded everything was exactly the same. A shell of potential sizzled into nothing. The Oikake resumed their scraping at the boundary between Verity Space and Teledice.

"What happened?" Sardon exchanged bursts of telemetry with the laboratory systems.

Yakini slowly sank back into her seat. "Maybe now you'll stop posturing and ask why we are here?"

"It doesn't matter. I still hold the advantage," Sardon ranted. "The ultimate deterrent. Never call the bluff of a man with nothing to lose. Tell them."

"They know. That's what I've been trying to tell you. You are why we are here. The event that decided humanity's fate is this. The Eidolon saw this moment. They saw what you were capable of, and they judged us all. You killed everyone with this insanity. Your ultimate deterrent is the reason none of us will have ever existed."

Sardon was still gulping air when a circular patch of wall exploded inwards with a shower of glowing shards. Julienne staggered through the sizzling aperture. One eye was stained with blood leaking from a wound on her temple. With a blast from a sonic pistol, she floored one of the agents guarding the door before he could even draw a gun. She stepped in close to the second guard, preventing him from levelling or firing his own weapon.

Mex felt the dislocation of being in two places, but this time he could see his own shocked and beleaguered face. He also saw a fist flash in front of Julienne's eyes and felt the shock of glancing blow to her nose. She reeled backwards, putting a hand on the wall as the room span.

Mex gathered himself to jump in and help, but his legs betrayed him. He slumped back into the seat.

Sardon was staring through the window into the laboratory as if Julienne was not even there. "You're right," he raved. "This is all down to me. Only I can bring us victory. The time for negotiation is over. This is war." He fired a message at the laboratory systems.

"He's going to detonate Teledice," Mex screamed. "Julienne, now would be good."

"Really?" Julienne grunted. She swung an elbow into the agent's face plate and followed up with a knee into the side of his abdomen. Julienne dropped her own weapon and deftly flicked the guard's out of his hand as he fell to the floor.

Her gun swung towards the table, but Sardon was already moving. Mex raised his clay arm as he realised the manic MynCorp executive was wielding a palm sized weapon. Through Julienne's eyes Mex saw the gun pin the raised hand to the side of his own head.

"Ms Garland, stand down if you please," Sardon instructed.

Shoot him, Mex thrust into Julienne's head. Her fingers tensed, then relaxed.

No, Sardon's weapon has an inverted trigger. It will fire automatically if he releases the weapon.

He's going to detonate Teledice, if you don't shoot him.

I can't sacrifice you. You'll find a way without me.

Julienne was already starting to lower her weapon. Through her eyes he could see Sardon's victorious sneer.

"It is long past time you died again Ms Garland," Sardon bombasted.

The pressure on Mex's head started to ease. Sardon was turning the gun away from Mex.

"No!" Mex screamed. He brought his spare hand up to the gun and stabbed two fingers into the wrist just as he had witnessed Julienne do. There was a noise like thunder in a mountain range and his body was flung sideways.

He watched through Julienne's eyes as his clay hand exploded in a shower of crystalline fragments. Mex's head snapped away from the impact, his face frozen in shock and surprise. The shards of glittering hand were still bouncing and dancing in the white light, when his body crumpled to the floor and lay still.

There were two more concussive sounds of shooting and at least one person screamed, before the view blinked and did not return.

Chapter 11

Care and diligence were the keys.

Nomia withdrew her tendrils of concentration and returned to the discontinuity. José had existed, then he did not. His past was fuzzy, slightly degenerate, but definite. The future contained plenty of rippling effects but a vacuum of causes.

José was not dead.

The death of a conscious mind was a decoupling from the Downey field. The remaining chemistry of the body continued to evolve, accumulating super-positional states, cruising towards higher entropy with a momentum like a downhill street car.

José was not dead.

Nomia exploded back into Verity Space. Her mind ran wildly down blind alleys in causality. Every ripple in the Downey field reminded her of José's presence, but none had his rhythm; the unique pattern Nomia provocatively called his soul.

Her distress echoed throughout reality. Sentient creatures on distant planets dreamt of a pale-brown skinned biped wrapped in layers of monochrome fabric. On Earth a few people of particular sensitivity, cocked their heads slightly as if listening to a secret message carried on the breeze.

Thump. Thump. Thump.

The sound bouncing around the room seemed crude and intrusive compared to the delicate intricacy of Nomia's distress.

"Nomia?" someone called.

A door iris opened a small portal. Several concerned faces squeezed into view. Nomia instinctively brushed tears from her cheek, but her skin was dry. The door opened fully, but her Nymphs did not enter. Their minds touched the patch of unshielded reality and recoiled.

Questions built up in their faces. Questions Nomia did not have the strength to answer.

"Nobody enters this room," she declared as she left. "How're we doing?"

"It's all falling apart," Cretheis blurted, her voice reduced to a creaking stammer.

Chania coughed his voice back to life. "The Suparna shielding is back in place and holding, but TC's group were exhausted before they started. The team on Earth haven't been relieved today. Nobody wants to go. Kaamil is here. He wants to speak to you."

Nomia's will threatened to buckle, but held long enough for a group hug. Silence accumulated until Nomia relented. "We need to relieve the city team," she said.

"Who?" asked Chania.

"If no one else is strong enough, it will have to be us. Get something to eat. I'll talk to Kaamil. See what fresh disaster has befallen us?"

Kaamil was waiting in the vestibule. His damaged arm was encased in a sheath of blue gel. His eyes were cast down, pretending not to notice the wary looks from a huddle of bleary eyed Incognito.

"Kaamil."

A myriad of partially formed emotions flickered across his face. Hope, expectation, fear and guilt condensed and evaporated before Nomia could be sure of their existence. Kaamil's face settled on concern.

"Where's José?"

"Gone," was all she could manage. "I have to go down to the city. What do you need?"

Kaamil stepped closer a hand half raised towards her. "The refugee council is meeting. There is a lot of shouting. We're worried somebody will do something counter productive."

Nomia hunted in her body for a hidden reserve of energy but found only pools of lethargic loss. "Can't you handle it?" she begged.

Kaamil looked panic stricken.

"Okay. Okay. I'll talk to them."

The council was made up of representatives nominated or persuaded to speak on behalf of the different groups of refugees. In as much as was possible given the limited possibilities of their predicament, they made decisions for everyone on the Suparna, except for Kaamil and the Satyagrahi. It seemed to be an intrinsic feature of human nature to form tribes. Division could be based on which shell of the Suparna they found themselves, which collection of shelters, what function they performed or common fears.

José had vetted the initial candidates until they had enough members to function. He had tried to select individuals with enough wisdom to be a reluctant spokesperson and rejecting anyone a corporation would see as a born leader. Still, the council had evolved and opinions could become entrenched.

Kaamil loitered at Nomia's shoulder as she stood before the buffeting of the council's consternation.

"We should leave orbit." The representative for Sphere1 Utilities raised his hand politely as he spoke over everyone else. "I say, we can choose to make a break for open space, or stay here and die."

"Kaamil," Nomia deferred.

Kaamil spoke evenly, masking his insecurity. "The Suparna has fully committed herself to humanitarian relief. She is not configured for significant flight."

"Then we stay here and die. I'd rather take my chances on the ground."

A few other voices murmured their agreement.

Nomia faced the bulk of the assembly. "You are, of course, all free to leave any time you desire, but have any of you been down to the surface recently?"

"You know we haven't," a woman. Her eyes were uniformly green, without pupils to betray whom she was looking at.

"I have. Things are bad. Even with the best efforts of the Satyagrahi, almost half the planet has been consumed by the Reset. Most of the population is in constant migration."

A short man with a gravel-like whisper dropped a sentence into a pause in the discussion. "Maybe we just need to be rid of your Satyagrahi."

Eyes locked around the room. Drawing conviction from others, several voices started to talk at once. Nomia let their ire burn itself out before responding in the following calm.

"The Satyagrahi are shielding you all from the Eidolons."

"They were just here attacking us."

"That was because we lowered the shield to fight the corporate intruders."

"But the spheres only attacked Satyagrahi. Maybe we would be safe without you here."

Voices rose as neighbours agreed or disagreed.

"Try telling my family," someone shouted. "The spheres killed them all without even leaving their bodies."

"And where were the Satyagrahi?" the gravel voice asked.

A woman with arms coiled around her chest like snakes said, "All I know is that every time I see a sphere it is trying to get at one of the Satyagrahi, and anyone who gets in the way is wiped out. I say we would be safer on our own."

Kaamil found his voice again. "You can all leave. The Suparna is here for you, but don't make her chose between you and Nomia."

"The ship will do what we tell it," the original speaker remonstrated.

Kaamil looked fragile but resolute. "She will not."

Nomia raised her hand. "Can we scale back with the rhetoric? The Satyagrahi did not start this war, but we choose to fight for all humanity. I beg the council to not give in to fear and prejudice. We survive or fall together."

The argument raged on, but Nomia found herself struggling to emulate José's patient wisdom. The more frightened people became the harder Nomia found to predict their behaviour; she might be better at seeing people's virtues, but José was perfect at untangling their demons.

Nomia sat down when she could not absorb any more debate and dissension. Kaamil drew closer.

"They will not leave," he whispered. "Fear makes individuals more cautious, but we may need to restrict mass assembly."

"Only as a last resort," Nomia warned.

"Of course. Whatever you think."

Kaamil was even closer. His hand touched her shoulder. "I'll never leave you. I will always be here for you."

She patted his hand. "Thank you Kaamil. You are a true friend."

Kaamil bent low and wrapped his good arm around Nomia. She leant into his chest and let him feed her warmth.

A minute passed.

Nomia sighed and gathered her strength to stand unaided. Kaamil continued to hold her tight. He was murmuring a sentiment too soft to form words. She pulled back with enough assertiveness to wake Kaamil from his daydream. He continued to hold her tight, pushing back against Nomia's determination.

"Kaamil," she pleaded into his shoulder.

"Ssh," he purred. "I'm here my love."

"You're hurting me. Let me go."

Kaamil's grip tightened again.

Nomia stabbed a bent knuckle between two of his ribs. "I said let go," she shouted.

Kaamil staggered back as if punched. The becalmed look on his face was replaced by one of devastation. "I'm sorry. I'm sorry," he started to repeat.

"It's okay," Nomia lied, taking another few steps back. Each step seemed to cause Kaamil physical pain. He continued to repeat his apology like a mantra.

Nomia struggled for anything to say. The last corner stone had just disintegrated from the edifice of her life. The room spun around her. She turned away and ran.

"Nomia!"

His voice gave chase matching her stride for stride. Finally, he stopped pursuing her, but he kept shouting; urgent but no longer pleading.

"Nomia. Please stop. I've just got a message from Earth. The Satyagrahi are falling. The Reset is at the city's edge."

*

"Sorry we couldn't find your name," Aisling lamented.

"That's alright. Maybe it isn't meant to be found."

Aisling considered the man with no name while giving her nose a dubious wrinkle. "I think I should stay here and look after my sister," she said.

Lesana was handing the younger sister over to a crèche volunteer. The youthful carer had a desperate smile fixed to his face, as if a momentary frown would bring the world crashing in on his sanctuary. He held one hand of the sister, but Lesana was not quite ready to surrender the other. Behind them dozens of children played, cried, sang or sat in contemplative huddles. Clumps of adults milled around the room. The air was thick with the same anxious conversations and trivial complaints as every building in the city. Here and there an adult would find themselves glancing at the children. The series of expressions was almost identical each time: wistful, sorrowful, then a final flash of determination.

"Thank you," the nameless man said to Aisling.

"For what?"

Her sister was already calling for Aisling. She held her arms apart as he bent down for a final hug. Her small arms and delicate hands left a trace of love under his skin. Aisling released him and trotted after her sister. The man rose to his feet, feeling lighter than he could remember.

"Thank you, for helping me find something more important," he whispered to no one.

Lesana and the nameless man stepped out of the moving building. The threshold carried them clear of the subduction zone and on to clear ground, but they had to trot to stay ahead.

The man searched for distraction from his protesting legs. "What were you before?" he asked.

"Data analyst," she said dismissively. "Still am, sort of." She pointed at the black towers ahead. "I've been pinning flags on a map for weeks. They tell me I'm helping the resistance, but it doesn't feel enough."

"So you care for waifs and strays in your spare time."

"Not deliberately."

"You can't fight your nature."

"Just surviving wasn't enough," Lesana pondered absent-mindedly. She was concentrating on running; favouring one leg, while the other moved in stiff lurches.

"Surviving is not enough," the man repeated.

She spared him a glance. "Does that seem strange?" she asked.

"No, but it reminds me of something."

"What?"

"I can't quite remember."

She was limping again. One shoulder sagged while the other was full of tension, pulling at the side of her head and completing the lopsided stumble.

"Well, I'm afraid you're on your own from now on," she panted.

The man's step faltered. It took him several strides to catch up. "What if I go walk about again?"

"Look around you. There are thousands of desperate people in this city. Millions more outside. I've brought you to the safest place on this planet, perhaps in the solar system. Grab a space in one of the leading buildings. Use it to find yourself."

"Perhaps I can be of use."

"Maybe. What can you do?"

"I've no idea."

"I suppose that's not much different to me a few weeks ago. Let's head for the Jefferson buildings. See if anyone needs a man with no memory."

The city was like a ship becalmed. Structural creaks and rumbles inhabited the spaces where the people belonged. Moving shadows flickered behind the few bidirectional windows, suggesting at the humanity cowering inside. At a glance it looked like a raft of polycrete towers cast adrift on a sea of dirt.

"I can't go any further," Lesana declared.

The man offered her a supporting shoulder. Suddenly, they were the thing becalmed and the city was flowing around them. The man scanned around for a building near enough he could realistically hope to carry her to.

"Sorry," she said. "There's a point where stim-conditioned muscles are a poor substitute for real athleticism."

The man knew she was protecting him again; rescuing him from the Reset had finally exhausted her reserves of energy. She had already overcome goodness knows what before finding him. She gave instinctively without holding anything back in reserve. Nothing she had told him about herself made sense. Apparently, a typically solipsist and narcissistic product of corporate society, and yet, totally remarkable and precious.

"We have to get you into one of the buildings," he pleaded.

"I wasn't proposing we lie down and die."

She put two fingers in her mouth and let loose an ear-splitting whistle, before sagging to the ground with an appreciative groan. The sound vanished into the city, the buildings harvested the energy and deprived nature of an echo. Lesana closed her eyes and breathed deeply while the man fretted around her.

"What's the plan?" he asked.

"Patience."

The ground grumbled beneath his feet, heralding the imminent arrival of an electric whine. A dart of silver appeared to their left. Its surface shimmered with electrostatic transducers, like bottled lightening. Banking hard to the left, it made a beeline for Lesana and the man, roaring to a halt with a crackle of energy dumped into the ground.

The top half of the dart flickered off to reveal Fez wearing an exuberant grin.

"You called m'lady?"

"Nice ride," Lesana said as the man helped her stand.

"What this old thing?" Fez mocked.

"Seriously Fez, did you do something stupid?"

"Nobody is worrying about a little wasted energy just now. The council are in meltdown."

The internal configuration of the dart adapted to another couple of passengers. The nose rose fractionally as acceleration tore at the ground. Fez slalomed the tiny craft through the lumbering buildings throwing up clouds of super-charged dust at the apex of each curve.

The final approach to the black towers Lesana called the Jeffersons was a straight dash. Fez showed no sign of slowing down. Lesana picked up on the man's agitation.

"Believe me, it's safer this way," she said without explanation.

The man picked out an oval entrance to the tower, strangely grey against the malignant black building. Fez held his hand over a red glow on the control display. The nose of the dart was already in the shadow of the cave when he finally thumbed down. Energy shorted against the ground and walls in spikes of blue light.

The couch relaxed its grip on the man, leaving him trembling. Lesana clambered out without comment, while Fez continued to grin.

They stepped through an iris into atria of jagged vaults. Gothic in proportions, the space had been crudely adapted to act as a logistics centre. Stalactites of black decay bristled from the roof, but the floor had been cleaved flat and the debris packed against one wall as a crude buttress. Men and women formed streams of dynamism between stacks of crates and a mishmash of antique ground vehicles. The sounds in the hall were of a completely different quality to the city: close, overlapping and intimate. The man wondered how long it had been since he had been inside a building. He felt like a Neanderthal stumbling into a shopping mall.

"This can't be good," Lesana shouted over the din. "Let's get upstairs and find out what's going on."

Fez and Lesana weaved their way through the noise and bustle without a ripple. The man followed in their wake, bumping and apologising for each clumsy collision. They stepped through a rough-cut archway into a scene from a baroque nightmare. The building's lobby was finished in mottled brass, wood aged to the colour of dried blood and yellowing lace. Proportion and scale were twisted to deceive, from the semi-circular dial above the gated lift-shaft to the oversized wedge of a reception desk.

Lesana nodded in the direction of the pair rustling sheets of paper at the desk and attacked the stairs. After three steps she turned and sat down with a thump.

"I've got you," Fez said rummaging in a pocket. He produced a translucent epidermal patch and offered it to Lesana. She shook it free from its sterile coating and pressed it to her chest. The fabric swallowed the patch.

Three minutes later she was clearing two steps at a time and the nameless man was regretting refusing his own stim-patch.

"This way."

Lesana trotted through a doorway held open by a climbing piton, and into a corridor that narrowed to a point a few metres in from the landing. A couple of doorways squeezed themselves into the available wall space. Lesana took the one on the left.

"John this is a man with no name, man with no name this is John," Lesana gibbered with a chemically enhanced flippancy.

"What?" said the man with an armful of folded paper.

"Hello," said the nameless man.

"Lesana, where the hell have you been?" John demanded. "Everything is falling apart and you were nowhere to be found."

"What's happened?"

"I think their getting ready to evacuate the city."

"To where?"

"I don't know, but something bad has happened. There's been no communications from the Suparna for hours. The Satyagrahi upstairs are starting to collapse. Their saying one of their leaders has gone missing."

"Without the Satyagrahi..." Lesana started.

"I know," John confirmed.

"So this is it," Lesana said with a look of stupefied horror.

Fez stepped back into the corridor. "I'm out of here," he said. "Who's coming?"

Lesana shook her head. "There's no point."

"The Satyagrahi, they're holding back the Reset?" the nameless man asked. An eerie feeling wandered out of the lost part of his mind, like deja vu but amplified. "They work in teams like a family of brothers and sisters. Fighting, resting, then fighting again."

John was giving Lesana an odd look. "Who is this?" he asked.

"I've no idea," Lesana admitted.

*

Something caught Talalelei's attention; a flicker of motion in his peripheral vision. The technician tensed, assuming Chimalsi had returned to add more unreasonable demands. There was nobody else in the small clinic. Uniform illumination radiated from every surface banishing shadows to the deepest recesses of cabinets and human minds. He could just make out other technicians hunched over splice terminals in the next lab. The semi-opaque walls made their forms lurk on the edge of visibility.

The room caught the direction of his gaze. It chose an image from his personal collection, and reproduced it across the wall. It was not the most flattering capture of his sister; she looked tired and just a little disappointed. Talalelei's nieces were running past her knees, their bodies flailing with surplus energy, like frozen dust-devils. Their miniature limbs were indistinct, despite the photon-perfect capture quality, as if their vitality could break the Plank scale.

Talalelei always kept the image close by for moments when freewill started to feel illusionary. It was the evening he had told his sister he was joining Durga. She had turned away for several minutes, but conflict was obvious in the intricate bones of her shoulders. Eventually, she faced him, and asked if he was sure a Martian corporation was the answer the planet needed. He had muttered an aphorism about fighting MynCorp's fire with Martian fire. She immediately quenched his bluster with a mother's scorn.

"Durga will make things better for Martians," he had answered sincerely. "The corporation's motives may not be altruistic, but it's the only way I can make a positive contribution."

Talalelei wished he could remember if the image was from before or after his confession.

The technician returned to the scans. It was decades of research to map and understand a consciousness existing in more than the usual three dimensions. Even developing the algorithm to manipulate the data could take years. He was being set-up to fail, but he pushed on with a mix of fascination and trepidation.

When he caught another flicker in the corner of his eye he ignored it as nerves. When he did look up, his eye's struggled to focus. His depth perception was scrambled. The walls had become completely transparent. All the other labs and offices were pushing up against his. His line of sight intersected with dozens of other people, each face mirrored the confusion he felt. The light changed from homogeneous white to sunlight diffused through a bed of green sludge.

The building controlled the privacy settings for the walls. Only Chimalsi had the authority to make a building-wide change. Maybe the open plan configuration was designed to increase motivation.

The technician looked up. The soles of someone's shoes were a metre above his head. The owner stepped to the side reducing the technician's urge to cower. Another floor up, Chimalsi was visible in his office. His body language suggested he was shouting at someone. He didn't look to be in control of events.

As Talalelei watched, Chimalsi left his office and headed to the stairwell. He took the steps two at a time, past the middle floor then turned towards the clinic. The technician barely had time to swear before Chimalsi burst into the room.

"Report," Chimalsi demanded. "Is it conscious?"

Talalelei hesitated long enough for Chimalsi to stab the Node in the leg again. A second point of red formed next to the scab of the previous assault. The Node remained inert, but a shadow passed over the room.

A spot of sunlight drifted across the Node's chest, across the floor and climbed to Talalelei's face. He blinked at the wall. Swirling shapes were forming in the algae as it flowed around the building. At first he noticed small clumps and feathery structures, but as his focus pulled back, he saw larger shapes. They almost looked like clawed limbs converging on something resembling a thorax. The technician pivoted on the balls of his feet, following the coalescing beast as it wrapped itself around the building. Near the building's entrance a featureless head punctuated a writhing neck.

"Sir?" Talalelei stammered.

Chimalsi glanced away from the Node and whatever private conversation he had been having with the building. "Don't get distracted. Focus on the task I have assigned you."

"But there's something growing."

"The shapes you are seeing are random coagulations in the algae flow around the building."

"Random?"

"Even if they prove to be manufactured, it's a thin layer of algae and growth compound. It cannot possible present a threat."

"It's moving, but the algae has no ability for self locomotion."

Chimalsi drew Talalelei's attention back to the Node. An impossible thought sidled up to the technician's mind. "Is the Node doing it? Maybe, some manifestation of his unconscious psyche."

Chimalsi turned to leave. "If you were doing your job you'd be telling, not asking."

The algae creature prowled around the skin of the building, gathering detail as it homed in on its quarry. Two rows of blunt spikes coalesced on its snout, circular domes condensed on either side of the head, above the beginnings of a mouth slit.

Chimalsi hesitated at the threshold to the room. He spoke without turning around. "I'm having the algae tank brought over. You will start the imprint process in parallel with your scans."

"I've no idea how to imprint a consciousness as complex as the Node's," the technician protested.

Chimalsi started to walk away again. "I have every confidence in your resourcefulness," he said. There was no menace in Chimalsi's tone, but Talalelei felt his pulse throb regardless.

Three minutes later a pair of technicians ushered a tank of green sludge through the doorway. They kept their heads bowed, but their eyes flitted upwards at every ripple from the beast on the building. The three technicians exchanged stilted pleasantries, as the gastropod tank settled into position next to the Node.

"Talalelei, do you know what's going on?" one of the new arrivals asked.

His colleague shot him a look of fearful surprise, which rapidly changed to expectation.

"Not really, but..." Talalelei allowed his gaze to drift towards the Node. The other two looked as if their worst fears had been confirmed. They retreated from the room without taking their eye's from the unconscious waif.

Talalelei dived back into his splice session, letting the sensory input smoother him like a comforting layer of sand. A lot of the R&D capability of the building had been dedicated to constructing a neural framework from the latest algae strain. Now the construct was complete and sitting next to Talalelei, he could draw on all the other technicians for the latest and final impossible task.

Dozens of other minds jostled at the edge of his awareness. They bobbed in and out of context like jostling ducks on a pond. Talalelei carolled them into squadrons, and assigned tasks appropriately. The project developed instant momentum, building towards the attempt to model the Node's mind using a malleable framework of algae-derived neurons.

Talalelei set himself the impossible part, letting the others achieve the merely improbably. Dogma dictated hard problems were simply a collection of easier problems, and Talalelei proceeded as if this were equally applicable to the Node. By compartmentalising data, he had different groups building identical models, but using different instances of the Node's neural scan; half a dozen examples of billion-connection networks and quantum states.

The Durga headquarters buzzed with mental activity. All of it building towards an inevitable dead-end. Talalelei was vaguely aware of Chimalsi's presence amongst the meta-data of the experiment. If Chimalsi was aware all the furious activity obscured a lack of real progress, he did not interfere to decry the fact.

The completed models of the Node's mind started to arrive in Talalelei data-sphere. Each model appeared to contradict the next, but must somehow compliment in such a way as to produce a complete mental map. In desperation, Talalelei simply stacked the models, creating superpositions of each definite state and connection. The result was an unintelligible quagmire of uncertainty.

Talalelei dumped the contradictory data into the algae lattice, and let the simple connection rules deal with mess. Software exceptions started ricochetting up the call-stack as the imprinting algorithms explored illegal code-paths and were rejected.

Any moment now the algae would be reduced to the inert sludge from which it had been grown. Talalelei prepared himself to admit failure, and accept the inevitable rebuke from Chimalsi.

The moment never arrived.

The imprint teetered on the edge of collapse, but failed to completely stall. Something complex was emerging from the chaos; a coherent and self-sustaining structure. Talalelei had no idea what it was, and it certainly did not resemble anything conscious.

He needed to focus; fight through the confusion and distractions.

Talalelei turned to admonish the scratching sound that clawed at his concentration. The dark-green head of a fearsome descendant of mythology was snaking towards him, teeth gnashing and dripping globules of green saliva. The neck and upper torso of the creature rose from the inner skin of the building's structure, like a basking shark breaching on Lake

Vanuatu. Coarse scales rubbed against internal walls as the head weaved its way towards Talalelei. The scratching sound was a portent of the approaching danger.

Talalelei turned to look for an escape. A posse of gargoyle creatures were harrying other members of staff. The monster leapt fully formed from the walls, and struck out at panicking technicians. People were already spilling from the building and staggering away; Talalelei was almost alone.

Something took a breath near Talalelei's ear. He turned and found himself nose to nose with the Node. Some small part of the technician's brain protested about their relative heights, and the improbability of the Node's stare actually making the back of his brain itch.

The Node formed words out of emotions."There's a sadness in you that is not your own," he said, before reaching forward with two fingers and plucking something from Talalelei's subconscious.

*

Kaamil floated at the heart of the nested concentric spheres that had once been his home. The data tethers that streamed from his skull and spine were rigid like quills. His fist was clenched and his head bowed as if the universe had nothing left he wanted to see.

A shell of matter was forming around him. Pieces of equipment broke free of the surface of the innermost sphere and soared up towards him. When they drew close, each slowed and shuffled into a predetermined position. A dozen sombrero shaped canisters slowly sailed into the air, smaller and less delicate devices buzzing past. The canisters took up positions near Kaamil. Threads of neural axons grew from each canister and other significant pieces of equipment. The bundles of fibres twisted together and grew into thick chords of connectivity. The chords coiled their way to Kaamil and melded with his tethers.

Kaamil managed a rueful smiled as he watched a midnight-purple cube of exotic matter nudge close to his chest; the soul of the Suparna. There had never really been any doubt. He might be anthropomorphising hideously, but the Suparna's loyalty and self-sacrifice contrasted his own failed attempt at redemption.

The makeshift structure was almost complete. The accumulating material finally obscured the diffused light of the Suparna's spheres. Kaamil switched to a purely telemetric view of proceedings. He relaxed his body as fibres grew from his suit and anchored him securely to the epicentre of his new pilot's bunker.

The moment of alignment was near. Kaamil could feel the five nested spheres micro-adjusting their spin to create a tunnel perfectly staggered to match his expected trajectory. All inter-sphere traffic was temporarily grounded.

Without giving himself time to think, Kaamil activated the co-opted nerves in his left hand and triggered the catapult sequence.

"Jeronimo!" he cried as the thump of acceleration pressed his organs against reinforced cartilage.

The bunker spun slowly as it flew, surface dimples disrupting eddies in the air before they could fully form. Everyone in each sphere would hear the thump of the bow shock refracting from each aperture, but he would be gone before they could turn and look or ask a loved-one what it was.

The bunker punched through the membrane separating the outer sphere from the unforgiving vacuum of space. The buffeting of the bunker instantly ceased, leaving the weight of acceleration divorced from Kaamil's other senses. The tranquillity was short-lived. The first tenuous wisps of the Earth's atmosphere made him feel suitably unwelcome.

A layer of nano-scale pumps sucked hungrily as friction heated the outer skin. The energy was commandeered to accelerate a kilogram of heavy ions in a series of magnetic tori. Regardless, the hull grew hotter. Kaamil reconfigured the skin to brilliant white and retracted external sensors. He lay in the dark of the bunker feeling his way through the familiar telemetry of a ship in flight: the containment state of the antimatter canisters, energy level of the ion accelerators, and the patient chatter from the virtual singularity he thought of as the Suparna's soul.

There would be no transition to calm. Atmospheric drag was pulling at the bunker but one-shot boosters epoxied to the hull did their best to push back.

There would not be time for glacial thought. Kaamil allowed his mind to enter and amalgamate with the Suparna. He became an entity of algorithmic perfection. Hubris, guilt, desire were left in the scared brain of his body. Only guile and determination translated into effective code.

A ruggedised optical sensor crept from its burrow and piped a forward view to the pilot. The Reset covered most of the northern hemisphere of the Earth. From his vantage point it was clearly oblate, a flattened sphere centred somewhere around the sixtieth parallel and reaching ten kilometres into the atmosphere. High enough for a storm front to have built up where global winds met the edge of reality.

The pilot did not bother fine tuning his trajectory. The box of exotic matter containing the virtual singularity migrated from his side. A chisel shaped protuberance grew at one point of the hull. The gradual rotation of the sphere stopped with the new snout pointing ahead. The bunker was now tipped with a material barely tolerated by the laws of this universe. The particle accelerators reached their maximum energy and held their stream of ions a hair's breath below the speed of light.

There was a millisecond spare for contemplation, in which Kaamil knew this was literally what he had been born for. He drew some satisfaction from choosing the who and the when.

The tip of the bunker touched the surface of the Reset. The reordering of reality was a finite process and the highly unusual configuration of physics gave it pause for thought.

The Reset was pierced.

The force of the impact caused the snout to sublimate, exposing the naked singularity. It was instantly annihilated by a universe in which it had never quite been real. The burst of gamma rays further disrupted the Reset but had a catastrophic effect on the rest of the sphere. The pilot observed with detachment as his body was vaporised. A counter ticked down the microseconds until the model of his consciousness within the workings of the machine would catch up with the physical world. It seemed an eternity, so he dismissed it.

The bunker was now more than half way inside the Reset. The pilot dumped the beam from a particle accelerator into each anti-matter containment bottle. The resultant annihilation generated a nanosecond of stellar energy outputs. Everything about the ship's design was dedicated to beaming the resultant energy forward and into the Reset; if anything material lay at its heart it would surely be destroyed.

The confirmation of the explosion should have been the last thing the pilot witnessed, but somehow a faint shadow of his consciousness lived on in the waves of energy tearing at the fabric of the physical universe and bleeding through into Verity Space. There was enough of the pilot left to feel the Reset heal the rift and close around him. Enough to feel his existence being unwound and undone. Kaamil knew he had failed to destroy the Reset, but he had tried; a redemption of sorts.

Chapter 12

Yakini watched as Mex crumpled to the floor and lay still. For a moment the only movement was the languid trickle of blood from the hole in his temple. She watched as incomprehension stupefied the muscles in Julienne's face. Sardon still held his gun against a missing head as intricate plans unravelled in the twitching of his eyelids.

A look of abject desolation consumed Julienne's face, taking control of her features in spluttering surges. Her eyes took on the glaze of a sleepwalker. She brought the gun level with her face. The muzzle swayed from side to side like a divining rod.

The first shot broke the enchantment and shattered the window to the laboratory. Sardon weaved left. Julienne's gun scanned. Yakini lurched sideways but was yanked back into position by the constraints in her seat.

Sardon strafed sideways. A second shot missed him by a fraction of a second, tearing a hole in the table. The furniture lost integrity and collapsed like a jellyfish on a beach. Yakini rolled into a corner and willed herself not to scream.

With a feint for the door, Sardon dived head first through the broken window and dropped from sight. Julienne's barely aimed shots peppered the floor with plasma burns, then she dropped to her knees. Her finger trembled as she traced the edge of the hole in Mex's head. Bringing her forehead down to touch his, Julienne spoke four words. Yakini could not tell if it was hope, denial or a prayer.

"He is not dead."

Julienne slumped on to Mex, her body loosing all resistance to gravity.

Yakini realised Sardon was now her responsibility. Her knees betrayed her exhausted body, but with a hand on the wall she found her feet. She could see Sardon moving towards Teledice. He weaved and meandered like he was crossing a minefield. Yakini could see the air shimmer around him with a patchwork of something like heat plumes.

Her shoes absorbed most of the impact as Yakini dropped into the laboratory, but Sardon still heard her. His head snapped round but he sneered when he realised it was not Julienne.

"You say the human race was condemned because of my actions," Sardon exclaimed. "I say I am humanity's only hope of revenge."

"I'm not going to let you kill Teledice. I told you I would kill you first, and I meant it."

"Such a small minded creature. Yakini Akida. The first Martian to make it as a pilot in MynCorp. Loyal and dedicated. Pitiful."

Yakini lunged forward. Something prickled at the skin around her left ear. On the edge of existence, an Oikake sphere clawed through the layers of reality, trying to consume her. Dropping to the right, she almost fell on another sphere rising through the floor.

Now she understood why Sardon was picking his way to Teledice with such care. On all fours, Yakini scampered forward. Two spheres converged on her path, passing through each other like shadows. Yakini leapt from a crouch, her legs unfolding like springs. Earth's relentless gravity dragged her back to the floor before she expected. Arms cartwheeling she teetered on her heels, trying not to look over her shoulder.

Sardon reached Teledice and started tinkering with a glowing panel on the side of her crucifixion constraints.

"Don't do it!"

"Make your mind up," Sardon jeered. "Either it's my fate or it isn't."

Teledice stirred, her arms and legs subconsciously exploring her bonds.

Yakini started to run, trusting luck and reflexes to keep her alive for long enough. Sphere's came at her. Some drifting almost randomly into her path, other making darting strikes. She bent and flexed as best she could, but never veered. A few strides from Sardon, she raised her arms and curled her hands into fists of intricate bones and slender tendons.

Teledice started to writhe and thrash every muscle as if her blood had turned to acid. Her eyes snapped open and through them something erupted into the room. Like a bright light it hurt Yakini's eyes, but still she could see. All her other senses shared the assault, while continuing to feel the world without interference.

Yakini pulled back her arm and struck at Sardon with everything she had left. Sardon recoiled slightly but the blow never fully landed. A finger width from contact a field of electrostatic charge mangled the signals to her arm muscles, turning most of the thrust inwards. Something small but vital snapped in her elbow. For a moment she was blind to everything except the explosion of pain beyond anything she had previously imagined could exist.

When her sight cleared she was crouching at Sardon's feet, cradling her damaged arm.

"It's done," he said calmly.

Someone was screaming. For a moment Yakini though it was her. It was in her head, but the source was Teledice. Yakini added her own voice to the cry. She sprung at Sardon. She made no attempt to coordinate an attack and just focused on pushing her body at him with as much force as possible. Her muscles convulsed, her jaw clamped down on the end of her tongue and her head sung, but her momentum won. Sardon rolled on his heel. He flung his arms forward but it was not enough. His head whipped round to guide his fall and then he saw the Oikake sphere behind him.

His arms flailed and his eyes flickered and through a thousand rejected strategies.

Sardon's shoulder hit the sphere first. A mercurial sheen flickered across his whole body. His mouth opened to form a scream, but his lungs ceased to effect the air trapped within. Teetering on the edge of existence, Sardon's body became translucent. Yakini watched in fascinated horror as the most powerful person she had ever encountered was unwound from the universe. She imagined his atoms strewn across the planet, restored to virgin soil, as if he had never existed. Yakini's sanity creaked with the contradiction. Sardon was erased from history and yet she was surrounded by the consequences of his actions, the most immediate of which hung naked and emaciated above her. Teledice's wrists and ankles were dwarfed by the industrial grey of her constraints. As she convulsed splinter-thin bones flexed and pressed at the scuffed skin.

Teledice screamed again.

Yakini dumped the charge from the cuffs. The young woman looked more like a child clasped to the Martian's body. Yakini rocked and murmured soothing nonsense, teeth gritted against her own pain. Yakini closed her eyes to trap the tears. Teledice shone brightly, like the after-image of a star. Yakini's eye's flashed open again. Teledice was limp and her skin looked mortuary-grey in the white light of the laboratory. Back behind her eyelids, Yakini could clearly see Teledice fighting a frantic battle to contain an explosion that had already happened.

Someone shouted Yakini's name; a woman's voice creaking on the edge of cataclysmic collapse. Opening her eyes felt like abandoning Teledice, but Yakini managed to push her sight across the laboratory and up to Julienne framed by the broken window of the observing lounge. The image swayed in and out of focus.

"You've got to get out now," Julienne cried.

Yakini understood in a juddering change of perspective. The laboratory was alive with Oikake, jostling like bacteria under a microscope.

"There's too many," Yakini pleaded cradling Teledice tighter to her breast.

Julienne swung one leg over the lip of the window then hesitated before retreating. "There's no possibility I can get to you. Yakini, you have to wake Teledice."

The Oikake pushed closer, slowly overcoming whatever barrier MynCorp or Teledice had erected in Verity Space. The rigid structure of the MynCorp apparatus pressed into Yakini's spine, punctuating her lack of options.

"Please wake up," Yakini whispered into Teledice's ear. "I can't do anything more. You have to save yourself."

Yakini closed her eyes and repeated the words to the image of Teledice in her head. It was the internal Teledice who responded. She opened her eyes and mouth, and Yakini could see the raging energies inside. "I can't keep it in," she roared.

"Teledice, we have to go now. The Oikake are everywhere. I can't do anything."

In Yakini's arms, Teledice's body shook like a sobbing child. In her head, Teledice was raging. A strangled roar grew into something like the last battle cry of an ancient warrior. A flash of incoherent energy erupted into Verity Space; a super causal shockwave in the Downey field, spreading faster than causality. Nothing bound by reality could escape and the intensity only increased as the shockfront grew.

Squatting at the epicentre with her senses heightened by Teledice's presence, Yakini watched in horror. In the first instant all the Oikake in the laboratory fizzled from existence. The destruction reached the edge of the laboratory and the extent of Yakini's sight. Beyond lay Julienne, Mex or at least his body, then the remnants of the human race.

Teledice tensed and the extinction of reality switched into reverse. The causal shockwave flipped direction and started to converge its source. Somehow her tiny body absorbed all that havoc and it faded to a whispering echo. Breath escaped Teledice's body and she became becalmed. Yakini could feel both of their pulses. Her own ragged and shredded by adrenaline. The other the languid beat of comal exhaustion.

Julienne called her name again. This time it was questioning.

"I think we're okay," Yakini ventured. She tried to ask after Mex but the question truncated itself to just his name.

"He's alive," Julienne managed. "His artificial hand took the brunt. The fléchette is lodged in his skull but it didn't penetrate."

"Are we safe?"

The question sounded absurd, but Yakini did not need to qualify it.

"Most of the staff surrendered to me as soon as they could. Sardon was pretty much on his own at the end."

Teledice stirred in Yakini's arms. Half opening her eyes, Teledice yawned. "Are we going home now?"

Yakini looked up. Julienne managed a tentative smile and said, "we're already on our way."

*

It felt good to be back in the open, with space for his thoughts to wander. The man tried to watch the Reset. It filled all the sky behind the city, forming a backdrop like the surface of a pond in a hurricane.

"Who are you?" Lesana asked from behind.

"I don't know."

"But?"

"I know this is all my fault."

"This? This what?"

The Reset shuddered. The distorted realities boiling on its surface jumped in scale. There was no way to be certain, but somehow he knew it had just jumped hundreds of metres in a heartbeat.

The nameless man spread his arms to encompass all he could see. "All of this," he proclaimed.

"From no one to a god in a single gesture," Lesana said sarcastically.

"Not a god, just a man. Just a blind and foolish man."

Amongst the people gathered on the terrace someone screamed.

The man saw devastation take control of Lesana's face. Her eyes were wet with defeat. "This is it. Here it comes."

He felt it too. The same sensation of ionised air he had felt on his death-walk.

Above the city a flash of sunlight burst through the storm-front perpetually rumbling ahead of the Reset. At the exact moment the Reset engulfed the city, an angel appeared in a sphere of light. A young woman, so delicate it seemed perfectly natural for her to defy gravity. The Reset buffeted against her will, but she did not vanish. Her radiance increased, ricocheting off the Reset as it smashed itself against her essence.

A scream of anguish spread throughout the city like the first clap of thunder. It was followed by a single word. Desperation, betrayal and love embodied by a single word. The word was everywhere and was everything. All the people gathered to watch the end and all those who cowered in denial or terror, felt the word and knew it was the last word. The word embodied the first and last thought of the angel above them. It was a word and a name.

The word was José.

When the word was complete, the nameless man knew himself.

Emotions came first, rushing in to fill the vacuum. Love, regret and a thousand lives worth of guilt. Following close behind was the mental constructs to explain his feelings. The fabricated rationality of depression, the dislocation of existing away from society, the refusal to hear words of love and concern. He remembered the intricate premeditation of his betrayal. His failure and then being scattered across time and space.

There was a calm point of certainty. An absolute knowledge that he had been wrong. The beautiful simplicity of his redemption was a singularity in his being. Be it a nanosecond or a billion years, he owed her everything. He would never fail her again.

Another word radiated from the terrace crudely grafted to the side of the Jefferson building. A man rose into the air and flickered from existence. At the same moment he reappeared inside the sphere of light.

"Nomia."

Now there were two angels above the city.

The Reset cowered in their presence.

The city was silent as every mind added his or her own will to those of their champions above. A patch of sky flooded natural light back into the city. The rag-tag collection of buildings stumbled through the gap and back into reality. The Reset pressed at the edged of the city, but it could not enter.

*

"It's my friend."

Sera gave Ben a moment to explain his new-found affinity for irony.

A putrid-green gargoyle gibbered at her from the corner of the ceiling. Sera ignored the way its body tunnelled through the diamond hard surface and melded with the algae within the building skin. The creature sneered and writhed, but seemed disinclined to engage her or Bergur.

Another creature slithered past the room. Sera tried to look away but deep recesses of her subconscious were already rioting. The beast's tortured body could only have been gestated in the accumulated nightmares of an entire species. Limbs erupted from salivating orifices of indeterminate function. Its belly was lined with spiralling clusters of teeth. Coarse hair sprouted from between the teeth. Its skin boiled with tumorous masses the colour of ancient death.

Sera dragged her head back towards Ben. "Friend?" she repeated. "It's a tank on legs, not a Chinchilla."

"Foot," Bergur interjected.

Sera stepped back, bringing both men into her field of view, and keeping the madness at an arm's length.

"My friend doesn't have any legs," Ben asserted.

"Just a foot?" Sera gestured to cut off the conversation. "Well, if your friend can run or hop, tell it to follow us."

Bergur stepped to Ben's side. "Shall I carry you?" he offered.

Ben took a tentative step forward. "My legs remember," he asserted.

Sera examined the corridor back towards the way out. She tried to judge the prowling creatures, plotting a trajectory to avoid the most terrible and disturbing.

She held up a hand to prepare the others for the moment to run, but Ben was already in the corridor. The Node picked his way towards the exit like he was traversing a dune of delicate lichens. The mollusc tank followed in his wake.

"Ben!"

All across the building the creatures melted back into the walls and ceiling. The largest and fiercest gripped the roof in two taloned claws. It gave one last thrash of its tail and dissolved into the circulating layer of green algae.

Sera found herself cowering in the doorway of a deserted building. She stood and brushed imaginary dust from her knees.

Bergur was shaking violently. His mouth flaps hung open as air grunted in and out of his lungs. Each tremor of his chest produced a clattering bark from his exposed throat. He gripped his ribs with both hands, as tears streamed from his eyes.

It took several seconds for Sera to equate the reaction to something she recognised.

"What's so funny?"

Bergur fought for control. "This is some rescue. We crash a shuttle into Mars, wrestle our way across half the planet, while Ben has a little lie down. Then when we finally get here, he decides he's had enough rest, gets up and leaves."

"You think that's funny?"

"Tickled me purple."

Sera gave Bergur a half-hearted punch in the arm. It felt surprisingly good. He laughed louder. She punched him a few more times, as hard as she could. Each punch drained mercury from her nerves. Her frustration faded, and with it, her strength.

Bergur finished laughing. He put a purple hand on the side of her face. It felt brutish next to the delicate bones of her cheek, but clean determination flowed though the contact.

"You okay?" he asked.

Sera wasn't sure enough to answer, but she managed a smile.

Ben was standing a few metres away from the Durga building, his face turned to the afternoon sun. His head was cocked, as if the wind carried a distant voice. Naked and scrawny, he looked like a Martian child. A small crowd stood at a respectful distance. There were the orange jumpsuits of the general workers as well as the silver-grey of the Durga staff. A woman stepped forward and wrapped a grey blanket around Ben's body. It draped to the ground and drew curls in the sand as he rocked back and forward.

At the building's threshold Bergur grunted and turned back inside. Sera felt the conversation flow between Ben and Bergur without comprehending the details. As she stepped closer to Ben, he turned, smiled and looked her directly in the eyes.

"Are you okay?" she asked.

Ben opened his mouth to speak. A rasping sound crept to his lips before retreating to his throat. He prodded his lips with a swollen tongue. The cracked and scabbed texture bought a perplexed look to his normally slack expression.

Sera touched his cheek, but the clarity in his eyes was already fading. His focus was drifting back into whatever meta-space from which he experienced life.

Bergur emerged from the Durga building a second time. He was dragging one of the gargoyles by the shoulder. It's legs stumbled and lurched in pointless resistance to Bergur's irresistible will. A fist sized globule of green muck slid from one of its limbs. The skin underneath was a softer shade of hazelnut and distinctly Martian in tone.

There were sporadic hisses and clucks of disapproval from the on-lookers. There was a moment in which Sera feared the crowd was turning on Bergur; one strange sight too many in frightening times. Untroubled and unmolested, Bergur dumped the creature at the feet of Ben and Sera. Red sand rose up and began the metamorphosis of the beast from slime to stone.

With a very-human cough the creature dislodged slime from its throat, causing algae to ooze from its mouth, nose and ears.

"What do you want me to do with him?" Bergur asked.

The creature looked up, eyes wide with alarm.

"Chimalsi?" Sera finally recognised the cowering creature as the Durga executive. "What happened to him?"

Bergur held his hand up. "This is how I found him. Honest."

Somebody started stomping the ground in appreciation. The sound spread and grew as the crowd parted ahead of a tall figure. Tabansi strode into the heart of the crowd. Next to his physical presence, Sera felt tiny and fragile, but she could see a twitch of uncertainty where the corner of his mouth blended with his beard.

"Sera," he acknowledged.

A chant was growing under the sound of stamping feet. The acronym used by the Martian independence movement was being turned into a new word and a rallying call.

"MBT. MBT. MBT..."

Tabansi let the crowd brew its own energy, apparently indifferent to the implicit call for him to speak the first words of the new Mars. He looked down at the quivering remains of his former collaborator, then he turned to Sera.

"You've been busy," he said softly.

Sera was still considering her answer when the Durga building started to melt.

Green algae erupted in tumultuous rifts. Flowing across the surface to dissolve more of the structure. An occasional piece of building infrastructure resisted the corrosion, to jut from the putrescent mush like a rib bone.

A large fraction of the Martian colony stood dumbfounded as the building was reduced to a green puddle. Chimalsi did not react until the puddle became a hole.

"No, no, no," he pleaded with a coherency that caused Sera to re-evaluate his apparent incapacitation.

The algae bubbled and burped steam from the rapidly deepening hole. The crowd edged towards the shear sided sink-hole.

A series of smoothed explosions sprayed green high into the air. Several people screamed and scrubbed at their faces. Their neighbours ripped rags from pockets and necks to wipe away spots of green. A few people gasped, one giggled, but there were no cries of pain.

"Chemistry memistry," Ben mumbled.

"What was down there?" Bergur asked no one in particular.

"The heart and soul of Durga Corporation," Tabansi answered. "The accumulated intellectual property, and computing power to realise their ambitions."

Sera looked dubious. "They'll have a dozen off-site backups."

287

People were arriving all the time. Drawn ineffably to the epicentre of evolutionary change. They brought questions and stories with them. A woman with the green neck tattoo of a farmer, decided to share a revelation with the crowd.

"It's happening all over. Every Durga building is melting."

As the crowd rediscovered its voice, Bergur moved closer to Sera, dragging Chimalsi by a fist full of jacket. "Finishing Durga can't be a simple as destroying a few buildings," he said.

"There are copies of the knowledge," Tabansi continued. "Probably, in orbit. They wouldn't have paid the data-tax to use the Nexus."

"Plus we destroyed the Nexus," Sera stated.

Tabansi looked from Sera to Bergur. He seemed to physically shrink and age before Sera's eyes. "It looks as if your little revolution has claimed a second corporation in a few months. All the production and mining facilities are on their own. The central brain has been cut out."

Ben slipped between Sera and Tabansi. The tank of algae tried to follow, bumping to a halt at Sera's hip. Ben leant over Chimalsi. "You are a contradiction to me. Your mind seeks influence over the fate of all humans even when their very existence is under threat. Yet you draw reality inexorably to this point. A point where you are irrelevant, and the people of Mars are free to determine their own future."

The algae covering Chimalsi had dried to a crust. It flaked and peeled. The man underneath was less broken than his demeanour implied.

"I concede defeat," he said flatly. "I request deportation."

"Where do you think you have left to go?"

Sera didn't wait for an answer. The crowd were looking to Tabansi again.

The drama of the melting buildings had only added to the feeling of portent, and they wanted a definitive declaration. This time he raised his hands to concentrate their attention.

"People of Vanuatu City, citizens of Mars, today we have made a major step towards self-determination. We have already driven MynCorp from Mars. Today, Durga has been critically weakened."

The stomping of feet was joined by throaty ululations of appreciation.

Tabansi had to shout to make himself heard. His voice echoed back from the crater walls, adding layers to the cacophony.

"None of us understand the threat faced by all humans. We survived the first encounter, but we cannot know how close to destruction we truly were. However much we resent Earth's stranglehold over Mars, we understand the importance of solidarity. We understand we fight or fall together. But it has to be on our own terms. We must be masters of our own fate."

The noise from the crowd was a physical wave, beating against Sera's head. Ben clamped his hands over his ears, and cowered near his tank of algae.

"MBT has always strived for self-determination. Struggled in the best interests of the Martian people."

Bergur issued a guttural growled, which Sera could feel more than hear. It matched her own indignation. "He's going to claim this as a victory for the MBT, after all his collusion."

Sera was starting to push forward, when a clear voice arrived directly in to her minds. "Wait. World-lines are converging. This is a point of resonance. Wait."

Tabansi looked at Sera. Her anger seemed brutal when confronted by his tears. He turned back to the crowd before she could react.

"MynCorp is gone." Cheer. "Druga is gone." Cheer. "Mars is free." Cheer.

"We are entering a new era. New times call for a new approach. New ideas. A new ethos."

The crowd was less sure of itself now.

"As the leader of MBT, we have – I have – made compromises. The road to independence has not been straight. Some of you might say we almost lost our way. It has changed me in ways I could not have predicted."

Tabansi no longer needed to shout. The cheers ebbed even as his voice started to break apart.

"History has shown time and time again, the best revolutionary generals, do not make good peace-time leaders. To celebrate a new dawn, I hereby disband the MBT."

Somebody shouted, "No!"

"We have to chose a new way to be led. A new system of consensual government. If you will permit me one final request, I would like to suggest a new voice for the people of Mars."

"Who?" asked the same voice in the crowd.

"Someone who has done more to bring about today than any other Martian. Someone who has been at the heart of the fight. I nominate Sera Tamakautoga."

*

The refugee city looked even more bedraggled than Julienne remembered. The buildings were strung out along several kilometres, like oxen being lead to slaughter. The streams of people linking the buildings looked sturdier than the tethers swaying above their heads. Taunt and tattered, the vital umbilical swung in the eddies formed downwind of each bluff edifice.

Shreds of skin fell onto the migrating queues like a ticker-tape parade in hell.

Several towers were conspicuous by their absence. The rate of attrition must have increased dramatically while she and Mex were rescuing Yakini and Teledice from the last meaningful fragment of MynCorp. Julienne's eyes flitted across the city's backdrop searching for a sense of scale. The Reset hung over the city with the inevitability of a tsunami. It snapped at the heel of the city's stragglers, reaching from horizon to horizon and only limited vertically by the perpetual rolls of cloud, never producing any rain.

It was a homecoming of sorts. Julienne's emotions were too complicated and conflicted to trust to facial muscles, so she stood impassively on the conning tower of the MyncCorp building while those around her fretted or cheered.

She tried not to blink. Even a momentary darkness was enough for that moment to leap from the choppy waters of her memory. The expression on Mex's face with a gun pressed to his head as he realised Julienne was going to capitulate. The palm of his artificial hand grasping the gun muzzle and the knuckles buried deep in the hair above his ear. Instinctive but futile and he knew it. That moment was the source of her anger. He had no right. No right to give his life for hers. After everything she had sacrificed – given or taken - because of him, how dare he throw it away in such a selfish gesture. He had seemed perfectly calm as his free hand reached for Sardon's wrist. He had not winced or closed his eyes in anticipation. Mex's fingers pressed into Sardon's skin, feeling for the trigger finger tendons. As the muzzle flared and Mex's hand shattered into a million stars, he had held her eyes as if ensuring he could hold on to her image in death.

Even before Julienne had reached his side she knew he was not dead. There was blood on his neck at the end of a stream leading back to his hairline, but his chest was still pumping air and she felt the presence of his mind. Brushing fragments of shattered hand from his hair, she found the entry wound. The tail of the fléchette still protruded from Mex's skull. With luck the tip had not penetrated the meninges or brain. Julienne fingered one of the fragments of hand. It was crystalline and showed none of the malleable properties that made it a useful appendage. In response to Mex's frightened reflex the hand had saved his life.

When he opened his eyes and lay blinking in surprise, he did not seem to appreciate the depth of her anger. He just smiled as she berated his stupidity. He mumbled something unintelligible. She leant closer to hear and he stole a kiss. His arrogance was intact and through it her fears of serious damage receded. When he reached for the wound Julienne slapped his hand away, telling him to wait. Nanites were already collecting the fragments of bone and reassembling the hole in his skull. The fléchette fell from the wound after an hour and Mex was back on his feet by the next day, waving his empty sleeve in the air like it was the funniest thing conceived by man. He seemed absurdly happy considering their circumstances.

The remains of the building's staff surrendered to Julienne with no serious contention. They knew enough of what was going on elsewhere in the world to shed any remaining loyalty to the corporation. She squared up to the security teams she had fought and smoothed over any lingering animosity. The building performed a slow turn until it was heading north-west towards the refugee city.

They slowed after a few hours. An outrigger was launched ahead to the crashed cruise liner. When the marooned passengers saw Julienne step from settling vehicle many proclaimed they had never doubted she would return. Julienne identified the conspirators who had attacked her and Mex loitering at the back of the group. The skin healing under her arm tingled but Julienne did no more than catch the ring-leader's eye and hold it until he looked down.

Lesana gave the passengers fifteen minutes to grab essential while her team stripped useful equipment from the wreck. Walking wardrobes and travel chests started to collect outside the outrigger, jostling to get through the single doorway. Julienne let every piece of oversized luggage board. In the cargo space two of her team scanned each piece for anything useful. The majority were jettisoned through another hatch on the unseen side of the outrigger. Nobody questioned how so much luggage could fit in such a small craft. The passengers boarded with something approaching gratitude and sat fidgeting on dumb benches. Once they reached the MynCorp building they started complaining about the spartan and cramped nature of their assigned quarters. By the time they realised their luggage had been lost Julienne had already put several layers of impassive bureaucrats between herself and their petty complaints.

The building's speed climbed to almost a thousand kilometres a day. A routine of sorts evolved. Julienne spent much of her time overseeing conversion of the building from a centre for commerce and research into a refugee camp: food storage and rationing, a basic medical centre equipped for numbers rather than complexity, accommodation for hundreds with shared but sufficient bathroom provision.

She received briefings from research teams. All projects, however misguided, pertained to the Eidolons. The principle investigators prepared pitches to defend their projects to Julienne and Mex. If the researchers resented explaining themselves to civilians they mostly hid it well. Julienne axed a few projects but most related to Sardon's attempt to weaponise Teledice. Julienne rejected with revulsion a suggestion Teledice should be subjected to further experiment, but she did want to understand what had been learnt to-date.

They passed near a city. Scouts reported the settlement as occupied but in complete lock down. When they tried to coax residents out of the buildings, defence measures were deployed against the vehicle. From what Mex could glean remotely, the city's A.I. systems had entered an extreme paranoid state after the fall of the global communications network. The buildings were bunkered down on a war footing, effectively hiding their heads in the sand against the approaching Reset.

The MynCorp building continued its journey, passing under a shallow sea. The city and its stranded residents dropped beneath the horizon.

After a week the staff began to realise the building was heading directly for the Reset. They asked for a meeting, which Julienne denied. She issued a statement confirming their destination as the refugee city and its position at the leading edge of the Reset. One security team found a group of technicians attempting to steal supplies and an outrigger. Julienne had to send another security team when the first team joined the mutineers. She argued with Mex over whether people should be allowed to leave. Julienne insisted everyone was free to go but not with vital supplies and the building would not stop. Even when they disagreed Mex was infuriatingly content, disarming her with random hugs and kisses whenever the whim took hold of him. Despite herself, the anger she felt dissolved a little more with each embrace.

Yakini emerged from her vigil of Teledice, eager for distraction. Julienne gratefully handed the shackled of command to the Martian's slender shoulders. Julienne and Mex retreated into a world of Downey field theory and induced symmetry breaking.

Within a day, cynicism and self-interest amongst the staff evaporated on a wind of humanist fervour. Yakini shouted evangelical anthems, whispered emotive axioms and generally spread a conviction of humanity's inevitable victory. There were no more attempts at mutiny and a self-organising community started to emerge.

Julienne began to relax.

It started as a few minutes each day alone with Mex. They explored each others mind and body with fresh and uninhibited perspective. They fell into each other and their thoughts mingled. It was not simply a blurring of the boundary between them. They fused such that she was as much Mex as Julienne. She felt her own lithe hips engulfed through his hardy hands. Her head swam with the rush of blood as his hips rose and explored her incalescence.

One morning Julienne woke and his sleeping face was the first thing she saw. She remembered an evening of unwinding tension and sleep creeping in to consume her consciousness. The unique sense of vulnerability was exhilarating and comforting in equal measure. Her wave of emotion drew him from the edge of sleep. He kissed her with lips damp with slumber.

The world receded. She grasped the moment and erased the past and future. Mex chuckled and told her the strange sensation was happiness. She rolled the word around her mouth and said it back.

Moments are by their very nature transient. Watching the refugee city stumble its way south at the foot of the Reset, Julienne consigned the happiest days of her current life to treasured memory. Mex put a hand on her shoulder and said something cryptic like we'll always have Paris.

Yakini stayed in the MynCorp building just in case the staff reassessed their fighting spirit, while Mex, Julienne and Teledice took an outrigger to the Jefferson buildings. A council meeting was in session. The reunion was subdued as if they were all awaiting a fresh delivery of emotional energy. Nomia and Teledice embraced and held each other tight for several minutes. Nomia cried but the tears did not seem entirely happy. José smiled but kept to the edges of the room. Scrubby black hair sprouted from his skull like a freshly released Node. He had lost his demeanour of worldly wisdom and looked faintly lost, like a child trying to understand an adult conversation. Alyona was the only one who seemed unchanged by Julienne's time away. She enquired after Yakini and gave a satisfied whirr when she heard the story of the rescue. Julienne relayed Sardon's death and Alyona gave the slightest of nods.

Nomia described the calamities that had befallen the city and the Suparna. There were big holes in her description of José's period of absence and the chronology made no sense. After the description of the near demise of the city, Julienne felt drained and despair nibbled at the edge of her perception. Nomia clearly had more to say. She took Juliennes hands and sobbed a few words.

"I failed. Kaamil is dead."

Julienne just stared, unable to process the new knowledge. The pilot who had killed her once in some twisted expression of love, who she had tried to strangle at the lowest point in her second life, who had belatedly confounded her with his dedication to redemption, was gone. Once Julienne had wanted him dead more than anything, now without him there seemed less reason to care about humanity's survival.

The rest of the meeting washed over her. The MynCorp building was assigned to search and rescue. With its superior speed it was tasked with skirting the Reset to the east and west, plucking people from the edge of annihilation. The scientific staff would be relocated to Jefferson-B to work with Nomia and José on a defence against the Eidolons. Mex was urgently required to patch over some psychotic behaviour emerging in several buildings. Julienne was expected to resume her tactical support for a city of civilians with no resources and almost no hope.

So much for happiness.

*

"It's the only way."

Nomia suspected José was talking as much about proving himself to her, as fighting the Eidolons. Twice she had thought him dead. The first time was deliberate and, in retrospect, a necessary reaction to the triple threats of Julienne's boarding party, Bergur's pirate friends and the Eidolon searching eye. This time it had been involuntary. An instinctive reaction to extreme stress, and, maybe in small part, her fault.

José could not be blamed entirely for behaving irrationally; when the refugee city was about to be overwhelmed she had leapt to its defence knowing full well she could not push back the Reset on her own. Without a full force of refreshed Satyagrahi or José by her side, all threads of probability led to her death.

Deprived of any hope, she had done it anyway.

The people had cheered but Nomia knew it had been a defeat. The Reset had been temporarily repelled, but for her it had been a surrender. It was not in her nature to give-in without a fight, but she had not intended to win. José's deception was no different. Without hope how else could he react? He could save those he loved, but knew they would never give their consent.

He must have known the betrayal would be complete. The one thing Nomia valued above all else was her freedom to choose. After years of captivity in the Nexus, José knew she would rather die than surrender her freewill.

Was it a higher form of love to risk damnation, or the arrogance of an egotist?

"Otherwise we haven't a hope."

He used the word too lightly. José had changed. The world did not weigh as heavy on his shoulders. His intellect was intact but his perspective was more straightforward, less susceptible to moral ambiguity. Most of his memory had returned, but the period of overlap between his rebirth and the confrontation on the Suparna was missing. Nomia carried the burden of the betrayal alone, and so far she had not found the strength to share it. When he had appeared beside her above the city she had embraced him physically and emotionally. They had shared a mind state during the battle, but not since.

Joy, anger and forgiveness, each operated on their own time scales.

"We would never contemplate mutual destruction. Would we?"

He deferred to her more overtly than in the past. He still showed conviction but the intellectual arrogance was gone. She had felt her anger form part of his expulsion to the wilderness. She had worried she might have triggered his destruction, but maybe her contribution had been subtler, more surgical. Had she expunged the source of the betrayal from his personality? Or, was such a thought its own kind of arrogance?

Nomia turned her attention to the report being dissected by José. Sardon's horrifying discovery was laid out in mathematics and graphs. The Satyagrahi could be manipulated to render the Downey field tachyonic. The Langrangian describing Verity Space lost certain symmetries at lower energy levels, when the potential dropped to reveal the current local maximum. Given the right perturbation the vacuum expectation value could be induced to become a tachyon condensate. The resultant spontaneous breaking of symmetry would fundamentally change the nature of the Downey field and mediating particle. In short, the relationship between sentient life and causality would be irrevocably disrupted. It was unlikely the Eidolons would survive the transition. It was entirely unknowable what would happen to corporeal life in the Universe.

Given the inherent instability of local maxima, the symmetry breaking was inevitable but only if the causal potential energy naturally fell sufficiently for it to be exposed. The universe might inflate and compact a million times before its inhabitants had to worry about this new form of reality.

The Eidolons had seen Sardon Lucas was willing to contemplate using such knowledge. Their reaction was understandable, almost human. Nomia had one advantage. She believed emphatically that Sardon could never succeed. For every Sardon there would always be a Julienne, Mex or Yakini. Until proven wrong, Nomia would always believe the good in humanity outweighed the bad. Otherwise, why continue to fight?

Nomia took José's hand. Let her finger tips explore, tracing truths and futures amongst the creases and folds. Their foreheads touched lightly. She felt his desperation to be forgiven echo her own need to forgive. She had failed with Kaamil, she could not live if she failed with José.

"You're right, José. We should go to the source. Just you and I. We will face the Eidolons together."

*

Mr Gaverson cleared his throat with a carefully calibrated level of authority. The council members and interested onlookers settled into their chairs and collected wayward thoughts. Julienne received the first nod. She pushed her packing-crate seat back with one heal and stood with grace too instilled for simple exhaustion to completely mask.

"I've received a preliminary report from the crew installed in the MynCorp research building." Julienne winced at Mex's disapproving look. "The recently rebadged Edging I." Mex met Juliennes grimace with a trademark grin. "We are not alone. As far out as they've explored there is mass migration: customized buildings, surface vehicles, even a few attempts to ride domesticated animals. It's uncoordinated. A headlong exodus. Predictable topographical obstacles are causing chaos, with buildings abandoned in the foothills of mountain range and simpler vehicles littering beaches. There has been some piracy and extortion, but the majority of people seem to find a way to keep moving."

A hopeful murmur spread through the gathering.

"Based on simple projections there could be a few million survivors from the northern hemisphere on the move. Combined with the few examples of bulk migration we know of, we are looking at a four to five percent survival rate."

Julienne sat down. The rough wood of her crate scrapped the floor, underlining the stark truth of her figures. Her dangling hand accepted Mex's touch and their fingers entwined.

José felt the attention of the room turn to him. Distracting desires to run, cry and scream kept his mouth clamped shut. He felt every emotion with a ferocity not dulled by age or experience. He had finally become one of the Satyagrahi.

"Mr Sanchez, what can you tell us about the MynCorp research programmes?" the chair prompted.

"We've found nothing useful." José wished Nomia was back. "All the projects targeted mutually assured destruction. Sardon obviously believed emphatically in a partnership between the Eidolons and MynCorp. He clearly had no intention of fighting. We know a lot more about how the weaponisation process works. It's horrific. Inducing a phase transition that would irrevocably alter the entire universe. It's unthinkable. I'm sorry."

What was he sorry for? What was there not to be sorry for? It had all started with him. A lifetime ago rummaging around on Titan. Tinkering in his arrogance with an unfathomable alien artefact. Mostly he was sorry because he could not regret his actions back then. He treasured everything he had experienced up until his betrayal of Nomia. He had exchanged the time with Nomia for the human race. Mostly he was guilty of not feeling guilty.

"And the Satyagrahi?"

Words backed up in José's throat. He wanted to tell them it was all over, the Satyagrahi were finished. "Not good," he allowed himself to admit. "Reduced effectiveness has meant an increased team size of eight. We can only make three full teams. With one shielding the Surparna, one resisting the Reset and the other resting, we can no longer offer a team to defend the city against the Eidolon spheres. We have maybe a couple of days before we will have to chose between the Suparna or the Reset."

The chair moved the discussion on. "Ms Akida?"

Yakini further exaggerated her slouched posture bringing her head down to a Terran level. "We're starting to see cases of malnutrition particularly amongst the most vulnerable. I was going to propose another supply run, primarily for potable water, but in light of José's news maybe we have more immediate decisions to make. Also, I've heard from Mars. Bergur should be joining us remotely in a few minutes. Alyona should speak on the city's defence."

"Ms. Semanov?"

Alyona stepped forward, her body motionless above the waist. "Sphere attacks are stable at once every seven point four hours. Rotation of bioengineered ammunition is now effective against sixty-four percent of attacks. Without Node support we will be completely exposed to attack within three point eight days. Fresh strains of pellet should be considered the highest priority."

"And where is Ms Nomia?" Gaverson enquired.

José raised a tentative finger. "She's investigating a disturbance in Antarctica." Nobody seemed able to get enough traction on his statement to ask a question. "She's back now," he added.

Nomia strode into the room. Folds of white fabric beat at the air in her determination. She spared José a tender smile that he absorbed hungrily. "Sorry I'm late," she said.

"The floor is yours," Gaverson offered.

"We found another Reset. It's small at the moment and not growing quickly, but it is accelerating."

Mex found his voice first. "Can we resist a second Reset?"

Nomia glanced at José. "Not a chance," she said. "Whatever we're going to do it has to be now."

Mex still seemed willing to be the voice of the rest. "Do? What can we do?"

Nomia looked at José again, but whatever she was searching for was missing. "I really don't know."

"Hello," a voice barked from a crude vibrating membrane rigged above the council table.

"Bergur!" Yakini cheered. "Where have you been?"

"Yakini. It is good to hear your voice. Things got complicated, but we're coming home."

"Ben?" Nomia cried.

"Sera?" Yakini added.

"Sera received an offer she could not refuse. She's staying. Ben is with me. Say hello, Ben. No? Sorry, he's talking to his new friend. We have fresh bio-pellets."

Nomia smiled sagely. José wondered if she had known all those months ago in the cave on Mars that Sera was destined to become important, or maybe even before she suggested they hide on Mars.

Joy suited Yakini's face. Her smile started in her eyes and spread to her whole face. The upward curve of her lips was almost incidental. It did not last long. "Bergur, how far away are you?"

"We left Mars yesterday."

"It's going to be too late. We won't be here by the time you get back. You need to turn around. Go back to Mars. Hide and hope."

Mex interrupted Yakini. "We need those pellets."

"And we need Ben," José added.

"It won't make any difference by then," Yakini sighed. "If they can save themselves they should."

"Can I say something?" Bergur asked. Even over the crude audio system his determination carried. "We're coming home. Ben says his friend could change everything."

"But you can't make it in time," Yakini pleaded.

"Don't you dare give up before we're back," Bergur growled.

Static leaked from the speaker.

"Bergur?" Yakini asked. "Bergur!"

There was a sharp intake of breath from Nomia and José. The air above the table crackled with conflicted realities. There was a flump of displaced air. At its centre materialised Bergur, his skin a mottled patchwork of brown decay. Beside him crouched Ben and a slug-like tank of green gunk.

Chapter 13

With muscles tuned by serendipitous perfection, Teledice sprinted down the corridor. Even so, her lungs dragged oxygen from the lacklustre air and crystals of fatigue shredded her veins.

A man was screaming behind a door to the left. The door aged and started to crumble before Teledice hit it, forearms across her face. She collated the room through the haze of debris: one door (past tense only), four vertical walls (square, three metres on a side, peak reflectivity four hundred sixty-seven nanometres [blue]), one window (equatorial triangular, grimy), one Eidolon attack sphere (threat), three humans (one large, two small). Teledice could see enough of the children's faces to determine a genetic link to the adult shielding them.

Teledice put a thumb in each ear, waggled the rest of her digits and made a meep-meep noise.

The sphere had no surface details but she could feel its attention swivel towards her. The moment it started to advance, Teledice was back in the corridor and running with everything her physical body had to offer.

A circular bulge pushed out of the joining wall. The sphere phased through the polycrete and straight into her path. Teledice allowed herself a thin grin; if the stakes had not been so high, she might have called this fun. Against all reasonable odds the atoms in feet slipped through the crystal lattice of the floor. Her feet still pumping, Teledice dropped through to the corridor below. She skimmed so close to the sphere, her hair sizzled with static.

Teledice landed heavily on the floor, toppling forward and crushing one shoulder. She lay on her back for the time it took for the pain to reach her brain. The sphere dropped towards her and she was back on her feet and running. Nothing broken. Lucky, but she had made certain of that.

Left turn.

Open double door into empty mess hall. The sphere moved at a fixed pace, but Teledice was tiring. She felt it close behind, a hole in Verity Space. It would be so easy to slip inside and enjoy the tranquillity of oblivion.

Teledice jumped. Not far. Just enough to keep her ahead of the sphere. She re-entered reality and stumbled once before finding her stride. The sphere was two floors below, but it had already picked up her scent and was phasing through the ceiling.

Just a little further.

Two more corridors.

The sphere was too close. She should make another jump, unless, maybe, she could push her legs just a little further.

Teledice burst through another wall. The room was dark. More than an absence of light. Her senses at all levels of reality, floundered and flailed. With no sensory feedback, her legs twisted and she fell forward, without being sure if she landed.

Finally, she felt something. The sphere was there beside her in this unspace. She floated in sensory deprivation, aware of nothing other than the crackling as the sphere prepared to unwind her existence.

"Now!"

She was no longer alone. Cretheis, Ethemea, Chania and Oinoie formed a protective ring around her. Nomia's nymphs sprung their trap.

*

At times the entity was known by two names. When the stakes were highest and disaster loomed, unity was their biggest asset. No name was necessary for the unified being - there was nobody to use it where they had ventured – but NomiaJosé would be an option.

Their physical bodies were between states, absorbed fully into Verity Space, awaiting a conscious mind to bring them back into existence. For now NomiaJosé spiralled around a world-line, probing back through space-time for the moment of instantiation. The shattered remains of an Eidolon sphere marked their point of entry. They sniffed currents of probability, tracing the sphere back to its creators.

From a distance the pocket reality felt distinct and traversable, but the closer NomiaJosé approached the more it blurred. Like an atom for which the question where becomes more meaningless the more precisely you seek it, the Eidolons exhibited no definitive when.

STOP.

The Eidolon demand was direct and immediate. NomiaJosé obeyed as much from shock as a desire to comply.

We appreciate you communicating directly.

NomiaJosé allowed the thought to find its own medium of propagation.

IN MOST VIABLE REALITIES BEYOND THIS SPACE-TIME POINT YOU DO NOT EXIST. TO ALLOW YOU TO UNDERSTAND YOUR DEMISE IT IS NECESSARY TO INTERACT FROM A WORLD-LIKE PERSPECTIVE.

Most realities? There are those where you do not destroy us?

THERE ARE FAMILIES OF REALITIES IN WHICH TOO LITTLE CONTEXT IS LEFT FOR YOU TO PERSIST, EVEN A FEW WHERE YOU END YOUR OWN EXISTENCE.

So, there is no hope?

HOPE? YOU MEAN TO DESIRE A PARTICULAR OUTCOME WITHOUT CREATING IT? YOU ARE EVOLVED BEYOND SUCH LIMITATIONS.

Obviously not.

MAKE YOUR CASE. RECEIVE OUR VERDICT.

You know we have a weapon that to all intent and purpose would destroy you.

YES.

You also know we would never use it.

RECENT HISTORY APPEARS TO DIFFER FROM YOUR ASSERTION.

Certainly, there are a number of individuals capable of such an atrocity, but the vast majority of humanity would rail against such an act and do anything in their power to prevent it.

THIS IS A DIFFICULT THEORY TO PROVE.

It is already proven. It was not a Satyagrahi who stopped Sardon Lucas.

A SAMPLE OF ONE DOES NOT CONSTITUTE A PROOF.

Yet, humanity was condemned on the basis of one man's intentions.

POINT CONCEDED.

Anyway, we are not here to prove humanity's virtue. You know that any of the Satyagrahi have the knowledge and ability to induce the tachyon condensate, but none of us ever would.

WITHHOLDING A WEAPON BECAUSE ITS USE WOULD DESTROY FRIEND AND FOE IS NOT AN ACT OF KINDNESS.

Because the breaking of the symmetry in the Downey field would end the concept of sentience both in the physical universe and Verity Space.

INDEED.

But if the breaking of symmetry was directed rather than spontaneous? What if the new symmetry mirrored our current reality, constraining the Eidolon's to determinism and allowing humanity to ascend in your place?

The unified being NomiaJosé fractured with internal debate.

Tell me you're bluffing, José pleaded.

I'm not. The science is beyond me, but I can instinctively feel the symmetries around us. Can't you?

No, I can't. You know how to defeat the Eidolons and you kept it from me.

The burden would be no lighter shared. This is something I had to keep to myself, but I promise it will be the last secret I ever keep from you.

We can talk about this later, but you know I'll back you whatever you do.

I relish the possibility we might have an opportunity to argue it out later.

Unity restored, NomiaJosé confronted the Eidolon presence as an equal.

*

Bergur's mouth flaps dilated fully, revealing two circles of needle sharp teeth. A guttural roar boomed round the cockpit, half yodel, half battle cry. Yakini laughed with an abandon she would never reveal to anyone other than him. For a while she forgot the brown patches of dead skin flora starving Bergur of vital oxygen.

Trimming the aerofoils another few microns, the multiple gravities of acceleration switched to perfect weightlessness. Her stomach lurched high into sore ribs. Bergur gulped air as he struggled to spread his body over the tank. Green sludge squeezed from the corners and formed spherical globules in the air.

"Can we keep some of this gunk in the tank for the Reset?" Bergur barked.

"That's your job. I'm trying to get us there before it destroys the southern ring of mega-cities."

"Ja, ja. Let rip. I can take anything you can."

"Fuck! I love you. When this is all over..."

"Of course you do. Where else are you going to find such a specimen?"

Their trajectory levelled. Yakini pushed the hull to minimum drag. The wings truncated and slid back to form tail fins. She pushed the engines until alarms sounded and they smacked through a few more multiples of the speed of sound.

When there was nothing more she could trim, Yakini's mind wandered. "Do you think it's freaky this stuff is sentient and yet you can scope out a bucket full and fly off with it?"

Bergur scraped another smear of green from the rear bulkhead with a finger and flicked it back into the tank. "After the things we've seen I've lost sight of normal."

"Do you think it's now two minds or two copies of the same mind?"

"Maybe it doesn't need to all be in one place to think. It doesn't matter, as long as it works."

"As long as it works," Yakini prayed.

From ten thousand metres the southern Reset reflected the blue of the sky, making it look like an oval lake amongst a continent of ice. A rapidly narrowing strip of white separated the Reset from the ocean.

"If we don't get down there before it reaches water we'll have to wait until it makes landfall."

Yakini accepted the challenge with a roll in yaw that made the horizon spin. She pointed the craft's nose directly at the ice and powered into a vertical dive.

"All or nothing?" she screamed.

"All or nothing," Bergur growled in agreement.

Two hundred metres from the ice Yakini flipped the craft about its pitch axis and slammed the engines into explosive overload.

They hit the ice.

Yakini felt something tear inside and her lungs gurgled with each breath. She did not try to get up from the acceleration couch. She had done her bit.

"Fokk!" Bergur swore.

Yakini managed to twist in her seat. Bergur was squatting on the floor of the cabin. Green slime was running through his finger amongst the debris of the shattered tank. He moved to wipe more of the slime from his legs. Underneath the skin was radiantly purple, as if they had been transported back to the moment they first met on the Suparna.

"Does that seem ironic to you?" he asked with something close to a shrug.

The walls of the craft flickered once and then went transparent. Yakini shivered involuntarily as ice crystals battered the hull. The visibility cleared for a moment and they saw the shimmering wall of the Reset.

Bergur looked up at her. "All or nothing," they said together.

After weeks of watching the northern Reset advance at a trot, this wall seemed youthfully exuberant as it swept across the ice, free of the echoes of destroyed reality and much too fast.

Yakini was determined for Bergur to be the last thing she saw. She tore her eyes from the Reset. Bergur was already looking at her. Even without a human face or eyes, Yakini knew he was thinking the same.

Fear was gone. Fear of being alone. Fear of being together. Fear of failing. All gone.

The Reset ate the ice and sky until there was nothing else. Then the bulkhead was consumed and Yakini heard the first hiss of atmospheric equalisation. Despite her determination her eyes clamped shut and she was alone amongst the afterglow of too much light.

One breath.

Another.

Yakini opened her eyes. Bergur was still there. A snow flake settled on the purple dome of his head. Behind him the Reset pulsed and undulated but did not advance.

*

IT HAS HAPPENED BEFORE AND IT WILL AGAIN, BUT IT SHOULD NOT BE AT HUMAN HANDS.

NomiaJosé allowed the word-line to evolve for a few seconds.

Nor will it, they declared. We have the ability but we chose not to use it. This is our defence. We do not offer a threat. We give you a promise.

HOW SHOULD WE JUDGE THE VALUE OF SUCH A PROMISE?

Do you doubt our intent?

NO. YOUR AMALGAMATED MIND HAS GROWN IN DEPTH SINCE YOU HAPPENED ON THE EVOLUTION ARTEFACT ON THE MOON OF THE GAS GIANT, BUT YOU ARE STILL DEVOID OF MALICE. OUR DOUBT RELATES TO YOUR ABILITY TO SPEAK ON BEHALF OF HUMANITY AND ITS DERIVATIVES.

The proof lies all around us. The potential futures of each human twisting and looping around every other human. The tension between each word-line straining to evolve the combined cord of humanity's future towards a collective destination. Self-destruction, genocide, ascendancy, or infinite repetition, each potential path formed not by individual choices but by the interaction between such decisions.

OF THE FUTURES WE WOULD CONSIDER DETRIMENTAL WE SEE THEIR PROFUSION AND SEVERITY SIGNIFICANTLY DIMINISHING. IF YOU HOPE TO USE THIS TO DISSUADE US FROM A FURTHER CULL, WE WOULD SUGGEST THE EVIDENCE SUPPORTS OUR ACTIONS.

Look again.

EXPLAIN.

It is the choices of those left behind which is changing humanity's destiny. Woken from the stupor of their tiny cages, forced to rely on each other, humanity is emerging in its truest form. Let me show you.

NomiaJosé ushered forth memories collected over the last few weeks. Strangers picking up children and carrying them to safety. An old woman tearing a single piece of bread into two and offering half to her neighbour. Time and time again, a man, woman or child throwing themselves between a sphere and a loved one, knowing full well the futility of their action.

Faster and faster they replayed the precious memories until the individuals blurred and only the actions remained.

When NomiaJosé could no longer bear the pain of recollection, the torrent of sacrifice paused on a woman exhausted by perpetual fear. She stood next to a ground vehicle humming with impatient energy. A naked man, with the slack face of an amnesiac, lay at her feet. Without a single thought for herself she lent down and offered him her hand.

Altruism is the true face of humanity. Greed and selfishness is something they have learnt, and they can discard it.

YOUR POINT IS WELL MADE, BUT IT IS NOT ENOUGH.

Then we have only one thing left to offer. Take our lives. Remove humanity's link to Verity Space. The knowledge is contained within so few of us. It can be contained. Reset or remove the device on Titan. Give humanity a few more millennia. Without us they are no immediate threat. Now and then means little to you, but to a mortal race it is beyond value.

IT WILL MAKE NO DIFFERENCE.

So be it, but I still beg for the reprieve. There is still hope. Anything is possible.

DO YOU SPEAK FOR ALL OF THE, SO CALLED, SATYAGRAHI? ARE YOU ALL READY TO GIVE YOUR LIVES FOR HUMANITY.

We do and we are.

*

The spheres were coming thick and fast. Mex tracked each using a tactical unit in Julienne's head. Their ammunition was finite and the mission urgent. Six spheres changed tack, moving to intercept the party. Julienne was already generating firing solutions for the four spheres on her flank. Mex swept his good arm through an instinctive arc and fired a volley of bioengineered pellets. One sphere turned itself inside out trying to avoid contact with the fragment of pseudo-sentient bacteria. The second sphere performed a spiralling dance around the projectiles and continued to advance.

"I said we shouldn't have brought Ben," Mex muttered. His voice was lost in the thumping of pneumatic firearms, crunch of bare soil underfoot and grasping breath of exertion under stress.

Julienne heard him clearly. "He was unusually direct about staying with his friend."

"So, we just have to deliver a boy and his pet tank of sludge to a certain death while every Oikake between here and Andromeda galaxy is rushing to make friends."

"Sounds like your idea of fun," Julienne offered.

"Just how twisted do you think I am? Don't answer that. There's only one thing for it. Engage arcade mode."

Mex relaxed the few remaining barriers his brain maintained to operate in a vaguely normal manner around other people. Julienne adjusted his aim and fired two fléchettes in tight succession, finding the centre of the evasive sphere both times.

Mex settled back to watch. Focusing his attention on keeping himself upright on the uneven ground. Each time an ankle folded he searched for balance with a phantom arm to the side. One armed, he felt ungainly and unsure of himself.

Ben and the mollusc tank made slow progress. Even slower when they stopped to study a single poppy waving its red flag against the grey soil.

"I don't mean to rush you, but fate of mankind and all that," Mex chided.

A sphere sighed into existence directly in their path. Mex yelped involuntarily. Julienne was firing at two spheres gaining from behind. Without turning to check with her own eyes, she whipped Mex's arm through a quarter turn and fired. Before Mex could realise what had happened, the sphere was writhing through conflicting imperatives.

"Mex, we need you back here," a tiny voice chirped.

"Alyona, what are you doing in my head?" Mex said out loud.

"I am on the thirty-seventh floor of Jefferson-A. Only my signal is in your brain."

"I don't know why I bother," Mex lamented.

"The city is stopping. We're under attack by three hundred and forty-two spheres. The building's are refusing to maintain the pace. If we can't get the Jefferson A.I. to change it/their mind, well need to evacuate."

"Sit tight. We're almost at our objective. Julienne, we need to pick up the pace."

"I heard. In case you hadn't noticed we are being surrounded."

The noise of individual Oikake being born merged into a continuous sound-scape of escaping air and discharging energy. Julienne was firing fléchettes in pairs, twisting herself and Mex through an intricate waltz. Mex watched the clusters of numbers superimposed against each target, mostly times counting up and down. There were also faint lines showing the past and future positions of each target relative to their own faltering path. Many of the Oikake projections lay in tightly overlapping curves.

"What are they doing?" he asked.

"Their forming coordinated columns, sacrificing the head to advance the rest."

"That's devious."

"We're going to be overrun in a few seconds. Ben, we need help."

Ben looked up from the cloud of dust particles cavorting around his ankles. "We could wait here until the Reset arrives," Ben offered.

"I don't think we'll last that long. Could we maybe trying running?" Julienne fired a burst of shots to emphasise her impatience.

"I don't think my friend can run."

Mex felt he should contribute in a more meaningful way. "Have you not given it a name yet?"

"Time and place!" Julienne's voice was starting to crack.

"I only have one friend and so does it. We will choose a pronoun and name when social interactions grow to a suitable complexity."

The hiss and thump of Julienne's guns stopped. Mex forgot his connection and twisted round to see her holstering both weapons. She slid two wispy arms around the tank of Ben's friend and hoisted the entire thing off the ground. "Run!" she directed.

Green sludge slurped against the lip of the tank as Julienne staggered forward. After a second Ben started to trot as if he was attached to the tank by an elastic thread. Mex waved his gun left and right in a vaguely menacing fashion and fired a few shots for good measure.

Julienne jolted a message directly into his consciousness. "Mex, forward. Carve us a path."

Mex's legs burst into life, momentarily leaving his torso behind and rocking his chin towards the sky. He could not be sure if his legs responded to his own will, Julienne's tone or something more direct, but for once the contrary demon inside kept its thoughts to itself.

Mex lurched past Ben and Julienne, one arm pumping, the other shoulder rolling in exaggerated arcs. As he raised his gun directly ahead Mex found himself roaring a strangled collection of incoherent vowels, some sort of ancient battle cry.

The first half dozen shots were wild and wide of any useful target. The fléchettes sizzled through the air until they were silenced by impacting on the Reset. Expanded circles of destroyed realities marked the Reset's attempt to absorb the unexpected pellet of alien sentience. With the first impact the Reset was given scale and distance. Focus was close behind.

Mex allowed a tactical display to dance in front of his eyes and he started to carve a tunnel. The roll of his body made aiming hard, but his shots found their mark more often than not. The columns of Oikake tried to adjust their angle of approach to compensate for Julienne's burst of pace, but Mex had a moment to strafe fire broadside to each.

The Oikake faltered. Mex and Julienne burst from the trap with Ben half trotting and half gliding in their wake.

Julienne thumped the tank to the ground like she was planting a flag. Mex moved to take her place, but she put a restraining hand on his chest. "Close enough," she panted.

The manicured bob of blonde hair on her head had recently started to develop straggly clumps of neglect. Mex loved the breach of symmetry but had not found the correct form of words to tell her. Now it was starting to lift in unison, each strand pushing away from its neighbour. Mex rubbed his tongue against the roof of his mouth in a futile attempt to clear a metallic taste leaking from the impossibly dense air.

The Oikake seemed to have lost interest. They turned away from the Reset and headed for the city.

"Thank you," Ben said like a full-stop, putting a hand on the tank and turning to face the Reset.

"We need to go," Julienne demanded.

"Yes you should," Ben agreed.

Julienne stammered a few adamant rejections. Mex tried to judge the distance and speed of the Reset. There were precious few seconds to reach a resolution.

Ben remained calmly detached. "This will work," he stated.

"And if it doesn't?" Julienne asked.

"Then I should share my friends fate."

Julienne mouthed unformed objections.

Mex turned to the retreating city. An unfathomable wave of exhaustion swept through him.

A hand slid into his, locking finger to finger.

"I'm sorry," Mex said.

"Don't be."

Her voice was close to his ear, but he could not take his eyes from the besieged city.

"I love you," he said.

"That's enough."

Hands welded together as tightly as their minds, they turned back towards the Reset.

The mercurial wall crashed into Mex, Julienne, Ben and his friend. Mex tried not to close his eyes, but his body expected a physical blow like from a wave.

Moments passed.

Mex forced himself to look. The Reset was an arm's length from his nose. Reality crackled and sparked as the Reset strained impotently against the small tank of new life.

IT IS NOT ENOUGH.

We cannot give more than our lives.

WE CONCEDE THE POSSIBILITY HUMANITY HAS TURNED FROM ITS DESTRUCTIVE PATH IN RESPONSE TO OUR INTERVENTION RATHER THAN AS A DIRECT RESULT. EACH DECISION CLOSES THE DOOR TO INFINITE FUTURES AND OPENS THE DOOR A CRACK TO INFINITE MORE, BUT CAUSE AND EFFECT ARE IMPOSSIBLE TO UNTANGLE UNAMBIGUOUSLY.

We have proved the collective behaviour of humanity can change through the actions of individuals.

IT IS NOT PROVEN BUT WE CONCEDE THE POSSIBILITY.

That's a start.

ENDING THE EXISTENCE OF THE SATYAGRAHI DOES NOT EXCLUDE HUMANITY FROM CONSCIOUSLY INTERACTING WITH VERITY SPACE. OTHERS LIKE YOU WILL BE BORN.

The collection of mutations that have resulted in Nomia have happened time and time again throughout human history, but have never persisted. Human society tends to segregate anyone who deviates significantly from the behavioural norm. Procreation is difficult for individuals who are institutionalised.

NOT A TRAIT TO BE CELEBRATED.

No, but it limits their ability to evolve.

TRUE. MOST POTENTIAL FUTURES SHOW YOUR GENOME WILL NOT SUPERSEDE BASELINE HOMO SAPIEN FOR ANOTHER TEN MILLENNIA.

So, give us ten thousand years grace.

A PURELY TEMPORAL DELAY MAKES NO SENSE.

It does for an existence experienced moment after moment.

IT IS NOT ENOUGH.

You keep saying that. Other than erasing humanity, what is enough?

WHAT IS WISDOM?

The ability to direct future actions through an understanding of the past.

NO LONGER. WHAT IS WISDOM?

The ability to direct the future through an understanding of the future.

YOU ARE WISE. YOU AND YOURS SHALL GUIDE HUMANITY. YOU AND
YOURS SHALL FEEL THE PAIN OF EACH BETRAYAL. YOU AND YOURS SHALL
ANSWER FOR THE ACTIONS OF HUMANITY.

*

Alyona herded a group of two hundred people away from the Jefferson
building. Eidolon spheres emerged from Verity Space and descended
on the group sending waves of panic through the collective like sharks
attacking a shoal of fish.

Alyona amplified her voice to carry above the shouts of distress.

"Keep moving," she demanded.

The crowd moved past her, frightened faces imploring her to pointless
sacrifice. Eventually even the stragglers began to move, pushing nervous
fingers into the backs of those ahead. For a moment she could ignore
the bleating of the herd and enjoy a sky wider than her imagination. The
horizon was circular like the portholes on the mining ships of her youth, but
the scale messed with her peripheral vision making her head jerk this way
and that.

She would miss weather. Wind devils scampered across the plain and ran straight at her, but they did not stop a metre or even a centimetre from her face. No screen or visor protected her from a hostile environment. Eddies of cool, damp air whistled through her pneumatics and tickled the skin on her face.

The cries of the crowd grew more desperate. Alyona turned to face the wave of harrying Eidolon spheres. She drew a pistol from each hip. Tentacles grew from her wrists and engaged with the gun's firing mechanism. A tremor ran through her frame and the whir of accelerating gyroscopes swallowed her sharp intake of breath.

Alyona started to move with an unnaturally elongated stride. One leg shortened fractionally allowing her to prescribe a slow circle without necessitating her torso lean to one side.

She circled the crowd once. Her crowd. The group of people she had chosen at random or had chosen her. A few hundred people she had decided were her personal responsibility. She could not save them. She could not save herself, but for these few she would try.

By the end of the first loop her legs had developed an extra joint. Her toes grew small teeth so she could run with minimal contact. Inside her head everything conscious was dedicated to mapping the encircling swarm of Oikake. Her foot step became the beating of a war drum. Faster and faster, until it transformed to the heartbeat of a cornered animal.

The Oikake struck in waves.

To the humans inside her perimeter she was a blur, a protective wall of gunmetal grey and the ear-splitting complaint of mechanisms on the edge of destruction.

Alyona poured torrents of fléchettes into the advancing Oikake. Her consciousness was everywhere in her tiny universe; one small circle of existence and nothing was allowed to enter. Faster than the rest, one sphere tore towards the cluster of humans. Alyona fired once as she approached. On her next circuit the pellet was still in flight. She judged the trajectory was marginal so fired a second shot from the other gun.

Each loop she fired several dozen shots and then tracked their transonic progress on subsequent circuits. She could keep this up until she ran out of ammunition or her servos gave out. Neither was very far in the future, but she ran on.

The Oikake took time to writhe their way out of existence, gliding on towards the humans as they imploded under the conflict of their purpose and imperatives. They moved in columns, following each other to good hunting ground like ants on the march. Alyona struggled to get clear firing solutions and the Oikake pushed closer towards her line in the sand.

Leap frogging a fallen comrade, an Oikake drove into her path.

Alyona fired restraining bolts in her legs. She sprung high into the air, clearing the sphere and somersaulting head over feet. At the apex of her flight, fragment of her own body surrounding her like a cloud of metallic rain, she fired all her remaining pellets in a wide arc.

At a metre from the ground, the majority of shots had found their mark and another wave of Oikake tore themselves apart.

Alyona landed feet first and crumpled into a pile of mechanical and organic body parts. Fluids of red and blue leaked into the soil and formed oily globules of reluctant mud. Her head was tilted back towards the Jefferson towers. She could discern her herd of defenceless humans by their screams and the scrapping of jostling feet.

The towers were not moving. The rest of the city had lumbered on for a few metres, closing the gap between the buildings. It looked as if they had huddled together for safety before settling lifeless into the soil.

Alyona could not be sure if her faltering senses were deceiving her but the Jefferson towers looked to be leaning. The angle became greater. The two towers were falling.

With a shudder of crushed masonry the tips of the towers collided and stuck tight. After a curtain of black shards had fallen to the ground the two buildings had become one, a static inverted V of black decay. A monument or tombstone to humanity.

Time passed in a dull decline, punctuated by stabbing moments of pain.

The cries behind her stopped. There was a hush punctuated by the shushing noise of the wind. Alyona tried to move but was paralysed as much by what she expected to see as by her failing body.

A shadow moved across her, a dim silhouette against a grey sky. A male, one of the herd, knelt beside her head. Leaning forward he kissed her forehead.

"Is it over?" Alyona gurgled through a congealed throat.

"Yes. They're gone. I think we won."

"Good. Then I can rest."

Chapter 14

The silence was pernicious.

Lesana woke in the lull between a scream and its echo. Stretching her senses deep into the fuzz of urban tinnitus, she hunted for a tell-tale sign of an attack. There were no warning yells, howls from victims or wailing survivors.

The war was still over.

Lesana wrapped her blanket across her shoulders and crept to the window. Dawn was pushing against the horizon and burning away the night. The remains of the Jefferson buildings were already visible as a black wedge against the violaceous sky. The rest of the refugee city clustered around at a respectful distance, like mourners at a funeral.

No sign of the Jefferson minds had been found since the towers collapsed. The processing constructs were completely empty of intelligence. Lesana had heard many outlandish theories as to what had happened in the last moments of the war. Some said the Eidolons had tried to consume the Jefferson minds and had been infected by a dementia virus. Another variant maintained the Jefferson minds had achieved some sort of ascension and had smote the Eidolons with a god-like power.

The truth was more prosaic.

Jefferson A had commandeered a handful of pico-minds brought into the building during the war. They had given him a marginal advantage in the battle against his brother. The balance of mutual attrition had been broken and the battle became exponentially one-sided. The real mystery was why there was no victor. The brothers had probably been entwined for so long that they were symbiotically linked, such that a Jefferson mind was unviable in isolation. Lesana imagined the minds had so confused love and hate that the bereaved brother had simply lost the will to exist.

Lesana was startled by a knock at the entrance to her room. She pushed the door to one side without getting dressed; communal living had taught her the absurdity of excessive modesty. A girl in her late teens handed Lesana a scratch pad without superfluous pleasantries. The simple message was a meeting request from one of the city's new technocrat. Lesana used the stylus to accept the request and handed the pad back to the messenger. The girl mustered a partial smile before turning away.

Lesana walked across the disturbed ground between the buildings. She kept her stride as casual and lazy as possible, enjoying the clear horizon and feeling of space. The city was quiet. Most of the population had departed for intact towns in the southern hemisphere, leaving as many memories as possible in the tattered remains of the refugee city. Those who remained were attempting to define a constitution to fill the vacuum left by the collapse of the corporations. The need to consult and engage every community on the planet and beyond was the major driving force behind the rapid repair of global communication infrastructure. Something for which Lesana had little aptitude.

"I've been asked to offer you a position." The logistics manager was in disarray. Her tunic was inside out and back to front. The collar pressed into her larynx, forcing little gulps at the end of each phrase.

"Asked by whom?" Lesana asked.

"A senior member of the council."

"What kind of position?"

"Pretty much anything you want, but I would suggest something senior in the new analytics foundation."

"Why would they do that?"

"I asked the same question. It seems the council considers your contribution to the war effort to have been rather decisive."

"Me?"

"Apparently so. I can't offer much at the moment, but once we are back on our feet the benefit package will be significant. Obviously, the new way of things is a lot more egalitarian than what went before, but you should be comfortably well off. You've already been assigned a suite in the refurbished Trellace block."

"I don't know what to say. Can I have a little time to think about it?"

Lesana left the building in a dreamy daze of satin sheets and herbal infusions delivered to her bed side. A quad-bike with grossly over inflated tyres crunched to a halt by her side. A gawky teenager leant down and grinned at her from behind frosted googles.

"Found you," the boy shouted over the descending whine of ancient gyros.

"Fez, what's up?"

"I just wanted to tell you I'm sorry but I can't make our date."

"Date?"

"Dinner date."

Lesana vaguely remembered agreeing to see him in the food hall around lunch time. "Oh that date," she smiled. "No problem."

"I've met someone else." Fez leant one jagged elbow on the dashboard.

"Really? That's great. Is she your age?"

"Almost. Maybe a little older. She's a logistics manager. We're leaving today on a mission."

"That sounds exciting. Is it a secret mission?"

Fez looked slightly crestfallen. "Not really, but its important. We're going to one of the lost cities. You know there are still entire populations that have no idea the war is over?"

"I've heard. They must be scared and probably starving by now. It sounds really important."

"It is."

Lesana looked at the dust on her shoes. She tried to imagine her feet in footwear expensive enough to reject dirt; pristine white in perpetuity.

"Fez?"

"Lesana."

"Has the mission got space for one more?"

*

The taxi drone dipped slightly as the man eased himself through the opening. Sound bites and voting trends from the latest people's forum scrolled across his face. At full stretch he cleared the projection field and white clouds blinded him with reflected sunlight. A wind, completely alien to the planet's surface, savaged his skin and threatened to prize his grip free. A second drone manoeuvred closer and he leapt.

As soon as the man was in the grip of the transit couch, the new drone dived with an almost joyful abandonment. The vehicle's mind spoke to the man. "Mex, my darling. I really thought you were dead during all the recent unpleasantness. I should have known the universe would not deprive me of your loveliness."

"It's good to see you again. How have you been?"

"How have I been? Really? After you abandoned me to goodness knows what. Oh how I have suffered. Do you know they starved me? I had to squat on the ground for months with only enough energy to keep my mind alive. I barely recognise myself. I must look a right state. Am I still attractive?"

"You are as beautiful as ever."

"Oh Mex. You are truly a devil. A delicious devil."

"Only with you."

"Where shall we go? Somewhere remote, where nobody will interrupt us."

"Actually, I'm in a bit of a hurry."

"Mex, don't tell me you're being chased again."

Mex squirmed in the couch, squinting at their surroundings through the scrolling messages. "I'm afraid so," he admitted.

"Who is it? I thought all the corporations were gone. Who could you possibly manage to offend in this world of equals?"

Something clattered against the outside of the drone. A lump pressed against Mex's sternum as they dropped dozens of metres. A fist sized hole punched through the roof and a beam of pure sunlight landed between Mex's feet. A pair of delicate fingers pushed through the hole and peeled back the roof like it was made of paper. Without hesitating a woman dropped through the expanded hole. She was slender and delicate like a dancer but a look of murderous intent overlaid her artificially symmetrical features.

"Well I never!" the taxi exclaimed.

The woman touched her blonde bob like someone testing the stability of a wig. She flattened a couple of stray locks before sitting opposite Mex.

The hole in the roof healed, restoring the acoustic dampening of the interior, but the taxi continued to express its indignation. "Mex, who is this woman? Please tell me I can drop her from a very great height."

The woman raised an eyebrow. Mex gripped the seat with whitening knuckles.

"I'm detecting a lot of chatter between nano-scale implants," the taxi said. "Are you two talking behind my back?"

"Sorry," Mex said aloud.

"Say it," the woman instructed.

"Okay. Okay. You were right and I was wrong."

"And?"

"Julienne. You are blameless and I am an idiot."

The taxi banked sharply to get their attention. "Mex, do you know this woman? She seems to know you."

"I do." Mex was speaking to the taxi but his eyes were locked with Julienne's. "I know her better than I know myself. I know everything about her, and despite knowing me completely, she loves me."

"And?"

"And I love her."

"Well really! Of all the barefaced cheek. I should drop you both right here and see how well you fly."

Mex's voice resonated with an inhuman level of confidence. "But you won't." Midway between a question and an instruction he offered and refused freewill in a single phrase.

The taxi's progress stuttered as if an unusually large fraction of brain-power was suddenly required to resolve conflicting sections of code. There was a pause unbecoming a machine intellect. "Oh Mex. I find it impossible to stay angry with you."

Julienne choked.

"Oh dear, maybe she's dying," the taxi chimed.

Julienne scowled.

"So, where are we going?" Mex interjected.

Julienne slumped back in the chair. "Anywhere free of committees."

"Aren't you enjoying leading a completely new police force?"

"We don't say things like lead any more. I'm consulting, but it all feels so backwards."

"How so?"

"We're implementing laws designed by the people, for the people. Each clause and use-case is discussed until every nuance is revealed. And everything has to be proven consistent with the constitution. It's a polite anarchy."

Mex laughed without constraint until a tear formed in one eye. With unnatural precision he removed the bead of saline with one rock-steady finger. The droplet formed a perfect sphere on his fingertip as the last convulsion passed from his body.

Julienne frowned deeply. "I don't see why you find it so funny."

"It reminded me of a drunken conversation with Sickle."

"Oh him." Julienne waved the memory away. "So, how's the new network coming on?"

"Slowly. This thing really is backwards. The infrastructure is designed specifically to prevent secrecy. Data is owned by everybody. The only security we're implementing is to preserve integrity and prevent concealment. We're rolling it out to a third and fourth city, but I've no idea how it's going to scale. Once we get everybody back online it's going to be a completely new kind of anarchy."

"Sorry to interrupt," the taxi said with heavy irony, "but where are we going?"

"We?" Julienne enquired.

"The least you can do is share him with me."

Julienne gave Mex a familiar look of disgust.

"North," Mex declared. "There's an entire hemisphere of unexplored wilderness. Four thousand miles of virgin forest, lakes that have never been swum in and entire mountain ranges without so much as a trail. Let's explore. Who knows what's out there."

"We could reposition one of the remaining satellites."

"Not the same," Mex sighed. "Let's play. Me Tarzan, you Jane."

Julienne gave him a suspicious look.

"Okay. Okay." Mex cringed. "You can be Tarzan."

*

Approaching from interplanetary space, the shuttle glowed gently against the star speckled backdrop. From orbit, a deceleration web deployed into space like the feathery tentacles of a filter feeding sea creature. The shuttle's engines bled heat into space, rapidly cooling and fading from human perception. A carrier laser painted an ultraviolet dot on the shuttle's hull. A few gigabytes of telemetry was superimposed onto the modulation of the light. The shuttle's mind digested most of the data, passing on a few bytes to its humanoid crew.

"Welcome to the Martian Cooperative. We invite you to take advantage of our orbital facilities. Due to the matrix structure of the Martian administration no dignitaries exist to greet you. We hope this will not cause inconvenience or offence. Enjoy your visit and remember to tread as lightly as you breath."

The shuttle drifted infinitely slowly against the backdrop but hypersonically with respect to the thin shell of gases covering the planet's surface. The deceleration web wafted towards the shuttle, shifting its configuration as more refined trajectory information became available.

Twenty kilometres from contact a stream of highly energetic particles erupted from the upper surface of the shuttle's nose. A second later an opposite jet emerged from beneath, but the shuttle was now broadside to the web, its prow pointing towards the planet's surface. With machine patience, the web rapidly reconfigured for the new profile and settled with a few milliseconds to spare.

Electromagnetic energy flared across the full range of sensed frequencies, leaving the orbital station briefly blind. Sensor pods scraped away layers of fried circuitry to expose freshly grown replacements.

The shuttle was gone.

It took forty-three nanoseconds for the orbital to conclusively exclude a catastrophic explosion. It cancelled the storm shutters that were already growing over all vulnerable subsystem and human habitation sections. The wave-front of the energetic burst was asymmetrical, a tail grew from the initial point of emission and jutted towards the planet.

High level of fusion products impacted on the web tendrils in an expanding cone. Extrapolating, the apex formed a trajectory rapidly approaching the planet's atmosphere.

The orbital switched to a communication laser with superior penetration through ion streams and painted a message between the engine cones of the receding shuttle.

"I assume you already know, but your design specifications do not extend to atmospheric braking."

This time the shuttle replied by reflecting a few of the photons back to the orbital. "Pray for me brother," it said.

The orbital had no way of responding to such a bizarre request. Its brain assumed the worst and invoked a mid-level paranoia mode. It cut the laser stream and purged the communications, without even checking for any suspicious data hidden in the exchange. Finally, it notified the planet surface that a potentially compromised ship of unknown intent was heading their way.

On board the shuttle Bergur was standing next to the pilot chair. His mouth flaps hung open, loose skin buffeted by deceleration and a battle cry. The pilot tried to join in, but, even with artificial strengthening, her Martian frame could not muster enough breath. Yakini gritted her teeth and edged the shuttle closer to total destruction. Darkness threatened to steal her consciousness, but she felt some satisfaction when Bergur grunted from the physical shock.

The shuttle stopped shaking and the view ahead lost the tinges of burning orange to reveal the true pink of the atmosphere. The externally generated noise dropped to the levels manageable by the noise-cancellation system. Bergur gave Yakini a look she had learnt to interpret as quizzical.

"The ship has religion," Yakini repeated.

"I get that, but why?"

"Mex claims it is the easiest way to get past the safe-flight interlocks, so I can fly the way I want."

"I can't see how belief in a god helps?"

A broad grin split Yakini's face in two. "It does when I'm the god."

The shuttle screamed across the Martian horizon, dragging grains of sand from the tops of dunes in its wake. Ripples and steam followed it across Lake Vanuatu. At the space port Yakini banked hard to avoid an automated mineral launcher.

"That explains the chirping from the nav system," Yakini said dismissively.

The shuttle flipped on one axis and landed hard on a pad of bare rock. The nose dipped as if kissing the ground and then melted to release the crew of two.

A Martian woman stood under the wing of a re-badged executive shuttle. She was slightly taller than Yakini and thinner boned, but otherwise they still looked like sisters to Bergur. As Sera strode towards them a smile wiped exhaustion from her features. She bent down to hug Bergur first and murmured her joy near where his ears should have been. Sera lingered longer with Yakini, as if the embrace was restoring her energies.

Eventually Sera stood back but her fingers still lingered on Yakini's arm.

"I assume the panicking orbital is your doing."

"I've no idea what you mean." Yakini tried to hold back her guilty smile. "Anyway, congratulations on being elected queen."

"I don't think queens are elected," Sera replied distractedly.

"Can we eat?" Bergur interjected. "And drink, but not for Yakini of course."

"Of course. What?" Sera stumbled.

Yakini gave Bergur a withering glare.

"Oops," he said. His head shrank deeper into the muscles of his shoulders.

"Tell me," Sera demanded.

"We're pregnant," Bergur blurted.

"Both of you?"

"Mostly Yakini."

"How?"

Bergur looked confused. "The usual way," he said tentatively.

Sera looked with bafflement from Bergur to Yakini. Yakini talked across Sera's confusion. "I want to give birth on Mars. I know it's a big ask, but I'd like you to be her godmother."

Sera repeated the female pronoun as if testing its suitability. "Is the baby going to be okay? Physically?"

Bergur let air rattle his mouth flaps. "With our genes how could she be anything less than perfect?"

Sera shuffled from one awkward foot to the other.

"Maybe we should pause this conversation for a bit," Sera offered. "How about showing us round you kingdom? Is there a nakamal tonight?"

The sun formed droplets of mercurial incandescence as it finally surrendered to the jagged rim of Vanuatu crater. The nakamal fire pit thrust back the thin chill seeping from the dusk and cast an earthy light on the faces of the gathered Martians.

Bergur barely waited for the music to begin before he started his barrel stomp impression of the Martian dance. The musicians tightened the beat to suit his stocky physique. A handful of locals joined him, struggling to make their languid limbs comply with the truncated rhythm. Other stared in disbelief or exchanged conspiratorial gossip, as if Bergur has stepped from an urban myth. Someone handed him a clay cup of thick liquid. There were gasps and cheers as Bergur dropped the cup, contents and all, into gaping mouth flaps. His skin flora pulsed pink and he let loose a roar of random bestial noises.

"What's he doing?" Sera asked.

"He's playing." Yakini chuckled. "He's having fun. Watch the edge of his mouth. That flutter is a laugh. He's happy."

"And are you happy?" Sera noted the effort it took for Yakini to drag her eyes from Bergur.

Yakini was still for a moment. The noise of the nakamal seemed to recede. "I'm getting there," she said. "The war has taken its toll on all of us. Even Bergur cries in his sleep. Don't tell him I said that; since I got pregnant, he's as protective as a swan. But the new democracy, cooperative-thingy is perfect for me. I get to fly almost anything I want, but even on the ground I'm more content than I used to be."

"So, what's missing?"

"You, Sera. Only you."

"You made your choice." Sera was surprised by the bitterness in her own voice.

"I did, but I've always been a have my cake and eat it kind of girl."

"What are you suggesting? Are we supposed to share you?" Sera waved away the thick air between them. "Anyway, I've found my calling. I have the opportunity to build the Mars my Dad always imagined."

"And what would he say about the importance of family? I want you and Bergur to be a part of my daughter's life. I've no idea what that really means, but with the three of us to nurture and teach her she'll be a force to be reckoned with. Come on, what have you got to lose? The one thing I can guarantee is your life will never be dull."

"Does Bergur even understand what we were to each other?" Sera whispered. "He seems a little naïve when it comes to sexual preferences."

Yakini cackled. "You underestimate him. Male or female, we all look alien to him, but I don't think it makes any difference to how he feels. What he cannot comprehend are repressed emotions."

Bergur bounded over to the two woman. He managed a shallow bow. "May I have this dance?"

Before Sera could react, he had lifted them both clear from the ground. She threw an arm around his neck as he started to spin. Yakini was howling with laughter, her head flung back to face the stars.

A shudder of caged tears erupted from deep inside. In its wake, Sera felt empty, then, in the freed space, something fresh started to grow.

Epilogue

They glide as phoenix shaped blurs in the plasma of the photosphere. They dance together, and they dance as one. They snare magnetic field lines as they fly, dragging and twisting knots of pure radiance; charged particles stream off into space, before diving back into the star's surface, like breaching whales of pure energy.

For many more orbits they float lazily in the chromosphere, letting the warm eddies bathe them in red light.

How do you feel, Nomia?

José, you can stop asking me that. I am content and complete.

Five other forms spiral over the horizon, creating helical formations that might be the genetic code of creatures yet to exist. Nomia mingles her essence with each, greeting them as she would a new day.

Cretheis, Teledice, Ethemea, Chania and Oinoie. My nymphs, show me all you have experienced.

We have blown bubbles in ice, to rebuild the lost colony of the Eridanian's.

Bergur will be so happy to know some of his kind survive.

We have tickled the orbits of asteroids, divided bacteria cells in faraway mud and swam along thermoclines under crusts of frozen methane.

Your journey has been a wonder.

Is it time to go back?

Yes, my nymphs, it is time we returned to Earth and relieved our brothers and sisters. It is time for us to teach and be taught. It is time to feel grass between toes of flesh.

The star settles back into its own rhythms and battles; the endless crushing forces of self gravity, and the balancing pressure of photons as they stream from the nuclear furnace at the core. Each photon performs a ten thousand year pilgrimage from its creation in the nuclear fusion of two hydrogen nuclei, to the freedom of open space. Sharing of themselves with innumerable stellar residents as they travel. They emerge from the photosphere as quanta of perfect yellow and head towards the void. Some travel for the rest of eternity, others land on leaves to trigger growth or reproduction. There is the tiniest of possibilities a few might flash though the eyes of a sentient being looking up to the stars and wondering why.

The End.

www.ingramcontent.com/pod-product-compliance
Lightning Source LLC
Chambersburg PA
CBHW060941030726
47503CB00003B/683